When Will My Morning Come

Shelly Kew

Shelly Kew

This book is a work of fiction. Names, characters, places and events other than those clearly in the public domain are a product of the author's imagination. Any depictions or resemblance similar to anyone alive or deceased are purely coincidental and not intended by the author.

Cover art by Germancreative

Published and printed in the United States of America

ISBN 978-1979795982
First print, 2017

CONTENTS

Title Page
Dedication

Chapter 1
Chapter 2
Chapter 3
Chapter 4
Chapter 5
Chapter 6
Chapter 7
Chapter 8
Chapter 9
Chapter 10
Chapter 11
Chapter 12
Chapter 13
Chapter 14
Chapter 15
Chapter 16
Chapter 17
Chapter 18
Chapter 19
Chapter 20
Chapter 21
Chapter 22
Chapter 23
Chapter 24
Chapter 25
Chapter 26
Chapter 27
Chapter 28
Chapter 29
Chapter 30
Chapter 31
Chapter 32
Chapter 33
Chapter 34
Chapter 35
Chapter 36
Chapter 37
Chapter 38
Chapter 39
Chapter 40
Chapter 41
Chapter 42

Epilogue
Acknowledgments
About the Author

This book is dedicated to my mother, Barbara Jean. My prayer is that you are looking down from heaven, with a proud smile, saying, "Great job, daughter."

For his anger lasts only a moment, but his favor lasts a lifetime; weeping may last through the night, but joy comes with the morning.
Psalm 30:5 (New Living Translation)

Sunshyne woke up wrapped in the arms of the man she loved more than anything in the world, so she the day was going to be good. There wasn't any other place she'd rather be. She thought back to the beautiful time she and Richard shared last night.

Dinner at Devon Seafood Grill in Oakbrook Terrace. Their scenic ride downtown. The view of the Chicago skyline. When they arrived downtown they parked in the garage attached to their hotel overlooking the Chicago River. After checking in, they walked along Michigan Avenue and Oak St. admiring the shops. The streets were busy with young people and other couples enjoying the beautiful summer night. They strolled through Millennium Park still buzzing with people and music from the street performers before returning to their suite.

Sunshyne couldn't wait until the day they were able to go home together.

Richard turned over and kissed her cheek.

"Good morning, baby. How is my sunshine feeling this morning?"

"I'm just fine. I'm waking up with you next to me. I'd be feeling much better if I could feel you inside of me," she whispered seductively as she rolled over and straddled him.

Richard stood over six feet. His lean, muscular body was chiseled, his fitted shirts often showed off the six pack he worked so hard to maintain. He had a fair complexion with soft curly hair and looked like he just stepped out of GQ or Esquire. She gazed into his warm, brown eyes, and was instantly mesmerized. He reached up and cradled her face between his hands, devouring her mouth with his tongue. Taking her hand, he placed it inside his boxers, on his manhood. She began massaging him, and could feel his dick getting harder and growing with each stroke.

He closed his eyes and let out a slight moan. The slightest touch from her always made his blood rise. She rubbed his shaft as he buried his tongue deeper inside her mouth. When he couldn't take it anymore he threw the covers back and flipped her over on her back. He unbuttoned her red lace teddy slowly, unfastening every button, while kissing the side of her neck. A sweet sensation ran through her body, straight to her secret. When the teddy fell open, he studied her body, taking in every perfect inch of it.

"You are such a goddess. I love you," he said, taking her erect nipples into his mouth.

He fondled her breasts tenderly with his tongue, slowly licking around her light-brown areolas. His lips moved down to her stomach, kissing her right above her pelvic area. Removing her matching red, lace thong, he slipped two fingers inside of her. A faint and sensual cry escaped her lips. Sunshyne melted into the bed. His fingers moved in and out rhythmically. Her hips matched the movement of his fingers, until she couldn't take it anymore and her secret juices flowed freely.

She wanted to feel him inside her. Grabbing his arms, she pulled him up to her. Her legs wide open, inviting him to enter. His two fingers parted her lips gently. His shaft slid into her nice and slow. Feeling the warmth of her swallow him, he began stroking it, unhurried, the way she liked it.

"Ooh, I love the way you make me feel. No one else can make me feel this way," he said, barely getting the words out.

"That's the way you betta keep it," she replied, right before her eyes rolled to the back of her head and her juices started flowing again.

They continued to make love until he could see that smile creep across her face, as it always did, letting him know he'd done his job. They laid there cuddling with him massaging her clit to get her excited all over again, but it wasn't going to happen. His phone continuously rang throughout the morning. He had ignored it for way too long, and they both knew who it was calling.

He reached over and grabbed the phone from the table, letting out a heavy sigh after going through his texts. Sunshyne got up to go get in the shower. She just had earth-shattering sex with her baby and didn't want to ruin it with an argument, but couldn't resist. Walking into the bathroom she asked him, "When are you going to ask for your divorce?"

"Come on, baby. You know it's not that easy. We just got to deal with it for a little while longer. Baby girl will be out of high school soon and I will be able to be with you, and only you," he said with his usual sad puppy face.

"I thought you were already only with me. That's what you keep telling me," Sunshyne said sounding disgusted.

"You know what I mean. I'm saying I will finally be done with her. Look, here you go letting that shit get to you. My heart is yours, baby. You are my future."

Was he trying to convince her or himself? She rolled her eyes as she slammed the bathroom door.

Richard decided to get the call out of the way, while Sunshyne was in the shower. He hoped it wouldn't take long because he didn't want to give Sunshyne any other reason to be upset. He unlocked his phone and dialed her number. Monica answered the phone almost immediately.

"Where the fuck are you?" she yelled into the phone.

"Keep your voice down. Who do you think you're yelling at? What do you want," he said with frustration building in his voice.

There was no need to play the game with her. They both knew their marriage was over, but she just wouldn't let go. She made it very clear. She was going to make his life miserable. She had given him fifteen years of her life, two daughters, supported him through school, and got his business up and running. No, she was not willing to give him to another female so easily.

"What time will you be here," she growled through the phone.

"I will be there in enough time to get her to rehearsal. I've always made sure she got to her piano lessons, so why would today be any different? Next time, don't blow my phone up like that for this. The next time you call me like this, it better be an emergency. You wanting to know what time I'm coming home is not an emergency. Goodbye, Monica," and with that he hung up the phone, switching his phone to silent.

Sunshyne stepped out the shower and grabbed the towel hanging over the toilet to dry off. She looked up and caught her likeness in the mirror. Any other time she would have admired the woman she saw in the reflection, but right now she wanted to cry. How could he tell her she was the best thing to ever happen to him? That he loved her more than any woman he has ever been with, including his wife, but couldn't seem to make a full commitment to her.

She knew he gave her all his time, but that wasn't enough anymore. They had been playing this game long enough. She wanted everything from him, but he couldn't give her that right now. He had things to clean up before he could make her a permanent part of his life, and she trusted everything he told her since she was his main focus, or seemed to be. He did everything he could to make sure she kept a smile on her face. Once he got his affairs in order they would be together for the rest of their lives... at least that's what she hope, but then again she wasn't so sure after times like this. The worst part was she had fallen in love with someone else's husband.

Regardless of what he felt for her or what she felt for him, he still belonged to someone else. If he didn't get it together soon she was going to find someone that could be hers — all hers. More and more she was starting to feel like a bigger fool every day. She just could not seem to let him go.

She snapped out of her deep thought when Richard yelled out to her, "Save some water for the fish."

She chuckled to herself and opened the door. She decided that she was not going to let her day be ruined by what she already knew. For now, she was in a hotel's luxurious suite, enjoying the time with the love of her life... for as long as it lasted.

When she came out the bathroom Richard was lying there in his boxers looking scrumptious. It didn't matter that she had just gotten out of the shower. She wanted to jump on him and ride him for the rest of the morning. However, she had other plans of her own today. She walked over to closet instead, opened the mirrored sliding doors and grabbed her bag. She pulled out her Levi skinny jeans, a white Levi t-shirt, and her white and silver Michael Kors sandals. When she walked back towards the bed, Richard tried to pull her to him. She resisted.

“Nope! We both need to get our day started. Plus, you need to get home to your *wife*."

She hated saying that out loud, but they both knew it was the painful truth.

Richard smacked her on the ass, "I'll leave you alone for now, but as soon as you’re done with your girls tonight, I need to see you."

"We'll see," she said in a sassy tone and Richard walked into the bathroom.

After leaving the hotel, they stopped at Golden Nugget for a quick breakfast before he took her home. They sat in her alley for a couple minutes saying their goodbyes.

"Baby, I'm going to try to make it out there to see you later. Maurice and his people are going to have a couple of tents out there and he told me and Tony to come check them out," Richard said hoping he could get her to cheer up.

"That's cool. You already know I'm going to help shut it down today. So hopefully I will get to see you later."

She needed to get upstairs to see about her children. She was shocked Mariah, her oldest daughter, had not called her yet this morning. Her niece, Trinity spent the night at her house with the kids. Trinity and Mariah were both fourteen. She must have had a lot of fun with her cousin because she had not texted or called, not one time.

Sunshyne reached over, kissed Richard, and ran upstairs to get things moving. Richard waited until she was inside then pulled out of the alley and headed home.

~2~

Jeanette Noelle Morris, more affectionately called Sunshyne, was 5' 7", 165 pounds, with a helluva body, as the younger guys told her all the time. She tried to keep it that way by making it to the gym at least four times a week. Some days she was at the gym twice a day to make sure her body stayed on point. Even with all that ass following behind her when she left the room, her most noticeable feature were her beautiful hazel green eyes. They seemed to put the fellas in a trance as soon as they noticed them. Her light brown skin was as smooth as caramel and amazingly flawless.

Sunshyne got her nickname as a baby. Her mother would sing, "You Are My Sunshine" to her beautiful, baby girl all the time. Her mom went through some hard times when she got pregnant with Jeanette, and from the very moment she was born, her mother felt the weight of the world lifted. Jeanette was the answer to her prayers. Sunshyne made her mother's days sunny after the loss of her first child a couple years before. So, for as long as she could remember, her mother called her Sunshyne except for the times when she had done something to really make her mom mad, and then she was Jeanette Noelle. She kept the nickname as she grew up and changed the spelling to make it her own.

She is the oldest of four siblings and was raised with her twin brother and sister, Damon and Desiree. The day after Thanksgiving, when she was eight, they found out they had a younger brother, Terrell. He was the spitting image of his older brother and their father. His mother basically dropped him on their doorstep and told her father, Mr. Morris, she just couldn't raise him anymore. Her and her siblings just knew that their parents were going to divorce, but their mother stayed and stood by her husband.

Sunshyne couldn't believe her father had kept it hidden that long in the small town they lived. Glenmont, a small suburb that bordered Chicago on the north, was the type of town where everyone knew everyone, so it was hard to keep anything in the dark for long. There was a single high school and everyone more than likely graduated with one another. Later in life she found out her mother already knew about the woman and the child for years, but she loved her father so much that she stayed and made it work. Their marriage weathered the storm. It took a lot of screaming, cussing, counseling, and praying before things got better, but eventually the family made it through. After some resentment and jealousy passed among the siblings, you would have never known Terrell was not a member of the family from birth. Damon now had a little brother to hang with and protect, and Sunshyne had another little knot-head brother to boss around.

Growing up, Sunshyne had to make sure her younger siblings were taken care of because her parents worked all the time. Her father owned a local bar and her mother worked as a nurse. She started on the intensive care unit until she could no longer handle losing most of her patients. She ended up returning to school to become a Certified Nurse Midwife. She soon learned bringing life into the world was much more gratifying than watching her patients lose theirs.

With her parents being away from the house as often as they were, Sunshyne was both big sister and mother to her siblings. She had to make sure they were fed, bathed, and in the bed at the time her parents instructed. This was up until she "started" a family of her own.

She was seventeen when she had her oldest child, Mariah. She often snuck out the house to see an older guy named Marcus while her parents were gone. He was not her boyfriend, but they saw each other regularly. They would usually just go back to his house and hang out while his mother wasn't home. After a while, he started coming by, bringing treats for her younger siblings, and from that day on she became Marcus' baby mama and nothing more.

He saw other women but always knew he could come back to Jeanette whenever he felt like it, and she would let him, even if she was seeing someone else. That was until she met Richard. He treated her like she should be treated. She knew he was married but didn't care. He made her feel like she was the only woman in the world when they were together.

***

When Sunshyne made it upstairs, she was glad everyone was still asleep. That meant she could hopefully get a little more sleep. She kicked off her sandals and lay across her bed, until she dozed off. When she finally woke up, she heard the kids in the front room. The alarm on her phone was buzzing, so she knew she had been sleep longer than she planned.

She quickly got up, went in the living room and made sure everything was still in place. Damon had already picked up her niece, and Mariah had fixed her and her siblings some waffles. She said good morning to the kids and went into the bathroom to get herself together. Her baby girl, Maia started to ask her a question, but Sunshyne closed the door. As soon as she opened the door, her baby girl was right there waiting.

"Good morning, Mommy."

"Good morning, baby girl."

"Mommy, we had fun with Trinity last night. She painted me and Mariah's nails for us. See?" Maia threw her hands up to show Sunshyne her bright pink nails.

"They're beautiful, honey."

"Thank you, Mommy."

"You're welcome. Go get in the tub so you can start getting ready to go with your dad today."

"Okay," Maia replied as she bopped into the bathroom and shut the door.

***

Sunshyne looked forward to attending the *Chosen Few* picnic every year. It was one of the biggest events of the summer in the City of Chicago. She couldn't wait to get out to Jackson Park to hear the soulful beats of some of the best DJs in the world. She hadn't missed a picnic since she started attending back in 2005. Even once they started charging — what her friends thought was an outrageous admission cost — she always managed to talk at least one of them into going with her.

This year all the people close to her would be there. None of them really cared for house music, but they didn't have a problem rolling with her because they knew there would be plenty going on to keep them entertained.

Just thinking about the mixes from Andre Hatchett and Terry Hunter as well as the other DJs she was about to be "jackin her body" to, gave her goose bumps. She was excited just thinking about it. She walked over to her tall, light oak dresser and turned on her iPhone. One of her mixes on Mix Cloud came up and she connected her device to the wireless speaker. She finished getting ready, as she bopped around the room full of energy. House music helped her forget all the negativity in her life, if only for a little while.

Her cell phone started ringing and the mix was interrupted right in the middle of Black Coffee's "Superman" merging with Rose Royce's "Love Don't Live Here Anymore." She looked over and rolled her eyes at the phone. She knew from the song playing, it was Marcus, the father of her children. They had three beautiful children together, whom he adored and would do anything for, but that was all they shared.

Even though they had no real relationship, he always felt the need to lie to her. Every time she asked him about the females she would hear about and caught his ass up with, his line was always, "Naw. It's not what it seems." He could never be honest about any of them. She told him he should change the name of his realty business from "The Home

Team...We're in a League of Our Own" to "Dream Homes... Imagine the Impossible" because he was always selling her a fantasy.

Marcus was one of the biggest loan sharks in their small town for a long time before he got his stuff together and moved to Vegas. He invested his money in a successful startup company once he moved out there before obtaining his license and starting his real estate business. He was only gone about a year and a half but had made enough money to return home and set up shop.

In the beginning of their break up — if you really want to call it a break up because they never had a real relationship — she made his life miserable. He had the usual baby mama drama. She would call him to talk shit about nothing, bothering him with unnecessary stuff just to make things difficult. She played the game. He wouldn't be able to see the kids as long as he was with "that bitch" whoever "that bitch" was at the time. She would even go so far as to drop them off at his doorstep and not return for a couple of days.

She always told her friends that she couldn't believe that he made three children with her and that was it. She felt he should have given her so much more. She should be enjoying the fruits of his real estate business. She should be living in his house with him and Prince, his cinnamon and white Siberian Husky. She should be the one going on all the fun trips. Not them other females who had given him nothing, but maybe some good head. She gave him so much of herself in giving him their children. It wasn't until she saw her cousin acting the same way with the father of her children that she knew she had to stop acting so immature.

She eventually moved on with her life and now their relationship was better, but it still wasn't the best. They fussed and argued a lot, but she didn't play the games as much. Today he was picking them up to spend the weekend. She just prayed as she answered the phone that today was not going to be one of those days where he was running late or he overbooked his showings and would not be done in time.

"Hello."

"Yo." Marcus responded sounding irritated. "What took you so long to answer the fuckin' phone, Jeanette? This is the third time I've called this morning," he hissed.

"Um, what do you want? Are you on your way? The kids are up and Lil Mama is ready to go. Please don't tell me you got something else to do. You know I go to the picnic every year," she pleaded with him.

"Then maybe this could be the year you stay your ass at home. You can miss a year."

He was talking to her like she was his fourth child.

“Or maybe you could just be on your way,” she snapped back.

"I was just calling to see if I could pick them up a little earlier. My last appointment cancelled, and I'm done for the day," Marcus replied.

She perked up, "Yes! They're dressed and they've eaten."

She walked toward the living room just to make sure Maia hadn't fallen asleep or gotten her clothes dirty. She plopped down on her lush, chocolate Chenille Fabric love seat nestled between two soft taupe chairs. A flat-panel television was mounted on the wall above the mock fireplace, lined with family photos. A beautifully designed rug covered the polished, hardwood floor, and there was African American artwork by Henry Lee Wright, Annie Lee, and Toni Taylor that accented the room.

Marcus was still on the line making requests, and she really didn't have time for it.

"MJ."

"Yes, mom," he replied from the bathroom.

"Come here. Your dad wants to speak to you."

As soon as Maia heard her mom say her dad was on the phone, she jumped up and ran over to her mother, "Mommy. Let me talk to daddy," she said eyes beaming and full of excitement.

MJ got ready to take the phone from his mom when Maia yelled, "Wait, I want to talk to him first."

Sunshyne reached down and handed Maia the phone.

"Hi, daddy," she paused in between responses waiting for Marcus to say whatever he had to say on the other end.

"Yes... Yes... I look very pretty... Trinity combed it for me this morning before she left... She's in the room getting dressed... O-k-a-y," she finally said with long exaggeration. "Here's MJ, love you too. Here," she said to her big brother and shoved the phone in his hand.

"Hi, dad," MJ said sounding less excited than his little sister.

Again, you could tell his father was asking questions and giving directives with the pauses in between the responses from his son. After he ended the call, he handed the phone back to his mom and yelled out to Mariah, "Hurry up and get ready."

Sunshyne popped the back of his head and gave him a hard, silent stare. He knew exactly what that meant. He walked over and knocked on the girls' bedroom door.

"Daddy is on his way and said he doesn't feel like waiting."

MJ sauntered over to the bathroom and finished getting himself together.

Ten minutes later Marcus was outside blowing his horn. He must have just left the car wash because his Black Ford F-150 was sparkling under the sunlight. The kids kissed their mom goodbye and went running down the stairs. MJ was carrying his baby sister and Mariah had their bags.

"Have fun," Sunshyne yelled down the stairs after them.

~3~

As soon as they were in the car, she picked up and unlocked her cell and sent out a group text, "I hope y'all ready cuz it's time to get this show on the road."

By the time she was dressed and had gotten her chair, insect repellent, sunscreen and alcohol together, everyone but Renae had responded. She should have known. Renae always wanted to get a *special* invitation. She craved attention. After Sunshyne took her stuff down to her car, she ran back upstairs to make sure the house was locked up. Jumping in her car, she commanded her Bluetooth to "call Renae."

On her first attempt, she got no answer. She tried again and still no answer. She was about to pull up to Michelle's house, so she texted her to let her know she was outside. Even though she was a few minutes away, she knew she would still be waiting for her to come out when she pulled up in front.

Michelle lived in a six bedroom, two-story bungalow in one of the wealthier cul de sacs of Glenmont about ten minutes from Sunshyne, with her husband, and four children. They have two children together, Chloe and Bryson. Her husband, Carlton, has a son, Jason, from a previous relationship. Jason's mom fell in love with some dude when he was about four years old and decided she didn't want to be a mother anymore. No one could understand how she could just up and leave her child, or what man for that matter, would even want a woman who would do that. Jason has been with them for the past seven years. They also adopted Michelle's niece, Krystalia, more affectionately known as Kay Kay. Michelle's sister passed away a couple years after Kay Kay was born, and no one knew who the father was.

Carlton works as a partner for Kohler, Johnson, and Bingham law firm. Michelle is the owner of a very successful toy manufacturing company. She makes fun, educational products, and acts as a consultant to some of the most popular toy companies worldwide.

As Sunshyne waited for Michelle to come out, she reminisced on their friendship, their sisterhood. They have been friends since elementary school. Anyone who knew them understood that they were more than friends and knew to never say they weren't sisters. Their bond was unbreakable, and in the entire twenty-six years of knowing each other they had never had a falling out. They had been inseparable, except for the four years Michelle was away at Rhodes College. Still then, they were together whenever she was back home or when Sunshyne could make it down to Memphis.

Lost in her thoughts, she saw Michelle and Jason walking to the car with chairs and bags in tow. She got out the car to greet them and rearrange her things in the trunk to make room for Michelle's items.

"Hey Auntie Shyne," Jason said, as he gave her a hug.

"Hey, baby. How are you doing?"

"I'm good. You know me," he said as he waved to a girl across the street and gave his mom and aunt a sly smile.

"What you got planned for today?" she asked as she made her way back to the driver's seat.

"Waiting on my dad to get back, so we can hit the Cubs game. Everybody else went to Great America with Uncle Butchie and Auntie Tina. So, it's just me and him today."

"That sounds good. I hear they're doing well this year. Hope you enjoy yourself."

Jason kissed his mom and ran over to talk to the young lady still standing outside with her little lap dog. Sunshyne and Michelle got in the car and headed to pick up the rest of the crew.

Michelle's beautiful cocoa brown complexion required very little makeup, if any at all. Her dark black eyes glistened like a starry autumn night. Up until the beginning of this year she was at Kuts and Kurls religiously, every week, keeping her hair done. However, one of her new year's resolutions was to stay away from "the chemicals designed to make us associate ourselves more with *them*." She isn't a Sista Souljah of the world, but she does love to embrace her African-American culture and is not ashamed to speak whenever given the chance. Now she sports a short naturally curly fro.

"Girl, I didn't think I was going to make it out with you today. I got a call first thing this morning from the plant in Des Plaines telling me they couldn't find the order we sent to Fun Time Toys on Thursday. They called looking for it because it should've been there last night. After several calls to FedEx, Fun Time Toys, and back to Kevin at the plant, we were able to track everything down," Michelle told Sunshyne over the house music playing in the background.

"Are Damon and them already out there," Michelle asked.

"Yeah, they've been out there barbecuing since 5:30 a.m. this morning. He sent me a text about an hour ago that his boy had finally made it out there to help finish up the meat."

Michelle reached for the knob and turned the music down so she could hear herself talk. She wasn't really a big fan of house music but her girl was. Since she had been busy lately, they had a lot to catch up on.

"So, what's up with you? How are the kids? How are things going with you and Richard?" she asked.

"The kids are fine. Enjoying the summer and getting on my damn nerves as usual. Richard and I are good when we're together, but I'm starting to get tired of all his bullshit-ass promises. He keeps telling me he is leaving his wife, but so far, he ain't done nothing to move any closer to making it happen. It's been over three years now and things are still the same. I know you are tired of hearing this, but I don't know how much longer we're going to last," Sunshyne said on the verge of crying.

Michelle reached over and patted her leg, "Stop this bullshit. I didn't come out to hang with you for this mess right here. I'm sorry I even asked. We can talk about it later."

Sunshyne got herself together and turned the music back up and the two ladies rode in silence for the next few minutes. Michelle's phone rang. She looked at the caller ID and answered it hesitantly.

"Hello," she said with distinct irritation. "Hello," she said a little bit louder, waited for a response and hung up the phone.

"Girl, you still getting them prank calls?" Sunshyne asked.

"Yes, and I can't wait to find out who is behind the bullshit. They keep using one of them apps because every time I block one number they call back on another, but these hoes are cowards. Bitch, say what you got to say and be done with it," Michelle hissed angrily.

"We both know they ain't going to do that. That's why they're hiding behind them fake ass numbers," Sunshyne said right before her phone started ringing.

She looked at the caller ID on the dash and answered using the car's Bluetooth. As soon as she pressed the answer button on the steering wheel, barely saying hello, her sister's voice came blaring through the speakers.

"How long before you get here? I thought we were leaving at 11:00 a.m. You know... "

Before she could finish Michelle blurted out, "Hey, girl. What you in such a hurry for?"

"Hey, Michelle. I've been ready for almost an hour and you know I get real antsy when I gotta wait," Desiree said breathing fast.

"Girl, we will be there in about two minutes. By the time you take your medicine and come downstairs we'll be in front," Sunshyne said as her and Michelle laughed hysterically.

"You ain't funny," she said right before hanging up the phone.

As they pulled up, Desiree was coming out the lobby of her building. Sunshyne pulled into the circular driveway and Desiree got into the backseat behind Michelle. Before she shut the door, Sunshyne asked "has anyone talked to Renae?"

"I tried calling her a couple times and got no answer," Desiree replied.

They all knew she had a lot going on with her worthless ass man Paul. He cheated on her with every female he could. She even knew it, but she stayed with his sorry ass anyway. No one understood why.

Renae was a petite, light-skinned sista, who people always said looked like the actress, Lisa Ray. Underneath all the make-up, weave, and designer clothes she wore was a beautiful young lady who did not know her worth. From a young age, she allowed men to determine her place in life. They all wished she would understand her value sooner rather than later.

Five minutes later they were pulling up to her house, she was standing on the porch looking like she had just lost her best friend. She put the blunt out on her step because she knew she could not get into Sunshyne's car smoking. She came off the porch and walked up to the car looking defeated and miserable. She was dressed in a light gray Michael Kors romper with a pair of silver logo gladiator sandals that covered her thick calves, and the matching Kors Fulton Logo bag.

Sunshyne popped the trunk as Desiree got out to help Renae put her stuff in the trunk.

"What the hell happened? You look like Muffin died," Desiree said referring to her dog. She could sense the hurt of her friend.

"Girl, ain't nothing wrong with my dog, at least not the four-legged one that lives here, but can we please not talk about it right now," she said and got in behind Sunshyne.

No sooner than she sat in the backseat and they pulled off Sunshyne asked her the same question.

"Girl, what the hell happened? Why weren't you answering your phone? I been calling and texting you all morning."

This time Renae couldn't hold back the tears. They began steadily rolling down her cheeks. One after another. She could barely get the words out, "I don't have a phone."

"What happened to your phone?" Desiree questioned.

"It broke. Right after I tried to bust Paul's fucking head with it," the words escaping through her sobs. "He woke up texting on his phone this morning. He couldn't even have sex with me for trying to be on the damn phone. I knew he was on bullshit when I tried going down on him and he wouldn't let me. What man turns down good head? Anyway, I'm sitting on the edge of the bed, and his phone started vibrating. Moni Love flashed across the screen. That was it. I couldn't hold back anymore," fury was in her voice now.

She went on to tell them the story she got from Paul on how him and that chick met, when they met and how he said she don't mean shit to him, as he always did. She knew Paul loved her and would do anything in the world for her, but he just wasn't ready to settle down and be with only her. But how much more of this could she take? When was enough going to be enough for her to see that she deserved so much more than what Paul could give her?

"I walked away from him and was standing by my dresser. The next thing I knew, I had thrown my cell phone and busted him upside his monkey head," she said and let out a evil laugh. "He grabbed some of his things threw them in a bag and left without saying another word. I followed behind him talking shit as he went from room to room, but he just grabbed his stuff and slammed the door behind him. It took me a little while to pull myself together and eventually I started getting ready."

"So now, let's stop talkin' bout his no-good ass and focus on what awaits us in the park," Desiree said drying her friend's eyes. "You never know. You might find somebody out there to get Paul off your mind and out of your system once and for all," Desiree said.

Desiree rarely let a man stress her out. She went through men almost as fast as she went through toilet paper.

No matter what they said to her, everybody in the car knew Renae wasn't leaving him. No one spoke the obvious. Sunshyne turned up the radio and headed down Sheridan Road to Lake Shore Drive.

~4~

Desiree called her twin, Damon, when they got off at 57th Street, by the Museum of Science and Industry. They needed help unloading and carrying the stuff from the car, before Sunshyne and Michelle found a parking spot at their usual lot. Damon and one of his buddies were at the picnic entry way when they pulled up.

The ladies got out helping unload as Sunshyne gave her younger brother instructions for the food and drinks.

"Hey, Damon," Michelle and Sunshyne said in unison.

"Hey, Michelle," he said as he walked over and gave her a hug. "Long time no see."

"Yea, it's been a minute. What have you been up to?" she said pausing for a minute as she took chairs and a cooler out the trunk.

"Y'all are bout to be in this park together for hours. You can catch up when we get back," Sunshyne said as she walked back to the driver's seat.

"Whatever girl," Michelle sucked her teeth, getting back in the car. "Let's go,"

They pulled up to the parking lot and Kevin, the usual guy in charge of the lot, got out of his air-conditioned Cadillac and showed them to their parking spot. When they got out of the car Michelle gave her speech to him on how they come and park here every year and he needed to give them some type of discount. He came with his usual reply, "Just give me your number and you don't have to pay a penny."

"Now you know I can't do that," Michelle flashed him her three-carat, white gold, princess diamond wedding set.

"I'm just asking for your number. I don't want to start a family. Everybody needs friends," he came back at her really quick.

"I have enough friends for now, but if that ever changes I know when and where to catch you," she flashed him a smile and they headed towards the park.

Walking down 63rd Street, the normal vendors were selling oils, t-shirts and CDs. The music flowing from the park had Sunshyne feeling some-kind-of-way already. She could not wait to get inside the park and feel the full effect. When they got to the gate to pay their entry fee the lady waved them ahead to the next person. When they got to him he must've assumed they had already paid and let them walk right in the park. They hurried up and put their money back in their pockets and kept it moving.

They spotted Damon's tent from the picture he sent earlier that morning and made their way to him. They couldn't walk more than ten steps without some dude trying to grab their hands, ask for their name or ask Sunshyne if those were her real eyes. They didn't stop for any of them. They just wanted to get to their family, have a drink, and chill. They knew they were in the right place because they could hear Lauren's high-pitched voice. When she talked she put you in the mind of the character Squeaky from *The Color Purple*. She saw Michelle pick up her pace once she got a whiff of the bud pouring out of the tent.

As soon as they reached the tent, Michelle said her hellos to Lauren, Damon's wife, and Damon's friend, Billy, while grabbing the blunt out of his hand. She took a long deep toke,

"Man, I needed this right now after the morning I had."

Billy stood there, staring at Michelle in amazement at the fact that she basically took the blunt right from his lips. They listened to the music being mixed by Alan King flowing through the speakers surrounding the park and talking shit to each other for a while, until Desiree set up a table for spades. Lauren and Michelle played against Billy and Desiree in the first game. Sunshyne stayed outside the tent by the grill talking to her brother.

"Have you heard from Terrell?" she asked Damon.

"Yeah, he said he would be out here a little later. He had some errands to run. You know what that means."

Even though Terrell graduated Magna Cum Laude from University of Wisconsin-Madison and was the Valedictorian at his ceremony, he could not leave the streets alone. His cousins from his mother's side of the family never let him forget that he was still part of the "family". They were all hood rich and always told him he could have it too. It was hard for him to resist when all he saw when he was around them were Benzes, Vettes and Range Rovers. No one on his mother's side drove anything common. They lived in big houses away from "The Town" as it was referred to, but they always made it back to do what was "right."

They gave back to the community that they grew up in and helped to cripple, but no longer sold anything in or around the neighborhood. No, they had found bigger and better clientele. That's where Terrell came in to the picture. With his clean cut, nerdy-boy looking self, his almost $200k computer science education and his cyber security position with Boeing, he was the best one to pull off fitting in where they were marketing their product.

He was only months out of college, and would always tell his siblings whenever they came to his house that "I'm only doing this until this job starts paying me more", or try to convince them with, "As soon as I get these loans paid off I'm done." Whatever excuse he gave, they knew he was trying to convince himself of it more than them. They knew it wasn't as easy for him to just to walk away because it was too easy for him to fall into it. They continued to pray for him and let him be.

Damon was just about to send Terrell a text when he heard his younger brother making his way toward them. He had a couple of his buddies and his older cousin, Larry with him.

"What up, Bro," he said as they greeted each other with the unofficial black man hand shake and hug.

"You got here sooner than I thought you would. I'm glad you finally made it because your sister was about to start buggin'," Damon said to his baby brother. "You know how she gets."

"I told her I was coming last night when I talked to her. I knew better than to not make it out here. I'd never hear the end of it, especially if the rest of y'all made it out here," Terrell said.

"Y'all talkin' about me like I ain't even standing here," Sunshyne said.

Everyone but Sunshyne walked into the tent, "Y'all want something to drink or eat?"

His boy Darius replied, "Grab me a beer."

"Ninja, you better come over here and grab it yourself. My name ain't Benson!"

"Who the hell is Benson, Dude?" Darius said looking confused.

Everybody in the tent started cracking up. They couldn't believe he had never watched or even heard of the sitcom, *Benson*. Their laughs were immediately interrupted by the commotion outside of the tent. All they heard was Sunshyne's voice snapping out on somebody. When they rushed out they saw why she was going off the way she was. Monica Harrison, also now known as Mrs. Richard Franklin had approached her. This encounter was long overdue. Monica had never taken advantage of other opportunities to confront Sunshyne when it was just the two of them. Maybe it was because she really wasn't a confrontational person, but today she got courage from her girls that were with her.

Sunshyne, Richard and Monica were all childhood friends, but while Sunshyne and Richard remained friends throughout high school, Sunshyne's friendship with Monica went sour many years ago. Monica and Sunshyne's friendship was so close that they would spend the night at each other's home until the day Sunshyne felt Monica had betrayed her. Sunshyne was infatuated with Jerry Ferguson. She had told Monica how she felt about Jerry and thought her friend was going to help her hook up with him. Instead, they went to a house party in the neighborhood. When Sunshyne was ready to go she started looking for Monica. She checked the house looking for her, and when she finally opened one of the bedroom doors she saw Monica and Jerry damn near having sex. Their friendship waivered after that because Sunshyne felt she could not trust her anymore. For the last five years though, Sunshyne and Richard had become a lot more than friends. Sunshyne had been seen in public with Richard plenty of times, but never by his wife. It was only a matter of time before shit blew up.

"Bitch, what the fuck you wanna do? You and your cousins can try the bullshit if you want," Sunshyne said with venom behind every word. Desiree and Michelle were out the tent now.

"It's ok, trick. There's gonna be another day. I'm going to catch you, and I hope when I do you're with him, Monica yelled back as Damon and Terrell made it out of the tent.

Damon grabbed Sunshyne as she spat back at Monica.

"Do you know how dumb you just sounded? You wanna catch me with your husband? That is the dumbest shit a woman could say."

Damon snatched Sunshyne into the tent. Desiree and Michelle came in right behind them.

"Why are y'all letting her act a fool out there like that?" Damon barked.

Desiree got ready to explain, "The heffa shouldn't have..."

Damon cut her off and turned to Sunshyne, "Why are you even out there arguing with that chick? Ain't it enough you're sleeping with her husband?"

"If I am sleeping with her husband...," she said as she rolled her eyes, "...then she needs to take it up with him and not me."

Damon stood back and shook his head as he went to grab him a beer out the cooler. He sat down at the table where the group was just beginning a new game of Spades. He did not have time for his sister's mess today. She was the one who invited everyone out here, basically threatened everyone to come out so she could make sure she had a good time. Now she wanna start with the bullshit.

Sunshyne wanted to step back outside the tent. She turned to ask Michelle to come with her, when she saw Michelle and Terrell in the corner having a very private conversation. He was bent over whispering in her ear. She walked over to them with a suspicious look on her face.

"What y'all two doing all hush-hush in the corner?"

"Um, well...," Terrell started and Michelle jumped right in,

"Girl, I keep trying to tell him that as soon as I can work out a position I will get him in at my company. I had to let him know that just because I am the owner doesn't mean I can just go making up positions. We still have a budget to adhere to, and plus he should have left his company when I first tried to get him over here."

"Awe, sis. Don't be like that. I just didn't think...," Terrell started to say and then Michelle interrupted,

"I know. You didn't think I was gonna get my company jumping' like I have. As soon as I can I will get you a position on the winning team."

Sunshyne was glad that her longtime friend was willing to help her little brother, but she had to wonder if that is what they were really discussing in the corner by themselves. She let them know she wasn't buying their story, but left it alone. Now she just wanted to do what she came out here for... walk around and see the sights while she enjoyed the music. She grabbed Michelle and headed out the tent to join Desiree and Renae. Terrell went over to the cooler, grabbed him a beer, and headed over to the rest of fellas.

~5~

Richard told Sunshyne over and over again that they would be able to live the life that they both wanted. He just had to make sure his daughter was at a point where she could handle it. Sometimes it looked crazy that Sunshyne continued to wait on him, but she did. It isn't easy to tell the heart who to love. It loves who it wants.

Sunshyne was mad as hell, and if Richard was there she would be ready to slap the taste out of his mouth. It didn't matter that she allowed him to do what he did. Before she had the chance to answer any of their questions, her phone started buzzing. It was Richard. She knew for sure what he was texting her about the incident that just went down.

She opened up the text. "Can you talk right now? Monica just called me, and I wanted to make sure you were alright," the text read.

Sunshyne sent back a simple, "I'm good."

She didn't feel like being bothered with him at the moment. Richard sent several more texts that went unanswered.

She finally responded, "I'll call you later."

She turned her phone off and got into the music she came out there for. She wanted to move around and see who she could see as she did every year, but everybody there with her forbid her to move from the tent area. They knew for certain that if she ran into Monica again things wouldn't go the way they did earlier. So she sat outside the tent kicking it with her girls.

This was not how she planned to spend the day, but just being at the picnic with her family and friends was enough for her, so she chilled. The afternoon was bright and sunny. The blue sky was nearly cloudless allowing the sun to beam down on the park. The soft, gentle breeze flowing through the air caused the leaves to flutter slightly. This was the type of weather Sunshyne loved.

After a couple of hours of eating, drinking, and chilling with her family, Sunshyne decided it was time to move around. She didn't care what any of them had to say about it at that point. She poured herself a cup of Tito's with cranberry and pineapple juice and told everyone she would be back. Of course, her brothers had a lot to say about the idea, but couldn't really stop her. She was a grown woman and not their child. All the ladies, except for Lauren, grabbed a cup of alcohol and rolled with Sunshyne. They were definitely not letting her go out into the park alone.

The four of them strolled through the park stopping every now and then to talk to friends they hadn't seen in a while. Finally, they made their way to the front of the picnic to listen to music and enjoy the atmosphere. Terry Hunter had made it to the stage and Sunshyne got lost in his old school house mix. She hated that she missed Andre Hatchett, but Terry kept her body moving.

They stayed near the stage listening to his mix until the sun started setting and then decided to head back to their tent. Walking back, Michelle noticed Paul standing between two tents talking to Monica and nudged Desiree. Two other people had stood in front of Monica and Paul but had just walked away as the ladies were passing not more than twenty feet away. Desiree was just arguing with their sister about messing with her husband. From the looks of things these two were really close, and her husband was the least of her thoughts. They knew for sure they were more than just friends when Paul reached down and kissed Monica in the mouth.

Desiree got ready to grab Renae so she could turn to see her no-good-ass boyfriend kissing and talking to Monica, but Michelle stopped her and mouthed, "Not now." Michelle knew it would only hurt Renae more and wanted to wait until a time when they knew for sure she was ready to be done with Paul. Not to mention if Sunshyne saw her over there with Renae's man things would definitely go up again.

Michelle was not the confrontational type, unless it was absolutely necessary. Neither of them said anything at the time, but Desiree hurried up and pulled her Galaxy out in time to snap a picture of the end of their embrace. There would be no denying what she saw when she thought it the right time to tell her friend.

When they got back to the tent, they each fixed themselves another plate and got some more to drink. Desiree decided she would revisit the subject of Paul with her best friend.

"Girl, so have you thought anymore about what you're gonna do about Paul's ass?" she said getting straight to the point.

You could see a distressed look come across Renae's face. Before she had the opportunity to respond Desiree added, "You know you need to leave him alone. Dude ain't nothing but trouble. When will you get enough of him tippin out on you? I understood you wanting to make things work the first time when he confessed his love to you and promised it would never happen again. Six children later by four different women, and who knows how many there have been who didn't get pregnant or decided not to have his baby is too much. You deserve so much better than what his triflin ass is giving you. You have stood by him through all this and he just keeps taking advantage of your love," Desiree said and she wouldn't let up.

Tears were rolling down Renae's face. She constantly prayed about her situation. In her quiet time talking to God, she always got the same answer from Him. She just couldn't get the words out. Deep down she knew she should leave Paul's sorry, cheating ass alone, but she loved him. Every time she thought about having the conversation with him to let him know they couldn't be together anymore it felt like someone was crushing her heart, like she was having trouble breathing. She knew she didn't have the strength to do what needed to be done, and that's when she prayed to God to do what she could not do for herself.

"Don't you think I know that? I know I shouldn't have to cry myself to sleep at night. Sometimes I do feel like I am the dumbest chick in the world. I love him though, Desiree, but what do you know about loving somebody when you go from one man to the next depending on who is gonna provide the most?" Renae said through her tears.

She knew she shouldn't have said those last words to her friend because Desiree was only looking out for her. She just couldn't take her riding her like that. You could tell by the look on Desiree's face, she had hit a nerve.

"What is that supposed to mean?" Desiree spit right back at her.

"I didn't mean that, Dee. I know you mean well, but sometimes you go too hard. If you must know I plan on telling him that it's over tonight," Renae said in an apologetic voice.

Michelle jumped in before the conversation went where none of them wanted it to go.

"Dee, everybody can't be as cold hearted as you are when it comes to men. We all know you're the player of the crew."

"Yeah, yeah. I can't help it that I want to be free to be me and do what I wanna do," she said trying to convince herself more than anyone else sitting around the table.

Sunshyne got up from the table and started packing up the remaining food.

"Let's start getting everything ready to go. It doesn't look like anybody else is going to eat, and I want to get out of here as soon as possible. Plus, I'm tired of hearing Dee beat up on Renae. We all have our own stuff to deal with, and when she is ready she will handle it. Nothing we say is going to change that."

The ladies got up and helped pack the food up. Desiree went over and hugged her friend and whispered something in her ear. A faint smile danced across Renae's lips. Damon stuck his head in the tent.

"Let Terrell and Billy know when you're done getting everything packed. They'll start taking down the tent while me and Lauren go and get the car." Damon instructed.

Once everything was ready to go, Sunshyne powered her phone back on. She immediately saw twelve text notifications and a few voicemails pop up on the screen. She had a few text messages from Marcus. The rest were from Richard. She felt bad about ignoring him, but she did let him know she was okay. If he was really worried, he would have made it out there to check on her. She wanted to finish enjoying the evening and whatever happened that night and resigned to call him back later.

Everyone said their goodbyes, after Damon's truck was loaded. Terrell invited them all out to *The Underground Bar*, a small club on the north end of the loop. It was always packed on a Saturday night. Hell, it was crowded on any night of the week, but since his boy owned the place there would be no problem with them getting in despite the crowd.

The kids were spending the night with Marcus tonight so Sunshyne was down. Michelle had to check with Carlton. She didn't see it being a problem, since she sent a text earlier to see if the younger children could spend the night at his sister's house tonight. When she called, she assured him she wouldn't be out too late because she wanted to make 8:00 a.m. service.

Renae wasn't feeling up to it, but Desiree refused to let her go in the house tonight sad and depressed about Paul. He was going to be out enjoying himself, so, why shouldn't she? Damon said him and Lauren were tired. They had been up since the crack of dawn getting everything ready for the picnic. They were going to pick up the kids and call it a night.

After leaving the park, the ladies wanted to freshen up before heading to the club. Sunshyne took each of them by their houses to grab what they needed and they went back to her house go get ready. It was like they were in their twenties all over again.

Everyone but Renae was in a partying mood. You could see it all over her face. She was stressing about something and her thoughts were a million miles away.

"Girl, snap out the funk," Desiree said as she nudged her with her elbow. "I know you're having a bad day, but maybe you'll find somebody tonight to turn it all around for you and take your mind off him."

"I'm not looking for anybody right now. I really just want to be home in bed," Renae said, sounding drained.

"I'm not telling you to choose your husband out of the crowd, but I'm sure there will be some fine ass brothas in there to help lift your spirits and say the right thing to get your beautiful smile back."

~6~

When they arrived, the club was jumping. The line to get in was down the block. When the ladies walked up, the security recognized Sunshyne and Desiree instantly, so he ushered them in the door with no hesitation. The crowd inside stretched from one wall to the next. The DJ was spinning the best of 90s rap. The music was loud and all you could hear was the Notorious B.I.G.'s voice blaring, "I got more mack than Craig and in the bed. Believe me sweetie I got enough to feed the needy."

As they made their way to the bar dancing, sweaty bodies rubbed against them. Long weaves swung widely about, brushing up against them, and at times, even slapping them in the face. Halfway across the dance floor Renae spotted Paul in the corner with his boys. She didn't say a word to anyone hoping they wouldn't notice him. He had his back to her so he hadn't seen her.

They made it to the bar and ordered their drinks. Sunshyne ordered Tito's with pineapple and cranberry juice, and a Pepsi for Michelle. Michelle could probably smoke Snoop under the table, but never had a drop of liquor. She had her mother to thank for that.

Desiree and Renae both ordered Hennessey with a splash of coke. That was all they ever drank. They liked their liquor like they liked their men, dark and strong. Desiree suggested they find Terrell. She was sure he would be in the private area at the back of the club. Renae couldn't wait to get back there. She hoped she wouldn't have to be bothered with Paul back there. It was enough that she was still letting him occupy her mind, but she didn't want to have to deal with it all, at least not tonight. She decided she was going to enjoy herself and wasn't going to let him spoil any more of her day no matter what.

They walked up to the VIP area.

"Hey, Desiree. Hey, Nette," a tall brotha said at the entrance.

It was Ruben Bradshaw. He had grown up on the same block with them, and was the only one who grew up with them that didn't call Jeanette, Sunshyne. Ruben was tall like a pro basketball forward with broad shoulders like a lineman on the Chicago Bears. His skin was dark, rich, and smooth like melted Hershey's chocolate. He put you in the mind of Michael Clarke Duncan. He and Desiree had a relationship at one time, if that's what you want to call it. It was more like they slept together a couple times and realized they were better off as friends.

"Hey, Ruben," they both said in unison.

"How did y'all get Michelle and Renae out the house tonight? I didn't think they knew their way around these parts anymore," he said as he reached down and gave the ladies a hug.

"You know Chelle has a husband and kids at home, but we wouldn't let her go in tonight, and Renae needed to come out for a little cheering up," Desiree replied.

"Maybe I'll be able to help out with that." He looked at Renae and winked his eye.

The ladies stepped into the room and saw Terrell with the same fellas he had with him at the picnic. The ladies made their way over to where they were sitting.

"I didn't think y'all were gonna make it."

"Well here we are. So, let's get this party started," Desiree said as she went to pour herself a drink.

Sunshyne shook her head.

"Always the life of the party," she said jokingly and found her a seat on the brown leather sofa in their area.

They were all dancing and drinking for about an hour or so. Sunshyne was dancing with Terrell's oldest cousin, Larry. Michelle was on the couch with some other ladies, and Desiree was up dancing with some guy she had been talking to all night. Ruben had just poured Renae a drink, and they were talking when Paul and his boys walked up to the entrance. One of the other ladies in VIP that was celebrating her birthday had invited them to join their party.

Desiree was the first to notice Paul. Then Michelle looked up and saw him walking in even though the room was kinda dark. He saw Desiree but didn't notice Renae standing behind Ruben.

"Hey, Desiree," he said walking in.

"What's up, Paul." As soon as Renae heard his voice she felt her stomach knot up. He scanned the room some more and finally met eyes with Renae. He started walking over towards her when Desiree grabbed his arm.

"Come on. Don't start that in here."

"Start what?" he said. "I just want to talk to my girl." His words were slurring, "Hey, baby. What's up?"

She didn't say anything. Neither did Ruben for the moment.

"Come here. Let's talk for a minute."

He tried to take her hand and bring her with him. She snatched her hand away. When he tried to grab her hand again and she backed away, Ruben stepped in.

"Man, homie, this is none of your business. You're gonna wanna back up and let me handle this with my woman."

"Dude, it's clear she doesn't want to go with you."

Larry and one of Terrell's boys saw things getting a little intense between the two men and stood up to see where things were headed. Paul turned his attention back to Renae.

"You not gonna come out here so we can talk?"

"No. You didn't think about me all day. What happened to the bitch Monica? Oh, she went home to be with her husband?" she said, waiting for him to answer.

His eyes got big. Sunshyne focused her attention on their conversation. Michelle looked over at Desiree with a look of shock. She wondered had she shown her the picture already.

"Guess you didn't see me when I was walking through the park earlier. Yeah, I seen y'all over at Gary's tent. Of course, your punk ass didn't see me, you were too busy all in her face," she said with a look of disgust.

Paul couldn't say anything. He had not seen them come through the park, and he wasn't sure what all she had seen.

"Come on out here so we can talk," he was frustrated and tried to grab her hand again.

"Get your hands off me. I'm not going anywhere with you, and I'm done talking. Now get the fuck out my face."

The words came out so forceful they made Paul take a step back. He got ready to snatch her, but instead, Ruben knocked him off his feet with one swift blow. Paul's boys jumped up and so did Terrell and his boys. That was when shit got real. Bottles were flying, punches were being thrown and a couple of the other bouncers came in and snatched Paul and his crew up. On his way out he barked in her face,

"We ain't done," and then pointed at Ruben, "This ain't the last time we gonna see each other with partna'." Ruben didn't respond. He just laughed and turned his focus back to the room.

Desiree, Sunshyne, and Michelle were consoling Renae. She was shaking. She couldn't believe Paul acted like that, but then again, she had seen him cut up worse.

"Girl, are you ok?" Desiree asked rubbing her arm gently.

"I'm good," she told her, but clearly, she wasn't.

"Well, I don't want you going home tonight. You're going to stay with me," Desiree told her almost pleading. "He's been drinking and definitely isn't thinking straight." She didn't want her friend to go home to face any repercussions.

Ruben walked up to make sure everyone was ok. "Are you ladies alright?"

"We're fine. How's your hand?" Sunshyne asked. “You almost looked as good as Tyson.” She joked.

"Awe, this ain't nothing. His face was soft so it didn't hurt for real," he said with a little laugh behind it. "Are you ok, sweetheart?"

"Yes, I'm good," Renae said with a somber smile. "I'm just ready to get out of here."

Terrell came over and offered to walk the ladies out to their car.

"That would be great," Renae hurried up and responded.

Ruben looked dejected. He wanted to be the one to see her home that night. Renae noticed the look on his face. She took him to the side.

"I think it would be best for everyone if Terrell walked us out. Paul ain't gonna do nothing to her brother. I'm not saying you can't handle yourself, but there has been enough excitement for one night."

"No problem. I don't want to cause you anymore problems. I just hope...",

Before he could finish his sentence, she grabbed his iPhone out the front pocket of his shirt, pressed the button to unlock it and punched her number in his phone. She was glad he didn't have a code on the phone. That would have messed it all up.

"I'll let you save it under whatever name you choose. Just make sure you use it," she reached up to kiss him on the cheek and left with her friends.

Ruben walked them through the club so they could get out quickly. When Renae got to the door, she turned around and waved to him. He gave her a nod and turned to go back to make sure everything was straight inside.

~7~

They were silent until they got off Lake Shore Drive. No one wanted to bring up the subject until Renae was ready to talk about it. They weren't sure what they were more shocked about. The fact that Paul tried to hit her in public the fact that he went out with one punch or that Renae finally stood up to him. Maybe it was her drink that gave her the courage or that she had Ruben standing there with her. Whatever it was, Desiree was definitely proud of her friend and couldn't hold back anymore.

"I'm so proud of the way you handled yourself tonight. I couldn't believe it when you busted him out like that. Neither could he for that matter. Did you see the look on his face? And when were you going to say something about him and old girl at the park?" she got it all out as she shattered the thick silence in the car.

"When were you going to tell me?" Renae said as she turned to look at Desiree.

In her mind she was replaying the scene in her head over and over again.

"I wanted to tell you, but we didn't think it was the right time," she said feeling as if she had betrayed her best friend. "I wanted to wait until the right time. I did get a picture of them though so he couldn't deny it when you did eventually bring it back to him," she said trying to correct the situation.

"I know it. I saw everything. I saw Michelle nudge you, saw her grab you before you could tell me and saw when you grabbed your phone. So I knew you was on something."

Renae was starting to sound less fragile in her tone. She even let out a chuckle behind what she said.

"I knew you had my back and it would only be a matter of time before you brought it to me. In a way I'm glad you didn't say anything. Then I would have been forced to say something to him and don't think I would have had the courage," Renae sadly admitted.

Sunshyne interrupted the conversation, "I can't believe y'all seen that heffa with him and didn't say nothing."

Michelle looked at her like she was crazy. She couldn't believe she was being that insensitive right now.

Desiree checked her really quick, "Is that all you can think about right now? Tonight is not about you and your wife-in-law. What were you gonna do anyway, run up and start a fight with her about *her* husband? Don't go looking for shit if you don't have to. Plus, we didn't follow your ass out to that picnic to watch you make a fool of yourself all day."

She hated she had to be so harsh with her big sister, but she really needed to hear it. It was one thing for somebody to run up on you, but why put yourself in a situation unnecessarily.

"First of all, I don't have a wife in-law. And no, I wouldn't have fought her about him. I'm gonna beat her ass about fronting me like she did," she responded with a half-ass excuse.

"I would've fronted you too if I heard you were sleeping with my man, let alone my husband. Just leave well enough alone. If she come in your face again then get at her ass, but until then leave it alone," Desiree said sounding as if she was the oldest.

Michelle simply chimed in, "Exactly."

Instead of arguing, Sunshyne surrendered, "Maybe y'all are right. It does sound stupid of me to be running up on her, but you can best believe if the bitch ever run up in my face again, I'll molly whop her ass."

Renae broke from her thoughts, "Do you ever feel guilty knowing that you are breaking up someone's home, someone's family? You're sleeping with somebody else's husband. After all the hurt you saw your mother go through when she found out about Terrell, how can you do that to another woman? I just don't get why you feel the need to hurt another woman to be happy."

Sunshyne didn't respond.

"I'm not trying to make you feel bad, but I know the hurt first hand when you've given your all to a man, and he is giving himself to someone else. But that bitch Monica ain't no better, cause she is fucking with my man. You may say that I'm weak for allowing him to do what he does, but you can't tell the heart who to love. It just does," she said sounding like a wounded bird.

Before Sunshyne had the chance to respond, Renae turned to her best friend,

"I AM tired of his bullshit!" It sounded as if she had an epiphany, like the light bulb went off in her head. "Come tomorrow his shit will be packed up and on the front porch. I'm glad you all were there today. I think it was the fact that I had all of you around that gave me the strength I needed to do what I should have done a long time ago. Dee, I really don't want to be there if he comes home, so I will come stay with you for the night."

Desiree celebrated in her head but didn't say it aloud to Renae. She was definitely glad her friend was taking the first step, one she had never taken before. She just hoped she stood her ground for good.

"You know I got your back whatever you want to do," Desiree said with excitement in her voice.

"We all got your back," Michelle chimed in.

Sunshyne sat there in silence considering the words Renae had just said to her. She knew what she was doing was wrong, but what was she gonna do. She didn't want to be that woman, but she had fallen in love with Monica's husband and couldn't leave him alone. At least that's what she told herself. Eventually Richard would have to live up to his word or she would have to give herself what she knew she deserved.

They swung by Renae's house so she could run in to get clothes, and then drove to Desiree's place. When she pulled up to Desiree's building, her and Renae walked to the back of the car and grabbed their stuff out the trunk. Sunshyne watched as Desiree and Renae walked to the door to make sure they got in safe.

Before they went inside, she called out to Renae.

"Hey, Renae, hold up a second."

Renae turned around and met her back down the walkway. Sunshyne grabbed her and gave her a hug.

"I just want you to know I don't have any hard feelings about what you said tonight. It's something I needed to hear a long time ago. I'm glad that one of us has the strength to move on and truly be happy. No matter what happens, I got your back too. I love you, girl."

Renae hugged her back.

"I love you too, Nette."

Renae's phone had vibrated a couple of times while she was in the car and was vibrating again. She took it out her purse and saw a text from an unfamiliar number. She opened it and a huge smile illuminated her face after she read the text. It was Ruben making sure she made it home safely.

"Is that his sorry ass?" Sunshyne asked.

"Naw. It's Ruben making sure everything is okay," she said still grinning.

"Well, you better let him know you're alright. He seems to be smitten already, and he is very protective. He will keep trying until he reaches you," Sunshyne said as she turned around to walk back to the car.

She drove off as Renae walked back to the building almost doing a two-step. She got in the elevator with Desiree and texted Ruben back as they went upstairs.

~8~

After driving for a few minutes, Michelle said "I need to get something to eat before I go in the house."

"What about IHOP?"

"No, I want something quick and easy. I don't want to stay out any longer, and I don't want to wait a long time for a to-go order."

She knew this time of night IHOP on Howard St. would be packed. Everybody and their mama went there on their way home from clubbing. They decided to drive out to Taco Burrito King instead and grab a couple tacos. They both just needed something on their stomach to hold them until morning. When they arrived, there was no line and they placed their orders quickly. Michelle ordered two chicken tacos. Sunshyne ordered four regular tacos and a side of rice.

"Damn, girl. You hungry ain't you?" Michelle said sarcastically.

Sunshyne didn't answer her.

"You know Renae was right."

There, she said it. She knew Michelle wanted to say it, but she said it first.

"Right about what?" Her best friend asked looking puzzled.

"Right about me and Richard. I think about it all the time. I don't know how or why I let myself get so deep into this situation. I should've never messed with him. She was right. I know first-hand how it hurts and tears a family apart. Mommy almost left my dad behind his infidelity, but I couldn't stop myself from falling down that rabbit hole. I love him, Chelle and can't seem to leave him alone. Honestly, I don't really know if I want to, and to top it off I found out the other morning that I'm pregnant."

Sunshyne sat down at a table, and Michelle sat across from her. She didn't know what to say, and it was written all over her face.

She finally asked, "Does he know?"

"No, I haven't told him because I am not sure what I'm going to do," she said.

Michelle felt bad for her friend, but she really didn't know what to say. They had several conversations about her relationship before, so now was not the time to beat her up about it. She could see that Sunshyne felt bad as it was.

"Look. I don't know what to tell you now that I haven't told you before, but you know whatever decision you make I got you. Remember, this is not all about Richard. This is your baby too, and you don't need him to have it. You're going to have to stop drinking until you make up your mind about what it is you are going to do," Michelle said as the man behind the counter told them their food was ready.

Michelle started eating her tacos as soon as she got in the car and closed her door. She wanted to be done eating when they got to her house so she could go in and go straight to bed. She took a bite out of one of them and stopped chewing, "When are you going to tell your family? Have you at least told Desiree?"

"No. You're the only person I've told so don't open your mouth to anyone. I was going to tell Desiree, but I wanted to be sure about what I'm going to do before I did. I had to tell someone, and that someone is you," Sunshyne replied.

They pulled up in front of Michelle's house.

"Alright, Chica. I won't say a word, promise. I'm going to leave my stuff in your trunk. I don't feel like carrying it all in the house now," she said as she was getting out of the car.

"No problem. I'm going to try to make it to eight o'clock service, but I'm not gonna make any promises.

Sunshyne drove home thinking about all that had transpired over the last couple of days. She was glad she finally shared her pregnancy news with Michelle. It was a relief to get it off her chest. The more she thought about her situation, the more the tears started rolling down her face. She couldn't believe she had gotten this deep, but she knew things were going to have to change.

She had known it for a long time, but she had never been able to let him go. He had a hold on her heart that was indescribable. She knew he loved her. That was undeniable, but he did not love her the way she needed to be loved. Still, she loved him with all her heart, one minute she was willing to wait on him and live together happily ever after. Then the next she was ready to leave him and move on with her life. No matter what her thoughts were on any given day, her heart ached thinking about whichever decision floated in her head.

She couldn't imagine living her life without Richard in it to share the precious moments. At the same time, she knew she deserved better and it was only a matter of time before their love affair would come to an end. Now her biggest dilemma was if she would keep the baby and whether or not she would tell Richard. She wanted him but didn't want his reasoning for being with her to be because of their child. She wanted it to be because he had finally chosen her and wanted to spend the rest of his life being her knight in shining armor.

The day had been draining, so for now she would go home and not worry about any of it. She had checked her phone. Richard had called and texted her several times wondering where she was, if she was ok, and letting her know he was thinking about her. She also had a missed call and text from Desiree making sure she made it home. She sent her sister a text letting her know she had just dropped Michelle off and was turning onto her block now.

She went upstairs, hopped in the shower, and got straight in the bed. She couldn't fall asleep, so she laid there and had a conversation with God. This time her prayer was different. This time she asked Him to give her the strength to do what He has commanded her to do so many times in their talks, and if she could not she prayed and asked him to fix the situation Himself. She read her Bible for a little while and knew she wasn't going to make eight o'clock service. She set her alarm to make sure she made the eleven o'clock service. After setting the alarm she laid there thinking until sleep finally came.

~9~

Renae was out the bed early the next morning. She tossed and turned throughout the night worrying herself over Paul obsessing about his cheating and all that happened over the course of the previous day. She knew when others looked at her they couldn't believe how dumb she was for staying with this man. A man that claimed to love her, but who constantly brought her heartache and pain. She saw her staying with him as being loyal. She saw it as not giving up and fighting for what she wanted, but love wasn't supposed to hurt the way their love had crushed her.

Today she had no more fight in her. Yes, she knew she should've left him a long time ago, but she wanted what she wanted and there was no telling her anything else. She knew that they were meant to be. With all they had overcome in their relationship, she couldn't understand why he couldn't, or wouldn't, fully commit to her. She couldn't understand what made him continue to do the shit he does. He would do anything he could for her. She could depend on him for financial support, and if she needed to talk about anything with him, she could. He was her best friend. Only when it came to giving her his heart, he could only offer her a piece of his love. He was not able to give her his all.

She had been willing to do whatever was necessary, go through anything to keep him in her life. Now it was sucking the energy from her being. She woke up every morning thinking about his unfaithfulness and went to sleep at night, crying about all that he had put her through. Some days she even had his foolishness for lunch. Last night she decided she was done with it all.

She said this several times before and always fell right back into their lopsided relationship, but she felt something different this time. Her chest did not feel like it was about to explode. Her heart did not feel like someone was choking the life out of it. It felt like a ton of bricks had been lifted off her back. She realized she was worth more than being constantly hurt by someone, and now it was time for her to move on to discover what was yet to come.

Before she rolled out of bed she asked God to give her the strength to make it through this time.

"Thank you for waking me up this morning, Lord. Thank you for keeping me sane when I was doing things to make my life crazy. I ask you to give me the strength I need to make it through this day. Even though I have always leaned on you for direction I have rarely gone where you told me to go. Now is the time for me to follow you wherever you take me. Show me where that is and I will go. Also, watch over Jeanette. Open her eyes to show her that she has everything inside of her so that she doesn't have to look for it in a married man. One last thing I ask of you this morning is to allow everything to go smoothly when we are at the house today. I ask all this in your son's name. Amen"

That afternoon when she knew Paul would be at work, she was going to get her dad and brother to change the locks on the front door. She would pack up all his belongings and let him know they would be in the garage for him to pick up. There would be no need for him to have to come back into the house at all. She understood that it was *their* home, but he blew that when he decided to share their relationship with whoever the hell he chose.

She decided that this was the one thing she wouldn't let him take from her. He had taken her dignity and abused every bit of it, but now she was ready to take it back. She did not like to get her family involved in her relationship issues because she knew, as well as they did, that a couple days later she would be right back with him. They would come if she called, but she didn't want to be the girl who cried wolf. Any other time her and Paul had gone through their antics she dealt with it herself. However, this time she needed her family.

Her mom passed away in 2011 from breast cancer. All she had was her dad and brother. She grabbed her phone off the night stand and saw several texts from Paul. She ignored them and texted her brother to tell him she needed him to be around when she got out of church. It was the summer time so she knew he might have something planned with his wife and kids. She didn't need to prepare her dad because she knew after his weekly breakfast with his two Marine buddies he would be sitting on the couch watching whatever sports team was on television. She would stop by after church and let him and her brother know what was happening.

Renae hopped out of the bed in Desiree's extra bedroom, used the adjacent washroom, and brushed her teeth. She started the shower and went to knock on Desiree's bedroom door to make sure she was up for church. Renae could hear Desiree talking. Desiree's voice grew louder as if she was arguing with someone. As Renae got closer to the room she could finally make out what Desiree was saying. It sounded like she was arguing with herself.

Renae pushed the door open gently and saw that Desiree was still asleep. She realized Desiree was having a bad dream. She was chastising herself for one of the many unhealthy relationships she had been in. She was reminding herself that her life was the way it was because she allowed things to happen, nobody forced her to do anything. Not only was she reprimanding herself for the relationship she blamed it all on, she went on to get on herself about most of her adult life.

Renae knew she should've left back out of the room, but she couldn't. She was a little shocked to hear her friend talking like that because she always had an IDGAF attitude about everything she did. As she stared in awe at her friend sleep talking, Desiree started crying. She couldn't continue to watch her friend suffer like that, even it was a dream. She finally entered the room and shook Desiree to wake her out of the torment she was going through.

Desiree woke up shaking and sweaty. She looked at Renae with shame in her eyes, but the look on Renae's face assured her not to worry about a thing. She didn't expect her to explain anything right now. Renae sat on the bed and hugged Desiree while she cried on her shoulder.

"You don't have to talk about it now, but whenever you're ready I am right here for you," Renae said as she listened to her breakdown and cry uncontrollably.

"I can't do this anymore. I need to get my life together. I'm getting too old to keep living the way I am," Desiree used the moment to pour her heart out.

"How about you get up, get dressed, and let's go to church. I was just about to get in the shower before I came to wake you. We can go get breakfast and make the second service," Renae said.

Desiree really didn't go to church, but today she felt she needed to.

"Okay. I'll get my clothes together and start making us some breakfast instead while you're in the shower."

Renae gave her friend one last firm hug and headed to the shower.

Desiree sat there for a minute thinking about the way her life was going and decided to cry just a little bit more.

~10~

By the time Sunshyne made it to church, she could hear the worship team singing as soon as she got out of her car. They were singing, Ricky Dillard & New G's *Amazing*, and it was flowing down the street loud and clear. She put an extra step in her walk so she could get in the church as fast as she could. It already sounded like *New Light* was going to have an awesome service. She had been attending *New Light Baptist Church* for almost fifteen years. Kevin Collins had taken over the church almost ten years ago after his father passed. The church had an excellent mix of members. Ever since the junior Collins had taken over leadership, the church grew rapidly.

As soon as she stepped through the door she felt a chill come over her body. Once the worship team finished singing, the choir sang *I Still Have Joy.* Then turned around and sang *For Every Mountain.* At the start of that last song the sanctuary was filled with the spirit. You could tell Sunshyne was carrying a heavy load. Hearing, *For Every Mountain* always put her in a mood, but today was especially rough for her. She had so much going through her mind.

This morning she was struggling with a lot. Yesterday had put a lot on mind. She laid in bed earlier thinking about the way she performed yesterday, the things Renae said to her, and the baby she was carrying in her belly. She was in shouting mode by the time Pastor Collins took the podium.

Pastor took the podium and told everyone to go with him to Psalm 30 verses four and five. The ushers took the floor.

"The song says late in the midnight hour when all hope is gone you can call on the Lord and He will give you joy. How many of you know the God who will comfort you and give you the joy no one else can?" Pastor Collins shouted from the pulpit.

The congregation responded with several "amens" and "preach Reverend".

"That's four of you. Can I get six? I'm sure there are more of you that know the joy of Jesus," he announced.

There were a few more “amens” while he read the scripture.

"Psalm 30 verse 4 says 'Sing praises to the Lord, you who belong to him; praise his holy name.' David continues in verse 5, 'His anger lasts only a moment, but his kindness lasts for a lifetime. Crying may last for a night, but joy comes in the morning.' Today I'm going to speak on the subject, "What Should We Do with Our Tears."

There were no seats in the back of the church where Renae usually sat when she and Desiree got to the service. So today they sat closer to the front next to Sister Johnson. Renae really enjoyed Sister Johnson. She was a traditional church lady, but she wasn't like the rest of the mothers in the church that turned their noses up at every little thing the younger generation did "wrong" according to their standards.

She had a funny way of handling things, and she was never judgmental when talking to them. If she felt a young lady dressed inappropriately for service she would look at her with a scornful look, but the young lady would never see it. By the time she reached her to talk about it, she would have the most loving, concerned tone.

Renae thought back to the first time she had a conversation with Sister Johnson. It was her third visit to *New Light*, and she wore a short skirt with a blouse and sweater. During offering, Sister Johnson grabbed her by the hand as she walked back to her seat.

"Hey, Baby. I've seen you at the church a couple times and seems like you are enjoying the service. I notice every time you come your skirt seems to get shorter and shorter. I used to wear my little minis back in the day as well until one of the elders in the church pulled me to the side and whispered something in my ear. Now I can understand if this is all you got, but by the way you dress it looks like you got some pretty sharp clothing in your closet. So before Sista Morton gets off her high horse to come down and say something to you, maybe you wanna pull out your longer skirts on Sunday," she said and chuckled to herself.

Renae laughed a little herself. "Yes ma'am." The next time you see me my skirt will be the proper length," she said looking the funny old lady in her eyes.

As she turned to walk away Sister Johnson grabbed her hand a little tighter and said, "And welcome to *New Light*. Hope to see you back next Sunday."

Renae walked back to her seat, and as she sat down she noticed Sister Morton eyeing her. She was glad Sister Johnson got to her first.

Pastor Collins was still preaching when Sunshyne came out of the washroom.

"According to the text, weeping is not a permanent condition. It's an uninvited guest. In biblical times, it was the custom of the elders to welcome a traveler coming through a city as night was approaching to welcome him into their home. That is how David wanted people to view crying; not as something that would be with you at all times, but as an issue that you were under obligation to house only just for the night. Stop crying over the same thing and use God's power to get rid of the tears being shed."

After the service ended everyone gathered in front of the church. Michelle went downstairs to get the younger children from Spiritual Adventures while Carlton and Jason went to get the car. The assistant Ministers and Deacons "had service" for the children ten years or younger. After Michelle grabbed Chloe and Bryson she met up with Sunshyne outside.

"What's up, Girl?" she asked as she walked up. "I guess last night was just too much for you to make it to 8 o' clock service."

"Yeah. I didn't get much sleep last night, or should I say this morning, when I got home. Now it's time to go to my parents, but I really don't feel like being bothered with the Morris clan today, but you know Barbara would have a heart attack if any one of us did not show up for Sunday dinner. I would have liked some time to myself today, but Marcus is meeting me at the house soon to drop the kids off," she continued. "Anywho, service was off the chain as usual. Collins knows how to bring the word right to where you are," she said as a little smile warmed her face. "So, what are you getting into today?"

"I don't have much planned. I was thinking about going down to the warehouse for a couple hours after I cook dinner. Carlton is going golfing with some guys from work, and I was gonna let the kids hang out at the job with me and then go back home," Michelle said.

"That plan sounds boring as hell. Y'all should just come over mommy's house with us. That way the kids can hang out. I can't remember the last time they all got together. You know Damon will have the kids over. They will have plenty to do in the backyard over there," Sunshyne said sounding excited.

"Okay, but do you think they want us all over there? Plus, I still need to go home and make Carlton something for when he gets home," she said as Desiree walked up.

"Dee, tell this chick mommy lives for company and won't care if her and the kids come over," she said trying to convince Michelle to spend the afternoon with her.

"Yes. Mommy would be highly upset if she found out you didn't come because you thought you weren't welcomed," Desiree chimed in.

Turning back to Michelle, Sunshyne said, "If it makes you feel better I will call her right now to let her know. Then you can just have your hubby meet you at the house when he's done," she took out her cell phone and called her mom. After a couple minutes of back and forth with her mother, she hung up and told Michelle,

"Mommy said if you don't come you will have to deal with her the next time she sees you. She has not seen you and the kids in a minute and would love to have you over for dinner."

Just as she as she was finishing her mom's message, Jason walked up, "We going to Grandma Morris'? Yes!!! Granddad said he would show me his gun collection the next time I was over. Man, I can't wait," he said with pure excitement in his voice.

"Hello to you too," Sunshyne said as she gave him a light punch in his arm.

"Hey Auntie Shyne. Hey Aunt D. I'm sorry. I just can't wait to get over there to see them guns," he said before he hugged them and ran off to get back in the car.

"Alright. I'll check you in a minute," Michelle said and walked to her car.

Sunshyne, Desiree and Renae stood there and chatted for a little while.

“How are you today? Sunshyne asked Renae.

“I’m doing okay. How are you?

"I'm good. I know what I've gotten myself into so I have learned to deal with it," she said to convince herself more so than Renae.

"Yeah. I know what I've put up with too, but it doesn't make it easier," she said as she felt the tears burning her eyes.

Desiree noticed it too and hurried up and changed the subject.

"You wanna join us for dinner today too? Looks like everyone else is going to be there and you don't need to be alone."

"Naw. I'm going to take my dad out today and hopefully my brother, his wife and the kids will join us," she said with excitement in her eyes. She loved spending time with her family and especially her two nieces and nephew since she had not been able to have any children of her own.

"Cool, but if you change your mind..." Desiree started.

"I know.

“You know where we'll be." They both hugged Sunshyne and walked to the car.

Sunshyne pulled out her cell phone and decided to read the texts she had. They were all from Richard. This time after she was done reading she sent him one back, "If you can. Call me." No sooner than the text said it was delivered, her phone rang. She answered the phone dryly.

"Hello."

"Hey, baby. How was church?" he asked trying to get a feel for how she was feeling today.

"How do you know I was at church? You stalking me?" with a serious tone.

"Naw, baby", he said with a chuckle. "You always go to church. I figured you were just getting out. What do you have planned after your family dinner?"

"Not sure what time I'll be leaving my parents. I'm still pretty tired. I had a long day yesterday. I'll probably go home and watch a movie with the kids," she said with a hint of disdain in her voice.

She noted disappointment in his voice. "I thought maybe we could talk about what happened yesterday."

"I'm really not in the mood for much talking right now. Matter of fact, I think I need some time to think about everything. I know I love you and would like to spend the rest of my life with you, but we can't continue the way we are. It’s been weighing on my mind for a long time now. I can't go on sleeping with a married man. I embarrassed my family at the park yesterday acting the way I did with your wife. There should be no reason for me acting like that."

She went on as he sat silently on the phone, listening.

"You need some time to figure out what you're going to do. I'm not going to wait on you any longer. Be a man and decide. Either you love me, and we will make it through whatever happens together or you don't and you will continue to stay in the marriage you say has been miserable for years."

She thought about telling him what she had found out yesterday about Monica and Paul, but she didn't want to be the one to tell him what was going on with his wife. She wanted him to find out on his own. If he did choose to leave her it wouldn't be because she came back and told him.

"Baby, I don't want to lose you. I want us to spend the rest of our lives together, but I can't leave my baby girl right now either. I know if I divorce Monica right now she is going to make sure I reach deep in my pockets or keep my baby away. I told you. I just needed two more years and we would be good. I think if we take time apart I will lose you. Maybe that's it. You have somebody else," he said half proclaiming and half questioning.

"Really, Richard? I've waited for you all this time and let you handle things the way you say needed to be handled. Now that I tell you I'm going to figure out what I need to do you wanna talk this shit about another man. Fuck you. We need to end this conversation now before we both say some other shit we don't mean," Sunshyne yelled before Richard interrupted her.

"Naw, Baby. I'm sorry. I didn't mean that. I just don't know what I'm going to do if I can't see you and be with you. The last twenty-four hours have been hard enough," he said sounding anxious.

"That's fine and dandy, but if that's how you feel you need to make it so you don't have to worry about not seeing me. I'm at my parents' house now so I'll talk to you later," she said as she cut off her car to go in the house.

Richard wanted to keep her on the phone a little longer, but he was sounding desperate. He would let her have whatever time she needed. He knew she loved him, and that love seemed to keep her with him through everything. He just prayed that love would make everything right this time as well.

"Alright, sweetie, you do what you feel you need to. I'll do my best not to pressure you during this time. I want you to be happy no matter what happens. I do hope and pray that your final choice is us. I just hope you don't take long, and I hope we can get it right when it's all said and done."

Before finally saying his last goodbye and hanging up the phone, he said I love you and Sunshyne ended the call.

~11~

Desiree dropped Renae off at her dad's before heading over to her parents' house. It was right around the corner. Renae's family moved to that house after her mom's job relocated and she and Desiree were going into the sixth grade. They didn't immediately become friends because Renae walked around with a chip on her shoulder mad that her mom took her away from all her friends. Renae's brother did not have a problem making friends. He was actually glad to leave Milwaukee. After joining the dance club and becoming walking buddies after practice, Desiree and Renae learned they had more in common than just dancing.

As young girls, they argued over who was going to marry LL Cool J or who was going to be the first to purchase a Range Rover. They both wanted to go to Chicago College of Performing Arts once they finished high school, and they both thought 227 and Different World were the best television shows ever.

That's how their friendship began, and they remained friends ever since. They saw a lot of friendships end, but they had only had one disagreement that caused them to stop speaking to each other. It lasted less than forty-eight hours. They had a code, and they stuck to it. Renae was there for Desiree whenever she needed her, and the same went for Desiree.

Now Renae felt like she needed to start doing things for herself. She knew it wasn't going to be easy, but she had made up in her mind that Paul's sorry ass was history. She just prayed her heart would follow the game plan.

When she walked through the door her brother was already there. They were in the TV room watching some football game that was on. Whatever team they were going for was losing because she could hear them yelling cuss words from the porch.

She walked in the room, "Hey daddy. Hey Dougie."

"Hey Baby Girl."

“Hey Sis."

They responded without ever taking their eyes off the television.

"What did Ms. Loretta make for dinner," she asked walking into the kitchen.

"How do you know it was Ms. Loretta? I could have made dinner today."

Renae looked at him and smiled, "Daddy please," then walked in the kitchen.

Their dad vowed to their mother before she passed that he would never remarry, but she told him to never be lonely, if he ever felt the need for companionship to go on with his life. He met Ms. Loretta about four years after his wife passed. She reminded him so much of his wife that he couldn't help but be mesmerized. She was a beautiful woman with three children of her own, she had lost her husband several years ago, and she definitely knew her way around the kitchen. Her dad certainly fell into the old cliché about the way to a man's heart is through his stomach. Ms. Loretta had done her job to make sure his heart was overjoyed.

Entering the kitchen she saw trays and containers on the counter. There were no leaving pots all about. Ms. Loretta always cooked and cleaned up right after. Smothered pork chops were in a pan on the stove. The containers held candied yams, cabbage, fried corn, rice, and corn bread muffins. Renae didn't see dessert on the table, but she knew there was one somewhere. She opened the fridge and saw a homemade banana pudding sitting on the top shelf in between the eggs and sour cream.

Ms. Loretta did not use vanilla pudding or Cool Whip; she made her pudding from scratch. She was truly old school. Renae was glad Ms. Loretta had been by before work because she wasn't in the mood to go out anymore.

It was half time and her brother and father were talking about the plays and calls from the first half. She sat on the brown leather love seat and got ready to eat. She began eating her food, but put her fork down for a minute because she wanted to get the conversation over before halftime ended.

"I need y'all to come to the house and help me with something."

"What has this dude done now? What is it you want us to do? I was wondering when you were going to open your eyes and see what's really going on?" her brother kept throwing questions at her like a detective investigating an unsolved murder.

"What makes you think it has anything to do with Paul?" she asked with annoyance in her voice.

"First of all, this is Glenmont. It doesn't take no time for things to get around, you know this."

"Then you should already know what happened since this is Glenmont." Renae rolled her eyes.

Her dad interjected before things got out of hand, "Baby girl, you never said anything, but we knew every time something went down with you and your fella. Like your brother said, you can't keep secrets in this town. Whenever your brother heard about your troubles he wanted to do something, but I had to calm him down." She glanced over at Dougie.

"As long as the young man wasn't putting his hands on you, it was your responsibility to deal with the rest of the relationship," her daddy explained in a loving, caring manner. He continued, "So I'm guessing you have finally made it up in your mind that you're ready to be done. If so, you don't know how long I've waited for this day to come. No man wants to sit back while they know their child is hurting, but if you weren't ready there was nothing I or your brother could do to get you to leave him," he watched tears form in his daughter's eyes.

"You're right, Daddy. I understand everything you are saying, and yes, I am ready to make a change. I am done allowing him to control my happiness. It's time I do it for myself," Renae said wiping tears from her eyes.

Then Dougie sat next to her and put his arm around her shoulders. "So what do you want us to do?"

“I want to go to the house and change the locks, put his things in the garage and bring some of my things back to dad’s for a few days. I don’t want to be there when he does decide to show up. Now is the perfect time to do it all because I know he’s at work.”

Dougie was all in, but her dad was a little skeptical about changing the locks on the house she shared with him. He told her as much. She tried to convince him that it was her house and Paul didn't have one leg to stand on when it came to anything. She felt she earned it after all he had put her through.

She gave her daddy a sad, wounded baby bird look. His heart melted. He could not tell her no. He instructed his son to record the rest of the game. The three of them got in Dougie's Lincoln MKT. They stopped by Home Depot to get some new locks, and headed to Renae’s house to do as she requested.

***

Ruben woke up thinking about Renae. He enjoyed the short conversation they had at the club the previous night. Even though her guy came up trying to flex, he still wanted to see her again. Her deep-set mahogany eyes were warm and inviting. Her laugh was sweet and infectious. He had texted her last night just to make sure she was in safely and texted her a couple more times this morning just to make sure she was alright. It was almost three in the afternoon, and she had not replied to his texts from this morning.

He hoped everything was okay and that her guy had not done anything crazy. He didn't want her to think he was disparate or being obsessive. He didn't want her to think he was one of those crazies out there. As much as he would like to hear her voice he figured he'd leave her alone and let her call or text him when she was ready. He wondered if she had even had a second thought about him.

He went into his kitchen and grabbed the Hennessy out of his liquor cabinet. He poured him a shot. He was about to place the bottle back in the cabinet but decided to just take the bottle back to the living room with him. There was no need to keep making trips. Plus Johnny and Steve would be there any minute to watch the game. He sat on the couch and turned to Fox. The Dallas Cowboys and Washington Redskins hadn't started playing yet since the noon game had gone into overtime and was still showing.

He tried to keep his attention on the teams on the screen, but all he could think about was that fine brown woman he met last night, wondering if he would get the chance to take her out. He contemplated calling Desiree to try to get somewhere with her, but resolved to just letting the chips fall where they may.

***

While Dougie and her dad were taking care of the locks, Renae went in her room and started packing a bag to take with her. She also grabbed Muffin, her all white Shih Tzu, some food and toys. She put Muffin's bed and cage near the door so Dougie could load everything into the truck once he was finished. She then began putting all Paul's belongings into garbage bags and placed them near the back door.

She cried the entire time she was filling the bags. She knew deep in her heart that this was it. This was the last and final time she was putting up with his trifling ass. No matter how much he had hurt her she still loved him, and that's what the tears were for. She wasn't crying because she was losing him. She was crying because their love had not been strong enough for him to love her the way she wanted him to love her.

She continued to throw his clothes, shoes, jewelry, and anything else small enough into the bags through all the tears and moved them into the kitchen. She had Dougie unplug the 55-inch Samsung along with other devices he had connected to it. She contemplated keeping the Fire Stick, but she had three more throughout the house so there was no need to be petty.

She was not bitter and didn't want to play the role. She just wanted it over. She was sure he would blow her phone up once he was able to read the text she was going to send him after she left, but that was to be expected. She just hoped he didn't turn this into anything more than what it was. It was their time to move on with their lives. Time to make room for whomever God had in store for the both them because clearly this was not a match made in heaven.

After a couple hours, she finished packing up the last little bit of his stuff. When she walked in the kitchen she heard her phone buzzing. She realized she had not looked at her phone since early this morning. She had several missed calls and texts. The last one was from Ruben. She had been so involved in what was happening she hadn't had much time to think about him or anything else for that matter. She sat at the table for a minute to read her texts. She missed texts from Desiree. Paul had called and texted her, but she was more interested in reading the texts from Ruben.

A bright smile illuminated her ashen, tear-stained face as she read his texts. She was happy to see he was still thinking about her. That she wasn't just one of the random chicks he met at work one night and forgot about the next. She got a different vibe from Ruben than she got from most of the men she met in clubs. She definitely had a different feeling about him than she had about Paul, but it was still early. She knew not to play much into it. She started to think about Paul and regret the decisions she made in their relationship, but now was not the time for that. She just needed to dust herself off and not to depend on anyone else to make her happy.

She was in the middle of replying to Ruben's text when Dougie walked in the kitchen. She apologized for not getting back to him sooner and let him know she was cool. She told him she would try to call him later this evening if that was okay. He immediately texted back, "I'll be waiting."

Dougie interrupted, "I think we are done, Sis. Pops and I put everything in the garage. The locks are done and the windows are secure. All you need to do is change the alarm code and you're good to G-O."

He grabbed a bottle of water out the fridge and they walked to the front of the house. Her dad was putting her bags and Muffin's things in the back of the truck when she made it to the living room. She reset the code to the alarm, locked the doors and climbed in the truck.

Dougie cut on the radio. V103 was in the middle of the Battle of the Best. This week it was Rose Royce against Midnight Star. Herb Kent started talking smack as usual.

"You really think Midnight Star is going to win. They only had two songs, but Rose Royce will put you in the mood all the time. Like this next one. Produced by Norman

Whitfield of Whitfield Records and sung by Gwen Dickey, the B-side hit, “Love Don't Live Here Anymore” was released as the second single from their third album. Eat your heart out young man."

Renae continued to replay her and Paul’s relationship in her head as they drove down Ridge. She knew it was going to take time to completely heal, but she just wished she could fast forward it all. Paul would always hold a special place in her heart, but today there was a vacancy. He had not treated her heart with respect and she needed to let him go. It was time to fill her heart with a love she deserved.

She wanted to pursue whatever might happen with her and Ruben, but most importantly she wanted to find herself again and appreciate the woman she knew she was.

~12~

Michelle went by the house to drop Carlton off so he could meet up with his boys and let the kids change out of their church clothes. Jason was the first one upstairs. He was anxious to get over to Morris' house to make sure Mr. Morris let him see the guns in his collection.

On the way home Michelle told Carlton Mrs. Morris had invited the family over for dinner and he could meet them there when he was done golfing. While she was changing clothes her phone rang. She grabbed the phone and went down the hall to check on Chloe and Bryson.

"Hello. Yeah. I'm still at home. No. I can't talk right now. We probably won't be able to talk much at the house either. Your sister is already looking at us all suspicious and shit. If she or Carlton find out they're going to be mad at the both of us. We're still on for tomorrow though. I'll be able to get away from the office tomorrow about 1:00pm. We can talk more then."

She heard Carlton coming.

"Alright see you in a few," she hung up the phone as Carlton was entering the room to let her know he was leaving. He wondered who she was talking to that she was going to see in a few and that she had to hang up on so abruptly.

"Who you gonna see in a little while? You said you were going to Jeanette's parents' house."

"I am. That was her calling to make sure plans haven't changed." She told him without missing a beat.

He didn't have any reason to ever doubt what she said, but he felt a pang in his gut that made him believe something wasn't right. He didn't say anything because he just thought he was being paranoid. She kissed him goodbye and went back to the room to finish getting ready. He grabbed keys and headed to hang with the fellas.

Michelle enjoyed spending time with the Morrises. She didn't have a good relationship with her mother and she never knew who her father was. She was very close to her younger sister. When she passed during Michelle's junior year in high school it was difficult for her to deal with. That was when her relationship when her mother went sour. Her mother didn't know how to deal with the loss and took it out on Michelle. She verbally and mentally abused her, and once Michelle left to go to college she never returned. Carlton's family was huge, but most were far away that they didn't get to see them much. She was glad she decided to go hang out with the Morris family today.

She hoped she would get the chance to talk to Terrell while she was there. They hadn't been able to meet up too much lately, and she needed to talk to him. She just had to find the right time. She did not want Sunshyne to keep seeing them in their own conversation. They had played it cool this long and she knew that it would not be going on too much longer. So if she got the opportunity today, she would take advantage of it. If not, she would just wait until tomorrow to see him.

When they pulled up to the house, Jason jumped out the car and ran into the house. He gave Gi-Gi a hug then went straight to the basement where he knew he would find Granddad. Michelle and the rest of the children got out the car and went into the house to say their hellos. Mrs. Morris was so excited to see the kids. She said she couldn't remember the last time she had seen them. Krystalia told her how good she had done in school this past year. Bryson and Chloe told her how much fun they were having this summer. Michelle hugged Mrs. Morris as Terrell walked out the kitchen. They had a short conversation before Mrs. Morris excused herself to the kitchen, to check on dinner.

The younger kids went out to the backyard to play. Krystalia went on the porch to listen to her music. Michelle and Terrell were glad that Sunshyne hadn't made it there yet. That gave them a chance to talk.

"So how much longer are we going to do this? I don't know how much longer I can keep this to myself. I have never kept anything from your sister or my husband. It's killing me to do it now," she said.

A sensitive look came over Terrell's face.

"I know, Sis. I don't like sneaking around like this either, but give me just a little more time to figure things out. I will have it all right soon."

Michelle gave him that "Okay, but you need to figure it out soon" look. He understood that look loud and clear. Then he promised her he would make sure he got everything in order by the end of the week. They had been doing it long enough, and he couldn't keep putting her at risk.

"I appreciate all you've been doing."

He was just about to hug her when they heard Krystalia call out to her Auntie Nette.

Before Sunshyne could get in the house, Michelle was back in the kitchen helping get things ready and Terrell had made it to the basement with his dad and Jason.

Sunshyne sat on the porch for a couple minutes and caught up with Krystalia. She was going into her last year of high school and was excited about going away to college. She was also glad she was alone on the porch and could have a few minutes with her Auntie Nette. She had wanted to talk to her about college and her mom. Krystalia had been accepted to a couple schools but had not heard back from Virginia Commonwealth University. That was the school she really wanted to attend. Their forensic program was ranked among the top ten in the nation and had a large enough African-American population.

Her mom wanted her to attend Rhodes. She had gotten their acceptance letter, but that was not her dream.

"Auntie Nette I really feel bad about it not being my first choice. I don't want to disappoint mom."

She knew her mom really wanted her to attend her alma mater, but it just didn't fit with her future.

“Don’t worry about a thing. Choose the school that you want, and do your best. Your mom will be disappointed for a minute, but she will get over it. At the end of the day, she will be happy as long as you do your best and succeed. Plus, you don't want to have any regrets about what you shoulda, coulda, woulda done," she told her.

"Thanks, Auntie Nette," Krystalia said giving her a hug.

"Plus, if your mama starts acting too crazy just call me, and I'll be right over there to take care of her," she said over her shoulder as she went into the house.

Sunshyne heard laughing coming from the kitchen.

"Hey mama. Hey Shelly," she knew Michelle hated that name.

Her mom would call her that down the block when it was time to come in for dinner. Michelle would cringe every time she heard it.

"You play too much," Michelle said rolling her eyes.

"I just thought you needed a little taste of Noreen," Sunshyne said laughing.

"Girl, bye, you really on some sh...stuff today," she gave Mrs. Morris a sheepish look. She had almost slipped. Just then MJ came walking in the kitchen.

"Hi Gi-Gi. Hey Auntie Chelle. Hey mommy," he said, walking to his grandmother to give her a hug.

“Hey MJ” They all said in unison.

"Where are your sisters?" Sunshyne asked.

"They're out on the porch with Kay Kay. Is Granddad downstairs?"

"Yes. He's down there with Uncle Terrell and Jason," Sunshyne said, before he darted down the stairs.

About fifteen minutes later, Mariah and Maia walked in the kitchen.

"Ooh, I didn't think I was going to ever to see you. It took you long enough to make it in to see your granny," Mrs. Morris joked with the girls.

"Your brother came straight in the house to say hello to his grandmother."

Mariah and Maia said their hellos.

"Granny, daddy said hi. He would have come in, but he was running late for a meeting." Mariah said rushing as she hurried back out on the porch with Krystalia. Maia went out to the back to play with Chloe and Bryson.

A few minutes later, Damon came walking in the house with his children.

"Hi, Granny," they all blurted out. Trinity went to the front with the other girls, Tony, Damon's step-son went down to the basement, and his youngest daughter, Kendall went out back.

"Hi, Ma. Where is daddy? Some man named Jesse Porter is outside asking for him. I told him he could come in and wait in the living room while I got him, but he said he'd wait outside." Damon said.

Their mother's eyes got big, but nobody noticed the surprise look on her face. She turned to look out the window as if she was checking on the kids.

"Your daddy is downstairs, but he probably doesn't want to be bothered with him right now," she said never turning around.

Damon went downstairs to get his father. After a couple minutes Mr. Morris came up from the basement.

"Hey daddy. Hi, Mr. Morris," Sunshyne and Michelle exclaimed.

His wife gave him a distressed look from behind their backs. He looked back at her with a 'You don't have to tell me' expression on his face.

"Let me go see what this cat wants," he said and marched out the house. He brushed past Desiree on the way out the door, and mumbled, "Hello, Baby Girl" to her.

Damon came up the stairs not too long behind him.

"Who is that man out there? I told daddy that the dude was outside for him, and he got this weird look on his face. So, I offered to go out there with him, but he told me to stay here. He got it," he said with concern in his voice.

Terrell followed him up the stairs.

"Pops alright?" Terrell asked looking around the kitchen.

"Yes. Your daddy's fine. That man is nobody to concern yourselves with," Mrs. Morris said as she started passing bowls and platters of food around, ordering anybody in the kitchen to take it out to the patio. “He is probably just trying to borrow some money. That is the only time he comes around”, Mrs. Morris hurried to explain. Michelle called all the children in to wash their hands so they could get ready to eat.

When they all got outside, Desiree just couldn't leave it alone though, "Can somebody please tell me who that fine brown man was in the front talking to daddy?"

Damon sucked his teeth, "Now you into senior citizens? You’ll end up giving him a heart attack," he said. Everybody laughed.

Everyone else just ignored her and kept setting the table. It was a beautiful sunny day, a great day to be out in the yard. Their parents had a deck put on the back of the house a few years ago. So they liked to use it as often as possible to entertain. The picnic table outside was set just as she would set her dining room table. She served the food in fancy platters, had bright sunflowers on the table, and used her best dinnerware to eat.

Desiree just wouldn't let the subject go.

"He looks familiar, like I've seen him before. Did he ever live in the neighborhood?" she said as her father came around the corner.

"What man?" Sunshyne asked.

She had been in the bathroom while everything was going on.

"We don't need to talk about that cat anymore today. He isn't important and won't be back around here. So, we can eat dinner now?" her father said to her as he sat at the table and waited for everyone to be seated so he could bless the food.

Desiree knew not to say another word on the subject, but her mind was working hard to remember who that man was.

~13~

After dinner the younger kids played outside, while the ladies put the food away. Mariah and Kay Kay went back to the front porch, and Jason and Marcus went downstairs with the older men. Jason was excited to finally get the chance to see Mr. Morris' gun collection. When Terrell, Sr. pulled out his collection, Jason's eyes got big.

Marcus wasn't really interested in guns. He liked playing with guns in games like "Grand Theft Auto," "Call to Duty," and "Resident Evil" but felt real guns were horrible. He went out on the porch with the older girls after a short while. Mr. Morris promised Jason when he was old enough, and if his parents let him, that he would take him to the gun range. That was all he needed to hear. Jason held a couple of the guns before he went outside as well.

Not too long after they had finished eating, Carlton called Michelle to tell her he was exhausted and on his way home. She told him she would fix him a plate and be on the way in a little while.

Everyone started saying their goodbyes as the sun set and it began getting dark outside. Desiree planned on going out after she left her parents'. Michelle and Sunshyne wanted to get their kids home and settled.

After everyone left, Mr. Morris locked up and headed to bed.

"What the hell did that fool want after all this time? He just can't leave well enough alone. He made it plain years ago he didn't want any parts of her life. So why is he here now?" Mrs. Morris said, all worked up.

"I know, baby. I asked him why he decided to come around after all this time. He said he found out a couple months ago he doesn't have long to live and wants to make it right with all his children. I told him I would talk it over with you, but not to hold his breath. Nette has been just fine without him, and there is no need to tear her life up now. I told him no matter what, he better not bring his ass back to my house again or I would fill it full of lead. He gave me his number." He said as he placed a piece of paper on the dresser.

"Daddy, I don't think I'm ready to tell her. I don't want her to hate us for keeping this from her for so long. Let me think about it for a couple days," she said almost at tears.

"You don't have to rush, but I think we should sit her down and explain everything. I think she would understand the decision we made, but no matter what you decide you know I've got your back, boo," he said as he gave her a kiss and climbed into bed next to her.

He held her tight. She laid there anxious, her mind swirling, until she finally drifted off to sleep.

~14~

Renae had dozed off watching the game with her dad. She wasn't a big fan of football, but she enjoyed spending time with him no matter what they were doing. She was still daddy's baby girl. Dougie had left and went home after he helped bring everything in the house and ate a healthy serving of banana pudding.

"Why didn't you wake me up, daddy?" she asked stretching, trying to get her bearings together.

"You were sleeping so peaceful. I didn't want to bother you. I almost woke you up a few minutes ago because your phone would not stop buzzing. Somebody is really trying to get you," he said through a slick smile.

Just then she remembered she forgot to call Paul to let him know that she had changed the locks and he needed to figure out what he was going to do. She picked up her phone and saw she had twelve missed calls, even more texts and a few voicemails. She called her voicemail and listened to Paul cussing on the other end calling her all out of her name. When she read her messages it was even worse. She was all kinds of female dogs, garden tools and he even threatened to kill her whole damn family if she didn't get him his shit and let him in the house.

She knew that last message was just because she was not answering her phone, but she still didn't trust what he might do, especially once it settled in that this was the end. She also had a couple messages from Ruben. He didn't have to work tonight and wanted to see if she wanted to hang out. His texts brought an instant smile to her face. She got up and folded the blanket her dad had tossed over her while she was sleep.

She headed into the bathroom, got herself together, and then went up to her room. She lay across the bed for a minute working up the nerve to call Paul. Before she made the call, she thought back to something her pastor had once said,

"God does not want you to stay in the place you are in, but if you want Him to do something miraculous in your life you have to do something miraculous for yourself," or something like that.

She dialed Paul's number. The phone rang a couple times.

"Where the fuck is all my shit, Renae and why the hell can't I get in the house? Did you change the locks on me?" he shouted into the phone as soon as he answered.

He didn't say hello or anything else.

She interrupted him, "If you give me a chance to talk you would know that your stuff is in the garage. You can go and get your stuff whenever you feel like it, and I would appreciate it if you get it all sooner rather than later. Yes. I did change the locks because you won't be getting back in the house anymore."

"What the fuck you mean I won't be getting in? That's my house too," he yelled at her.

"Well you should have thought about that before you did the shit you did. I have put up with you and your bullshit long enough," she said crying into the phone.

"I don't feel like arguing about it anymore. We're done. Now you can go on and be with Monica or whoever else is the flavor of the day."

When she thought back to the phone call the last morning they were together, she put two and two together. Moni Love was probably Moni-ca. She got more upset with the thought of it. It further confirmed that this was not the relationship for her.

"Alright, Nae. I'm sorry that I keep hurting you like I do. I don't want to keep hurting you. I'm gonna let you have your space for a couple days. When you're ready to talk you can let me know. We can work through this," he said with sincerity in his voice.

She had heard it all before and knew he wasn't gonna ever change. She let him finish.

"Paul, there is no more talking for us. The next time we talk we need to figure out how we are gonna split this stuff up between us. I'm done trying. I'm done being there for you when you don't want to be there for me. It's all take and no give with you."

She had gotten a little bit of her strength back. She was finally able to let go of the words she held onto for so long. Those were words she never thought she would be able to say to him. It was like he had some kinda spell on her, but now the spell was being broken.

"We can meet in a couple of days to figure it out," with that she hung up the phone.

As soon as she set it on the dresser and walked into her bathroom, she heard it buzzing again. She didn't know if it was an incoming call or texts, but she knew it was Paul and ignored it.

After she came out the bathroom, she texted Ruben and told him she would love to hang out with him. She told him to give her a minute, and she would call him. Then she went downstairs to check on her dad and make sure he didn't need anything before she got ready to leave. He was in the kitchen fixing himself some banana pudding when she got downstairs.

"Is everything alright, baby girl? You look like you've been crying again," he said as he pulled her in to give her a hug. She started crying into her father's shoulder.

"Daddy, I don't understand why he just couldn't get it right. As much as I love him and have sacrificed for him, he just wouldn't love me and only me. He just couldn't stop messing around with these chicks in the streets," she pulled out of his embrace and wiped her eyes.

"Sweetie you put all your faith and trust in that man, and you let him do what he wanted for far too long. Once is a mistake. More than that is a pattern. If you didn't have enough respect for yourself to put your foot down and let him know you weren't going to tolerate his mess, you couldn't expect him to respect your relationship," he went on to tell her.

"You made it too easy for him to have his cake and eat it too. You didn't do anything to force him to make a choice. But no matter what, don't hold a grudge and don't walk around holding onto any anger. You won't be able to get past it until you let it go. Get him out the way to make room for next one," he told her with deep sincerity.

She saw him drift away for a second.

He knew all too well how he had to deal with his own anger from a cheating mate. When she was in high school his marriage went through a rough patch. Her mother cheated on him. She felt he wasn't giving her enough time. Working all the time, hanging with his boys every free night he had and not spending any time with her. She went out and found someone who would give her the affection and attention she required.

He was angry. No. Angry didn't begin to describe his feelings. He left. He could not live under the same roof with his wife at that time, the woman he had given everything. He stayed gone for a few weeks until one of his older partners helped him realize his role in the situation and he couldn't run at the first sign of trouble. He didn't condone her unfaithfulness, but he knew he played a part in their problems. He decided from that day forward his wife and his family were his priorities. He didn't stop hanging with his friends, but his wife came before anything else. He had made a vow to her and God and nothing was going to come between it again.

Before he could move forward completely though, he had to let go of the anger he was holding onto. During a conversation he had with his pastor at the time, he was told that he had to forgive her if he wanted to save his marriage. The pastor told him he could not dwell on her offenses or he would not get what he needed from God to heal. So he worked through it, expressed his feelings to his wife and eventually let it go.

He didn't want his baby girl to miss the true blessing God had in store for her because she was holding onto hate in her heart. He came back from his thoughts.

"You let this man take enough of your happiness. Don't let him steal your joy too. Even though you will always be my baby girl, you are grown so I can't tell you what to do. All I can do is give you this and let you do what you feel is best. If a man continues to mistreat you he is not the one for you. No man should want to be with a woman if he is not willing to keep a smile on her face. And you, young lady, shouldn't want that man if he is not up to the task."

He kissed her on the forehead, took his banana pudding and went back to the TV room to finish watching the game.

Renae stood there for a minute soaking up her daddy's words. Then she unlocked her phone and dialed Ruben. Hopefully he was still up for hanging out tonight. She thought about calling Desiree to see what she was getting into, but she knew she would have to talk about Paul and for tonight she didn't want to have to think about any of it. She just wanted to have a good time.

Ruben answered on the second ring. She could hear a lot of noise in the background.

"Hello, Ms. Lady. I didn't think I was gonna hear back from you today," he said with excitement in his voice. "Hold on, let me go into the other room."

"Hey. Is this a bad time?"

"Oh no. Just have a few of my boys over watching the game. I hope you're not calling to tell me I won't be able to see you tonight," he said with a hint of disappointment in his voice.

"Not at all, I was calling to make sure we were still on for tonight. What time do you want me to be ready?" She beamed, trying not to sound anxious.

"They'll be leaving soon. How is 7:30? Text me your address, I'll come scoop you. Is there anywhere in particular you would like to go?" he said not hiding his excitement.

"Nope. I'll let you decide. I'm just looking forward to seeing you and enjoying the night."

"Okay. I'll see you in a little while."

She really was looking forward to seeing Ruben and hoped the night would turn out to be a good one. Renae got her clothes out and hopped in the shower right after she sent her daddy's address to Ruben.

***

Renae was upstairs putting the finishing touches on her hair and makeup when she heard the doorbell ring. Ruben was early. She could hear her dad giving him the third degree. She quickly finished getting ready and hurried downstairs to rescue him. When she walked into the living room she saw Ruben and her dad standing together in front of his wall that held precious pictures of various African-American baseball players. Her dad was fascinated with baseball, and it seemed that Ruben was also. Her dad had been so fascinated he gave his one and only son the name of his favorite player. Dougie's real name was Douglas Ernie. He combined the two and always introduced himself as Dougie. They were having a lively conversation about the Chicago Cubs.

Renae wasn't used to hearing that much happiness in her dad's voice other than when he was around Loretta. She often heard him and Dougie have spirited conversations watching sports, but she knew how much he loved his Cubs. Paul could not stand baseball, so they never connected in that way.

Ruben had just scored a few brownie points with his knowledge of the game, with her and especially with her daddy. They hadn't noticed her at first when she walked into the room. As she got a little closer to them they both turned around simultaneously.

"Baby girl, your friend, umm Ruben, knows his sports, especially baseball. We won't hold it against him that he is a Cowboys fan though," her daddy said smiling.

"Yeah. My grandfather used to take me and my cousins to the games when we visited. He shared his stories and pictures with me, and I got into them at a real young age and never stopped being a fan," he said with softness in his eyes remembering his grandfather.

"Well come back anytime you'd like. Her brother doesn't have the same enthusiasm, and I always love talking baseball. Now you youngins go ahead and enjoy yourselves," he kissed his baby girl on the cheek and went back in the TV room.

After they drove for a couple minutes, Ruben finally broke the silence.

"I thought maybe we could grab a bite to eat and then go listen to some disco music at *The Den.*"

Renae smiled at him, "That sounds good. Like I told you, I really don't care what we do as long as I have a good time. Listening to disco will definitely be good. I love to dance."

"I'm not a good dancer. I can get out there with you and do the Carlton dance." He joked.

She laughed out loud real hard, "We can just sit and listen tonight. Maybe next time we can get on the dance floor."

Their conversation was easy and pleasant. Their drive downtown on Lake Shore Drive in his metallic gray drop top Camaro SS was great. They talked about their childhoods, parents, siblings, and their mutual love of music.

"I've always thought you were beautiful, but didn't want to step on anyone's toes."

He pulled into the Water Tower Place parking garage.

"They have a nice urban buffet in here called Foodlife. Have you ever been?" he asked.

"No. I've heard its pretty good, but I've never been," she said as they pulled in to the parking space.

"Well let's go in and enjoy," he said as he got out going around and opening her door.

~15~

Desiree was sitting in her living room, racking her brain, trying to remember where she had seen that man that was at her parents' house earlier. She knew she had seen him somewhere before. He looked a little different now, but those eyes. His grey eyes were like thick clouds on a stormy afternoon. She was going to figure out where she saw those eyes before.

She knew her parents were keeping something from them and was gonna find out what it was. For now, she was going to chill before she went to see what she could get into or who could possibly get into her tonight.

Desiree called her big sis to see if she wanted to hang out.

"I'm going to pass tonight. I'm not really in the mood to party and wanted to stay in and watch a movie with the kids." Sunshyne replied.

So Desiree put her clothes on and headed to the city. She decided she wasn't in the mood for too much excitement tonight and opted to go to one of the laid-back lounges out south. She ended up in *The Bar*. She had dated the owner for a little while and knew most of the regulars so she felt comfortable hanging out by herself there. She and the owner had remained very good friends, and she still had carte blanche whenever she hung out there.

There was a new, young bouncer on the door tonight though that she didn't know. He was about six feet tall, very dark complexion, and sported a short, clean fade. He kind of put you in the mind of the actor Derek Luke. Desiree got ready to walk through the door when the Antwone Fisher lookalike asked her for her ID. Darnell saw her walk up and quickly intercepted her and took over.

"Hey, Desi, how you been? Ain't seen you in a minute," he said escorting her past the long-mirrored wall at the front of the club and over to the bar in the back.

"Hey Darnell. I been good. How about you? How is Jerome?"

"I'm good. You know he misses you. He still looks for you on Monday's to come through the door. You really broke that man's heart, but I understand we all have to do what we think is best for us," he said calling for Romie, the bartender, to come over.

Darnell was Jerome's right-hand man. They had been friends since elementary school, and Jerome didn't trust anyone as much as he trusted Darnell. Jerome opened *The Bar* on 79th Street soon after moving to Chicago.

Desiree thought back to when she had first started coming here for karaoke just a few months after it opened with co-workers. Jerome fell in love at first sight. He made sure every time she came in, she got whatever she wanted. While she was there he would come and talk to her and he eventually asked her out to dinner. From that day forward they spent as much time as possible together. He always wanted to be with his Baby Bear, and she couldn't live without him. She had practically moved into his lakefront condo. He had finally met her family and was coming around to more and more family events.

She was head over heels in love with Jerome too. Then after two years of dinners, holidays, and trips she finds out he had a 17-month old daughter named Sienna he never told her about. She was crushed to the core by his deceit and betrayal. He tried to call and sometimes he waited for her at work or her parents' house to explain and apologize, but she would not let him. She even stopped taking his calls and did not go back to the lounge for more than six months.

Finally, one day he caught her in the parking lot at work and did everything short of get down on his knees to beg her to let him explain. She gave him the opportunity over dinner. At dinner, they talked, cried, and eventually laughed. She allowed him to finally tell her everything.

He explained that the young lady was someone before her, who he had cut all ties with before he had gotten serious with her. He did not find out about his daughter until she was eight months old. The mother showed up to the lounge and dropped the news on him out of the blue. He admitted he did not know how to tell her and kept it a secret because he didn't think she would understand. She had voiced so many times that she wasn't ready for children, and on top of it he wasn't even sure if the child was his.

She eventually accepted his apology, but she could not get pass the fact that he was not truthful with her. She thought they were bigger than the secrets he kept from her. She would never have thought he would do it to her, but she learned that she could not put her trust in another person like that. He was the second man to break her heart. The real reason she couldn't forgive Jerome wasn't that he had hurt her so bad but that she let the pain from her past relationship affect their relationship at the time.

So here she was at *The Bar*. Darnell came back up to her and snapped her out of her trance.

"He is back in his office if you want to say something to him. He has somebody in there with him, but we know he is never too busy for his Sweet D."

"Naw. I'll just wait for him to get done and then...," before she could get the rest of her sentence out she saw Jerome emerge from his office with that same man she saw outside her parents' house earlier that day. She never believed in coincidences and she wasn't going to now. She thought about going up to him and questioning him about his presence earlier and now him showing up here. Instead, she turned back towards the bar so he wouldn't notice her. She would ask Jerome about this mysterious man later.

~16~

Sunshyne sat at home with the children watching *Dream Girls*. This was Mariah's favorite movie. So everyone knew when it was her turn to pick a movie, they were going to be watching *Dream Girls*, *Love & Basketball*, or *Bad Seed*. Today Sunshyne wished Mariah would have chosen to watch the evil little girl because she couldn't stay focused on the movie. Every love song Jamie Foxx, Beyoncé or J-Hud sung reminded her of what she wanted with Richard. Something that looked like it may never happen.

She loved him. She would love so much to have that beautiful baby boy he longed for, but lately she was feeling as though his promises were empty. She felt his daughter was old enough to handle the truth about her parents. She would be a junior in high school after the summer and was not a baby anymore. Sunshyne was starting to believe he really didn't want to leave his family and was using his daughter was an excuse.

She wanted and needed him to get it together, and figure it out either way. She knew it had been long enough and now was the time for her to focus on herself. She felt her belly and decided she would call Desiree. Her younger sister always had a way of making her laugh and taking her mind off whatever had her down. Then she remembered she was going out.

She picked up the phone to call Michelle, her line went to voicemail. So she sat there with the kids trying her best to watch the movie. After the movie went off she went to her room and turned on Spotify, she grabbed the latest book by JaQuavis Coleman to read. As she started dozing off, she heard the song "Husband" by Shirley Murdock coming through the speaker.

"They say be careful what you ask for because He will show you what you need to see, but it is up to you to accept it or not." Sunshyne laid there and let those words soak in before dozing off listening to Chris Michaels and the Quiet Storm.

***

Renae and Ruben were having a great time together. He was intrigued with her conversation over dinner. When he had asked her about what went down at the club the other night, she was very open and honest about her past relationship and what she was looking for moving forward in her life. She told him that they had been together for over ten years and how during that time she had loved him with all her being. She shared what she had gone through with him but that she couldn't do it anymore, and now was the time for her to be happy.

She was upfront with him about not wanting to jump right back into a serious relationship. She didn't want to become a hermit sitting around in the house stressing or becoming depressed about what didn't work either. She didn't want him to feel like she was expecting him to commit, but she did want him to know what she was looking for. They could hang out and see where things went, but if he just wanted it to be sex they didn't need to waste each other's time.

When she got to the point where she felt the emotions rising inside her, she quickly changed the subject and asked that they not ruin their time talking about Paul.

After dinner Ruben took her to *The Den* as promised. DJ WyldChyld was cuttin' up when they got there, and Ruben even shocked her and got on the dance floor for a hot minute. He didn't want to embarrass himself, but he didn't want her out there dancing with anyone else either. He wanted her all to himself. He wasn't sure where this was going to go, but he felt an immediate connection to Renae and didn't want this to be their only date.

Before they left, she excused herself and headed to the restroom. She took a minute to check her phone. She hadn't looked at it all night. A couple missed calls and texts from Desiree, her brother and, of course, Paul. By the time he sent his last text she could tell he was mad as hell, but that was not her concern anymore. She texted Desiree and Dougie to let them know she was straight and they could talk tomorrow. She went back out to Ruben and they walked back to his car. As they were pulling out the parking lot, he offered to take her to grab another bite to eat, but she said she was still good from dinner earlier. He wasn't really hungry either. He just didn't want their night to end yet.

He hopped on the Dan Ryan, and it didn't take long before they were on her dad's block. When they pulled up her chest tightened and her face became pale. Paul's car was sitting right in front of her dad's next-door neighbor's house. She turned to Ruben, and he immediately saw the worry on her face.

"What's wrong, baby girl?"

She just looked out the window as they rolled past his car, "That's Paul's Impala right there." She didn't know how this was going to end, but she knew something was about to go down.

"You don't have to get out if you don't want. You can pull into the driveway, and I can just go in his side door. I don't want you to be involved in any of this. It's enough he acted a fool at the club the other night," she said almost begging him not to get out.

"Don't worry, sweetheart. It will be alright. I am not going to let you walk to any door by yourself," he said adamantly. He pulled his car into the driveway and went around to open the door for Renae. By the time they reached the walkway to the front door Paul was standing there waiting for them.

"What the hell is going on Renae? This the motherfucker from the club the last night? Your knight in shining armor?" his speech slurred with every syllable.

Renae knew he had been drinking.

"Go on, Paul. I don't have time for you and your bullshit tonight. Take your act over to Moni Love's. Oops. You can't because she is at home with her husband," she spat in his face and turned to walk toward the house.

Paul got ready to come at her and Ruben stepped in the way.

"So what. You captain save-a-hoe again tonight?" Paul said getting louder.

"Naw, but it doesn't look like you're in your right mind, bruh, and may just want to walk this one off," Ruben responded nice and calmly.

That's when Paul got belligerent and louder. By this time, Ms. Connor, the next-door neighbor had brought her nosey ass on the porch, and Ms. Loretta was in the doorway calling for Renae's dad.

"I think you should go on and leave now while you have the chance," Ruben said as he continued to walk Renae to the door.

He could tell Paul was a coward and really didn't want a replay of the other night. Paul just kept following behind them talking shit and making a fool out of himself. By the time they reached the stairs Renae's dad was at the door telling Paul to get away from his house with his nonsense. He told him if he didn't leave he was going to call the police.

Paul turned in Renae and Ruben's direction, "This here is far from over. I will be to holla at you," he bellowed with complete rage in his voice.

Ruben didn't want Renae and her family to think he was a punk, but he also didn't want to disrespect her dad. So he just told Paul, "Get at me. You know where I'm at."

Paul held up his hand using two fingers like he was pointing a gun and shot at Ruben. Then he got in his car and sped away.

Renae turned to Ruben, "I am so sorry you had to go through this again. I understand if you don't want to be bothered with my drama," she apologized.

"Don't sweat it, mama. The man is hurt and doesn't know how to express it, and I don't scare that easy. As long as he doesn't put his hands on you then we good. Now go on in there and get your beauty rest, and hopefully you and I will talk tomorrow," he said as he hugged her and then watched her go in the house with her dad and Ms. Loretta.

He got in his car and texted his boy Rufus, "I'm gonna have to watch this nigga Paul. Get at you tomorrow." and drove home smiling thinking about the wonderful night he just had despite the ending.

Renae's dad checked to make sure his baby girl was alright and told her they could talk in the morning. She went upstairs, changed into her pajamas and got in the bed. She texted Ruben to let him know she had a wonderful time in spite of how the night ended. Then she texted Desiree to tell her she had decided to go out with Ruben and for her to call her tomorrow. She had so much to tell her. She laid in bed thinking about her weekend and sighed. She knew it wasn't over with Paul but didn't know how the next episode would play out.

~17~

Desiree stayed until closing. She was going to make sure she had a conversation with Jerome about the mystery man he was talking to. She knew something was funny because he had been avoiding her all night. Whenever he came by the bar where she was sitting, he kept the conversation short and acted like he had so much to take care of around the club. Normally he would sit and talk for a little while. Desiree had caught Darnell for a brief moment to find out if he knew anything about the guy Jerome had met with when she came in, but he couldn't tell her much.

Now that the bar was closed Jerome was not going to be able to avoid her any longer. She looked over at Darnell and he gave her the nod. She went back to his office and found Jerome going over the books from the night. When he looked up and saw her standing there she could see the concerned look on his face. She made herself a cocktail and got comfortable on the black leather sofa in the corner of his office. She couldn't believe he still kept a bottle of her favorite liquor in his personal cabinet, especially since it seemed like the bottle was the same one that was there the last time she was there.

It felt like old times to her. When they were dating she would sit with him and scroll through Facebook and Instagram, as she was doing now, while he went over whatever paperwork he needed to finish before they left to go home for the night. After she checked her social media sites she saw she had a text from Renae. She couldn't wait to hear all about her evening with Ruben.

It seemed to be taking Jerome a little longer than normal to finish what he needed to get done. So she poured herself another drink and walked over and sat in the chair by his desk.

When she sat down he asked her, "What brought you in here tonight?"

"What. I'm not welcomed here anymore?" she said in a playful tone.

"Naw, baby, you know you're always welcomed here whenever you want. I'm just not used to seeing you by yourself. You usually have a group with you," he said trying to prolong what he knew she wanted to discuss.

"No one wasted to hang tonight, and I didn't feel like staying in the house."

She cut it short and got straight to the point. "Jerome. What did that man want with you earlier?" She just came out and said it.

He paused for a minute before answering her, "Baby, I promised you when we broke up that I would never tell you another lie, but I think this one is not for me to tell."

Now she desperately wanted to find out what he was holding back from her. She moved the chair closer and leaned seductively on his desk.

"This is the second time I have seen this man in one day. I need to know what the hell he wants," she said raising her voice.

"What do you mean the second time?" Jerome asked.

Desiree briefly explained what took place at her parents' house earlier, and how her parents were being so secretive. She went on to tell him how she recognized him from somewhere but just couldn't put her finger on where.

Jerome wanted to tell her, if only for his own selfish reasons. He thought if he broke the news to her they could work it out together. He could be the one she would lean on and it would bring them closer. Ever since she left he had a hole in his heart. He never looked at another woman the same, but then he thought about her feelings. How could he drop this bomb on her? Would she ever forgive him if he didn't? So many things raced through his mind.

"Baby Bear," he started out.

That was the name he had given her so long ago. Before he got a chance to finish, Darnell poked his head in the office.

"Everything is cool up front. Tina doesn't have her car so I'm gonna drop her off and head home. You got everything else? Do you need me to take the deposit?" he threw several questions at him at once.

"Naw, man. I'm good. Go ahead. I got it. I may just lock tonight's earnings in the safe until morning," he said and then told him to make sure he locked up before he left.

When he was sure Darnell was out of ear shot he turned back to Desiree and asked her to pour him a drink. When she came back and sat down she gave him that stop stalling-and-get-on-with-it look. He got up from behind his desk and took her over to the couch.

He grabbed her hand, "This dude has been calling me for a couple weeks, and I have been ignoring his calls. So I guess he decided to take a different approach and come up here."

He was still making small talk and she knew it.

"Jerome, please just tell me what he wanted. I promise I can handle it," she said pleading with him.

Finally he just came out and said what needed to be said.

"This cat says that he is Nette's father, and your parents have kept him from her all this time. He says he has also been trying to reach your mom and dad but they won't take his calls either," he rushed to get it out as he felt the words getting stuck in his throat.

Jerome went on to tell her that the guy had been up to the bar a few times while they were still dating and saw them together in the lounge quite a bit. He said he had seen them leave together a few nights, so he thought he could get some information from him or at least get him to give Desiree his number so he could talk to his daughter. He left his telephone number and hoped she would eventually get it. Jerome had told him he wasn't sure what he could do for him but that he would look into it.

She sank back on the couch. She could not believe what she had just heard.

"Dude is lying. He is not my sister's father. Terrell Morris is our father. He is up to some other shit and just using that as an excuse to try to get you to feel sorry for his ass," she said as she jumped from the couch and started pacing.

She couldn't believe what she had just heard. Why would this man try to ruin their family? They had already weathered the storm so many years ago when Terrell Jr. came into their lives. Now this? Why were her parents being so secretive about the whole situation? There wasn't anything, at least as far as she knew that they didn't discuss, but now she wasn't sure.

"Baby, come sit back down," he held his hand out to her.

"Why did this motherfucker come to you? What the hell was he trying to accomplish?" She snapped at him.

She knew it wasn't his fault, but she was heated. She couldn't take it out on Jerome. He didn't invite the man into her life, into her parent's life. She thought about Nette. She knew how she felt, but she couldn't imagine how devastated her big sis was going to feel if this dude's story turned out to be the truth.

Why the hell had they kept it a secret? Their family had been through tougher times. Jerome took her in his arms and kissed her on the forehead. This had always made her feel better in the past when things weren't going right. Tonight her world had been flipped on its backside. She sank into his arms and just let his embrace console her. She felt her body react to his touch. She did not want those feelings to cloud her mind, especially not right now. She loved Jerome and she missed him, but she couldn't forget how dishonest he was with her.

"Jerome, I think I should go. I need to get home and figure out how I'm going to handle this," she said her voice cracking as she attempted to hold back the tears.

"Let me take you. You are in no shape to drive. I would hate if something were to happen to you," he said grabbing her keys. "Don't give me that 'I'm fine stuff' that you always give me. There is no argument. You will leave your car and I will drop you at home," he said giving her that stern look he always gave when she knew there was no arguing with him.

She finally agreed. He put the money in the safe, locked up the office and he took her home. They drove to her condo in silence listening to his Isley Brothers playlist from his iPad. Once they got to her building, he made sure she got in the doors safe and sound.

"I'm in," she texted him once she was in her condo as he requested.

He immediately texted back, "You know I am here for you whenever you need me. My offer still stands. Good night, Baby Bear. I love you."

A few people were going to have to explain themselves real soon. She undressed and just laid in bed thinking until she dozed off to sleep.

~18~

Terrell woke up around 8:30 a.m. despite the fact he had taken the day off. He had hoped to be at the bank earlier in the week, but things at work were too hectic. He wanted to get as much as he could wrapped up. Things between him and Michelle had gone on long enough. His sister was starting to get a little too suspicious of them now, and he didn't want her knowing what was going on. The less people the better. He didn't want to involve anyone else in their madness.

He got up out the bed, brushed his teeth and started making phone calls. He was able to get an appointment for that morning which worked perfect. He would meet with the banker with enough time to still make the lunch with Michelle. He wanted to give Michelle as much information as possible when they met to conclude their business.

He walked into Huntington Bank two hours later and asked for Mr. Beasley. The receptionist at the front desk called to Mr. Beasley's office and asked Terrell to have a seat while he concluded a current meeting. She seemed to be captivated with the young brother sitting in front of her. She could not take her cinnamon brown eyes off of him. Her face became flush when he caught her staring at him a couple times.

Finally Mr. Beasley came out to escort Terrell back to his office. He offered him something to drink and Terrell kindly declined. He just wanted to get right to it. Mr. Beasley was a long-time friend of his mother's family and had known Terrell since he was a baby. Mr. Beasley still kept in touch with his mom and tried to make small talk with him about her. Terrell didn't like talking about his mom and now definitely was not a good time. He knew he didn't have to worry that he would say anything so he spoke honestly about what he had done and what he was trying to accomplish at this time.

Mr. Beasley told him it may be difficult and that he could not move it all at once. He went on to tell him that as he was giving the money to Michelle to help "add" inventory to her business she should have been making regular deposits somewhere else. Neither of them had thought it all the way through. They were both concerned with just making the money look legit.

So now they would need to figure out how to make it work to their advantage. Mr. Beasley told Terrell to give him some time to find some options for him, and he would give him a call later this morning. Terrell thanked him and then texted Michelle.

Hope we're still on for lunch today.

May have some good news.

See you at Wildfire. 12:30.

Don't be late please.

Michelle had just stepped in the shower when her cell started buzzing. She got four notifications back to back so Carlton thought it was important and was taking her phone to the shower when he noticed it was Terrell. Why was he texting her so early in the morning? He wondered if everything was alright with Nette. Maybe it was one of the kids or her parents. He normally wouldn't, but he slid the phone to unlock it and read the texts.

He couldn't believe what it said. Why were they having lunch together, and why hadn't she told him? What else was she keeping from him? Was that him she was talking to the other day? He had so many questions to ask, but he didn't want her to know he had read the texts so he erased them and placed her phone back on the night stand.

He hurried and finished dressing. He hollered into the bathroom that he had gotten a call and had to get to the office. The kids were still sleep so he didn't wake them. He grabbed his keys off the hook, got in his truck and sped away from the house. His mind was racing still thinking about the messages he read in his wife's phone. He didn't know what was going on between the two of them, but he was going to find out — today. He would make sure he cleared his schedule today to be at Wildfire to get an explanation.

Michelle had not heard from Terrell all morning. He told her yesterday he would be going to the bank and wanted to meet today. So before she went into her last meeting for the morning, she called him.

"Hey. Are you calling to tell me you have to cancel", he asked?

"Cancel what?" she said puzzled.

"I texted you early this morning to tell you I might have some good news for us and to meet me at Wildfire at 12:30."

"I never got a text from you this morning. I was calling because I hadn't heard from you."

"Well, we need to sit down and talk. Can you make it to Wildfire by then?"

"I got one last meeting this morning, but I should still be able to make it by then. See you later," she said and hung up the phone.

She checked her phone again and there were no texts from him. Her phone had been acting up lately so she didn't think anything else of it. As she walked past her assistant's desk she stopped her. Her assistant, Esther, was an older lady who always had a story for her. She knew that it was going to be something when she saw the receptionist standing there with her.

"Michelle. I didn't tell you the good news. My niece is ba-nigh. Her results came back negative." She noticed the confused look on Michelle's face.

"She is ba-nigh," she said a little louder this time thinking Michelle didn't quite hear her the first time. Michelle still looked a little puzzled. This time Esther pronounced each syllable separately.

"Ba-nigh. The tests showed she doesn't have cancer." Michelle rolled her eyes and got ready to tell her the term is benign, but she knew it was useless. Her and Katie just looked at each other and shook their heads. They both have had these types of conversations with Esther before and knew what the outcome would be. She simply told her that it was good to hear and went on to her meeting.

***

Desiree pulled into Wildfire's parking lot about five minutes after she had gotten the text from Renae to see where she was. The host took her to the table she had seated Renae at just a short while before.

"Girl, I didn't think we were going to ever find time to get together," Renae said after they placed their drink order and the waiter left the table. They were supposed to hook up a couple days ago, but Desiree was busy at work. So this was the first chance they got. Desiree just came right out with what she needed to say. She had held onto this news for as long as she could and needed to tell someone.

"If I thought I was going to blow your mind with the news I had to tell you the other night. Humph. You're going to need a few more of those Tequila Passions." Desiree told her she went to the lounge the other night, broke down the events that went on at the house that afternoon and then ran down the whole story Jerome told her after closing.

Renae sat there in shock for a few minutes listening to her best friend tell her the story that could possibly tear her family apart before she moved her chair around to console her friend. Desiree was trying her hardest to hold the tears back but could not contain herself any longer. The waiter came back to the table with their drinks and stared at her for a minute until Renae gave him a nasty glare. He told them he would be back for their order.

After a couple minutes she got herself together, "Now I'm not sure what my next move is going to be. I'm not sure if I want to tell my brothers first so they can be there when I talk to my parents or if I just want to go to them alone. Jerome told me I should bring them with so I can have some support. He volunteered to go with at first, but I told him that we needed to handle this as a family first."

Renae's eyes were getting bigger and bigger as the conversation went on. She had not heard that name in a long time, and now she had heard it more than once in the past ten minutes. Desiree could sense she had questions, "Before you ask. Yes, Jerome and I have been spending time together the last few days. He has been a shoulder to cry on trying to wrap my mind around all this."

"What else has he been," Renae asked sarcastically.

"Girl, bye. You can go back to your side of the table now."

"Whatever. I saw the way your eyes lit up, and I know how much you still love the man," she said as she slid her chair back around the table.

The waiter came back for the third time. The ladies went ahead and placed their order. Desiree ordered the coconut shrimp and Renae got the steakhouse salad. Once the waiter left the table again, Desiree hurried to change the subject and ask about her and Ruben. Renae was a little hesitant to tell her because she didn't want to share all her wonderful news when she had just shared such heartbreaking news.

Desiree wouldn't let her hold back. She saw the big Kool-Aid smile plastered on her face as soon as she asked about him. Renae told her about the date, about Paul's being at the house when Ruben dropped her off, and that they had another date despite Paul's crazy ass. The whole time she told the story her face was glowing and Desiree was so happy to see her friend feeling this way. She had put up with enough of Paul's bullshit and knew she was due for some sunshine in her life with all the gloom and misery she had been through.

Renae told her they were supposed to be going out this evening and she was excited about it. They were both so into telling their stories and listening to the other's they had not seen everyone who had entered the restaurant until it was too late.

Michelle and Terrell had gotten to the restaurant just minutes apart. They sat at one of the tables in the back but only by coincidence. The waiter took their drink orders, but Michelle was ready to order her food. She had eaten here so many times she knew the menu backward and forward. Terrell went ahead and ordered the turkey burger and Michelle ordered the swordfish sandwich. As soon as the waiter was done taking their order and walked away, Michelle looked up to see Carlton standing there staring at her with fury in his eyes.

All Carlton saw was red. He couldn't think of anything else all morning besides the texts he read on his wife's phone and now he didn't know what to say.

"Are either one of you going to invite me to sit?"

Michelle and Terrell both looked at each other in amazement.

"Carlton, what are you doing here?" Michelle asked with a serious attitude.

"No. You need to tell me what y'all are doing here," he said getting louder.

She would not answer his question.

"What the fuck is up. I can't believe you are messing with Terrell. He is your best friend's little brother or maybe Nette knows what's going on too," he said about to explode.

Terrell jumped in, "Calm down, Bro. You think me and Chelle are... Oh no," he said full of anxiety.

Michelle finally slid over into the booth so he could sit before making a bigger scene.

"I can't believe you just accused me of fucking Terrell. He is like a little brother to me."

"Then tell me why the fuck he is texting first thing in the morning to meet you?"

People were beginning to stare.

Terrell interrupted him, "Man, Carlton. I know things look crazy, but you still don't need to be talking to her like that." Michelle grabbed his arm so he could let her handle it.

"Baby, look. I should have told you before, but let's go home and talk about this. I don't wanna do it here," she started softening her tone when she saw Carlton was not backing down. She waved to their server so she could get the check. By now more and more people were staring.

Renae noticed people moving in that direction when she saw Carlton and Terrell sitting in the booth. She nudged Desiree and they both saw Michelle sitting in the booth with them. By the time they got there, Carlton was storming out with Michelle following behind him.

"What is going on, Terrell?" she demanded.

"Not now, Sis. Now is not the time. I'll call you later," he said about to get up and leave.

"No, we need to talk about something more important. I need for you and Damon to come to my place this evening. We got some important shit to talk about. Then you can tell me what the heck was going on here," she said before she called for her server.

"I'll try, but I don't know if I'm gonna be able to..." she cut him off.

"This isn't a request. I'm not playing," she said about to cry again. Her voice was trembling, "Be at my house as soon as Damon gets off. I'll be home," she kissed him on the cheek before she paid the bill and left.

Terrell sat there for a minute trying to figure out what the hell had just happened and how all of this was going to affect their plans.

Desiree got in her car and immediately called her sister. She hit her with a barrage of questions because she just knew she was aware of what was going on and couldn't believe they were all keeping this secret and for how long. Sunshyne promised she didn't know anything and was just as shocked as everyone else. When they got off the phone she dialed Michelle's number and got no answer. She called her a couple more times with no success and then sent her a text.

Call me ASAP!!!

Michelle texted back a few minutes later...

Talking to Carlton. Will call you as soon as I can. I'm sorry I didn't tell you sooner," with a few emojis behind it and that was it.

So now she would wait for her friend to call and not jump to any conclusions because she just knew there had to be an explanation.

As Terrell pulled out the parking lot of the restaurant he noticed the same black mustang he peeped earlier at the bank. He didn't pay much attention earlier, but he knew it was the same one only because he was admiring it at the bank. Now here it was with the same guitar air freshener hanging from the rear view. He knew he needed to keep his eyes wide open now.

It seemed like everything was starting to fall apart. He would wait for Michelle to call him. Hopefully everything would be alright with her and Carlton. He called Damon and told him Desiree wanted them at her place when he got off work. He made sure to tell him she said it was very important. Damon told him he would meet him there at 6:30 p.m. Terrell texted Desiree and told her what time they would be by.

~19~

It had been a few days now since the fiasco at the restaurant. Sunshyne did not believe that her best friend and her baby brother were sleeping together. She knew Michelle was a flirt but she would never step out on Carlton, and especially not with Terrell. So when Michelle called her after everything went down to finally come clean and let her know what had been going on with her and Terrell, she was relieved that it wasn't what everyone thought. She still couldn't believe what they were doing and that she hadn't told her about it, but she accepted her reasoning and apologies. She wasn't going to harp on it and make her feel bad about it because she had enough going on in her marriage at the moment.

Carlton moved out right after everything went down and was staying with his boy, Jacob. He believed her when she told him that she was not having an affair with Terrell, but he couldn't get over the fact that she was willing to throw away everything they built to help him get his money clean.

Michelle wished she had told him, but knew he wouldn't have approved. At the time, it was the easiest way to get the help she needed. Her business was failing and the amount of money she was making was helping the company bounce back. Now it was costing her everything else. Her family and her marriage was in serious jeopardy, but at this point she was way too far in to come out now. There was no way she could pay Terrell back all the money he advanced her without the ship sinking.

She just prayed that when it was all done, and it would be done very soon, she would be able to make it all right with her husband. She knew it would be a rough road ahead, but she would fight. She would rely on the love that brought them together and has kept them strong over the years. For now, she needed to finish her business with Terrell.

***

Sunshyne had gotten up early that morning, cleaned the house, and was cooking breakfast. She was listening to her 80s R&B playlist on Spotify. It seemed like every song that played reminded her of Richard, *Betcha She Don't Love You, Save the Overtime for Me* and even *Murphy's Law*, flooded her thoughts with memories— good and bad. She knew she would never be able to get him out of her system. She couldn't stop thinking about him and now she was carrying a part of him inside her. She thought about all of their good times together while she rubbed her belly. There was no way she would be able to end the life growing inside of her. Even if he never left Monica and she had to raise this child without him, she couldn't get rid of it. She didn't do it with the others and wouldn't start now. The thought alone caused her eyes to well up. With tear filled eyes she fixed the kids plates, and as she walked back to her room she called them to eat. Maia came racing out her room to see her mother was crying.

She grabbed her by the leg, "What's wrong, Mommy?"

"Nothing baby girl. Go on and eat breakfast."

She put a weak smile on and hugged her youngest. She had not talked to Richard since Sunday. He hadn't called in a couple days, but he still blew her phone up texting her, it seemed like every hour on the hour. After she showered she sat on her bed rubbing her body with the last of her *Scrubfusions* lavender body butter. She couldn't hold out any longer and sent Richard a text...

Thinking about you.

He immediately responded with a barrage of texts before she had a chance to respond.

All I've been doing is thinking about you. So glad you finally responded. I miss you, Nette. Will you please let me see you? "I'm sorry for everything that has happened.

Finally he stopped texting and she was able to text back.

I'm still hurting. I miss you and want to see you too. I'll text you once I get to the shop and let you know my schedule.

She could not resist Richard. She was in love with the wrong man. This man supported everything she did and gave her strength but was also her greatest weakness. She finished getting herself together. She kissed her baby girl and told her she would be back later to get her so she could go over to Pa-Pa and Gi-Gi's.

Maia loved spending time with them. She was the only four-year-old she knew that would rather be sitting under her grandparents on a beautiful summer day than out playing with other children. She told Mariah that MJ was in charge and not to argue with him.

When she got to the shop her first appointment was at the bowl being washed. The young lady was a last-minute appointment. Renae's cousin was leaving to go on vacation and her regular hairdresser was sick so Renae told her to call Sunshyne and see if she could get her in. After she pleaded, Sunshyne put her on the books before her first appointment so she didn't mess with her regular clients' schedules.

Katrina was a loud sista. You could hear every word of her conversations. At one point while she was under the dryer, Sunshyne could hear her telling the person on the other end that some chick was pregnant and didn't know if it was her husband's or her boyfriend's baby.

"Girl, the chick is trifling," she tried to whisper into the phone.

Sunshyne and Meechie, her partner at the shop, looked at each other and just shook their heads. This was not the norm at Kuts & Kurls, and she couldn't get her in the chair and out the shop fast enough. She had to make sure she remembered to mention this to Renae. She took her from under the dryer and decided to blow dry her hair to speed up the process. She attempted to carry that conversation over into the chair with Sunshyne.

"I know you heard some of the conversation. My sister's friend is married and is cheating on her husband. She just found out she is pregnant and don't know who the daddy is." She kept talking even after the blow dryer came on, and Sunshyne just tuned her out. She did not have time for anybody else's baby daddy drama. She had enough of her own.

She figured she would be done by 12:30 p.m. today since Ms. Taylor had cancelled her and her daughter's appointments. She texted Richard to let him know she would be ready around 1:00 p.m. just to make sure she gave herself enough time. By mid-morning Sunshyne was tired. She had done two wash-n-curls, a highlight, and a keratin straightening treatment. Her last appointment was already ten minutes late and had not had the decency to call. She decided once she was done with her last updo she was going to call it a day until later this evening when other clients were due in.

At noon she texted Richard and told him she was ready. Ten minutes later he texted her and told her he was out back.

He had already stopped and gotten them some tacos. He figured they could go down by beach and have a quiet afternoon since she told him she only had a couple hours. He knew a part of the beach that would be secluded and they wouldn't have to worry about anyone they knew rolling up on them. He wanted to make it up to her for all that happened this past weekend, but he also had some more devastating news to share with her and wanted everything to be out in the open, even if it meant that he might lose the love of his life. He couldn't hold on to it anymore now that things were getting out of hand. He wanted her in his life, but he also needed for her to be happy. With all they had been through, he didn't know if they would bounce back from what he had to tell her.

They were both quiet the entire ride. He spoke briefly, letting her know what he had planned. When they arrived at the beach, he found a parking space close to the rocks. He got out and grabbed the blanket and little basket out the trunk. When they got to the spot he laid the blanket out and laid everything out. She prepared their plates while he opened the bottle and poured their glasses. She figured a little wine wouldn't hurt anybody.

They talked about what had been happening over the past couple of days with each of them. He told her about his daughter's' recital she had been practicing for and how well she did. Then finally they talked about what went down at the picnic. He apologized again for Monica coming at her like that and, more importantly, in front of her family.

"I really don't want to talk about your wife," she said.

"I don't want to spend this time worrying about that bullshit. It is what it is. It comes with the territory. I knew what I was getting myself into when I started dating you, but you have not stood up to word. You keep changing the game as we go along, but it stops now. Get your shit together or let me go. Matter of fact, you won't have to let me go. I will remove myself from the equation. I will tell you one thing though. If she runs up on me again, no one will be able to save her ass," she snapped at him harshly.

He got the point.

They spent the next couple of hours eating, walking along the beach and talking about more light-hearted subjects.

As they started walking back to where they had their blanket and basket, she noticed Richard's uneasiness. He was making small talk, but she could tell he had something more on his mind. Every time she looked into his eyes she could see the wheels turning, or at times he wasn't even there with her. She told him she didn't want to talk about what had happened, but if he wasn't going to be able to give her his full attention she needed to know why.

Every time she asked him what was bothering him, all he would say is, "Nothing. I'm fine." That was all she could get out of him.

She couldn't understand why he wouldn't tell her what was bothering him. The one thing they said they would never do and that was to hide anything from each other, to be honest.

She thought about that for a moment. If that was the case, why couldn't she tell him what she needed to tell him for the past two weeks. Maybe if she told him about what was keeping her from a peaceful night's sleep, he would move a little faster with what he needs to take care of. However, she knew she didn't want to use the baby as an ultimatum to be with her.

Still, she knew he needed to know the news about her pregnancy. She had been delaying because she wasn't sure how he was going to react. Would he finally choose her, or would he tell her it wasn't going to work? No matter what he decided, she had to tell him. It was now or never.

"Baby, let's sit down here. Since you don't want to tell me what's bothering you, I have something I need to tell you," Sunshyne said feeling her stomach starting to turn flips.

"What is it, my love?" Sunshyne was just about to tell him, when her phone vibrated again. This had been the 4th or 5th time it rang, and she couldn't ignore it anymore.

Sunshyne put up her finger as to tell Richard to wait one minute and answered her phone.

She put her cell to her ear to answer the call. After a few seconds, her face turned sullen and then a look of terror immediately washed over it. Mariah was on the other end of the line. She had been trying to call her to let her know her baby sister, Maia, had been hit by a car, and the ambulance was on the way to the house. Her baby girl? Just been hit by a car? Her knees buckled beneath her and she almost fell to the ground had Richard not caught her.

"What? Why weren't you watching her? What the hell were you doing?" She hurled several more questions at Mariah before she gave her the opportunity to get in a single answer.

More calls were flooding her cell phone. Every couple of seconds she looked at her caller ID to see who was calling, but she wanted Mariah to give her as much information as possible.

Sunshyne turned to Richard and said, "We gotta go now!"

As they ran to the car, Sunshyne listened intently, pure shock and panic consuming every inch of her body. She listened as Mariah recounted the story of what happened. Her voice was trembling with every word that escaped her mouth.

"We were outside playing with Kayla and Deshawn," she started.

"MJ ran into the house to grab her bike for her because Deshawn wouldn't let her ride in his car."

"What were you doing?" Sunshyne shouted.

"I was talking to Malaya and Brianna. I turned around to check on her, and that was when…" Mariah's voice trailed off.

Sunshyne heard a man in the background ask, "Who are you talking to young lady?" Mariah responded with a meek voice, "My mom." The officer asked for the phone from Mariah.

"Hello, Ms. Morris. My name is Officer Gentles. There has been a terrible accident at your home and you need to get here as soon as possible."

Sunshyne started firing more questions at the officer. All he said was "It would be best if you just hurry up and come home. That would be the best thing for everyone at the moment."

Sunshyne and Richard got in his car and sped away. It seemed like every traffic light was working against them as they raced through the streets to make it to her house. Sunshyne sat staring out the passenger window in disbelief. Richard did as many California stops as he could for every stop sign they came upon, until he stopped to allow a mother and her children to cross the street.

Sunshyne shot him an evil look. He knew she was stressed right now so he didn't say anything. A ride that would have normally taken fifteen minutes turned into a five-minute ride. When they pulled up to the block, it was mass hysteria. It looked like they could have been throwing a block party. However, Sunshyne knew it was not a happy occasion. Her baby was laying somewhere hurt and broken up. The first thing she noticed was the ambulance parked in front of her apartment building, lights still flashing. She could not, and did not want to, imagine what she would see once they opened the doors. With the car barely stopping, she swung open the door and jumped out.

Richard pulled over into a parking space as soon as he could. Once he got out of the car, he strolled over to blend in with the crowd. He did not want to cause her anymore undo pressure by being seen. Focused, she ran for the ambulance. As she approached the closed doors, she heard a soft, excited voice yell, "Mommy!!!" She whipped her head to the right to see Mariah standing there with MJ, Desiree, and her mom.

Everyone's face had the same look of terror. She could not stop for them yet. She had to check on her baby before anything else. However, before she could make it to the ambulance an officer blocked her pathway.

"Ms. Morris?"

"Yes, that's me," she said sadly.

"Can you please step over here with me so we can talk for a minute? We have a few questions to ask you."

She followed the officer closer to the parked police car away from the huge crowd that had gathered around the scene.

"My baby is in there. What is it that you have to ask me right at this moment?"

"We need to ask you why your children were left at home alone."

"My daughter is fourteen. She is more than old enough to look after her siblings. Can I please see my baby? After I let her know I'm here you can ask me all the questions you want."

The officer moved out the way to allow her to get to her child.

When they got to the ambulance the officer knocked on the doors and one of the EMT's opened it up. Once the family saw Nette going to the ambulance, they joined her. On the way over Desiree noticed the man that claimed to be Nette's father, standing down the street in one of the crowds. She started to go confront him right then and there, but Mariah grabbed her hand and brought her back to the priority situation, her injured niece.

The scene in the back of the ambulance was just too much for her to take. Sunshyne saw Maia lying on a stretcher. Bruises and blood were all over her body and she was wearing a neck brace. She could not believe her eyes. How could this have happened? How could she let this happen? As many times as she had done this before, she never thought anything like this would happen.

One of the EMT's were working on Maia, telling her funny stories to keep her distracted from the unfamiliar procedures she had to endure. Sunshyne asked the other EMT how bad things were. As soon as Maia heard her mother's voice she immediately started yelling for her mom.

"Mommy! Mommy! Where were you, Mommy?"

"It's okay, baby. Mommy is here now," Sunshyne said in a calm, soothing voice.

It took everything in her being to hold back the tears so she wouldn't upset her daughter. She just sat there rubbing

Maia's arm as they did what they could to make her comfortable before taking her to Lakeview emergency room.

"The cuts and bruises look worse than they are. It doesn't look like she has broken anything and the brace is just a precaution. "Your daughter was very lucky— this time, ma'am," the female EMT said while giving her a very cynical look.

Sunshyne rolled her eyes and continued to focus on her daughter. Before long, they were ready to move her. The male EMT opened the door and called the officer over. Sunshyne thought it very strange, but again her focus was on Maia.

"Baby, you go ahead and ride with Maia. I'll stay here with the kids and Desiree will be up there soon." her mother told her.

"Unfortunately, Ms. Morris, we can't allow you to ride in the ambulance."

A look of confusion contorted her face. "I don't understand why not."

"We still have some questions for you." The police officer said calmly.

"Are you kidding me with this bullshit right now? My daughter is hurt and needs her mother, and all you want to do is question me. Well, guess what? I'm going to ride in this ambulance and go to the hospital with her. Then I'm going to sit by her side until they are sure everything is okay with her. If you can't wait until after that then arrest me right now, and I will make sure my attorney meets us at the police station. Yeah, I said my attorney," she turned to hop in the ambulance without waiting for a response. The female EMT blocked her entry until the male officer gave her the green light. Sunshyne was getting tired of this bitch.

"Go ahead, and we will meet you there." The policer officer replied.

"That's what I thought." Sunshyne got in, and they drove away.

~20~

When they made it to the hospital, the nurses were very attentive to Maia. They kept her occupied while her mother got her registered in the system and signed the necessary papers. She had not seen the officers that were at the house yet and hoped someone higher up had instructed them to stay away. That maybe their superior had informed them the matter did not call for the police's attention, but she knew that was just too good to be true. She especially knew that was not case when she finally saw the two officers coming through the emergency room doors. They stopped at the door to talk to the security guard for a brief second before walking over to the vending machine and then into the security office.

Sunshyne finished up with the concierge and went back to the room with Maia.

A young man stepped in the room. "Is this cute little girl Maia?"

"Yes, it is."

Sunshyne looked a little perplexed, and the nurse noticed her facial expression.

"Ms. Morris, Calvin is here to take Maia up for some x-rays. Dr. Matthews has ordered x-rays just to ensure nothing is broken."

"Thank you. Can I leave my belongings here?"

"Sure. That won't be a problem."

Calvin made sure Maia was situated properly and locked the railings on the gurney, and they all went up to radiology to get the x-rays taken. Maia was back in her room and settled by the time Desiree made it to the hospital.

"Mama said to call her as soon as we know how she is."

"Hey TT. My tongue is purple," Maia said as she stuck her tongue out of her mouth.

"How did you get a purple tongue? Did you color it with a marker?"

Maia laughed. "No. The nurse gave me a Popsicle earlier. Mommy, do you think she will give me another one?"

"I don't know, baby. We can ask her when she comes back."

Sunshyne's body cringed when she heard the echo of Marcus' voice asking for their daughter's room from the hallway. As soon as she stood up to open the curtain he walked in the room with disgust on his face as he glared at Sunshyne. Now was not the time for him to have that conversation with her though.

"Hi daddy."

"Hi baby girl."

"Look, daddy," and Maia stuck out her tongue again.

"I want a purple tongue. How do I get a purple tongue?"

"We gotta ask the nurse for some more popsicles. Mommy said she might get me another one when she came back. Mommy can we get daddy one too?'

"Yes. We will get daddy one too."

As soon as the nurse returned, Maia asked her for a Popsicle for her and her daddy. The nurse left and returned with two of them and asked Sunshyne and Marcus if they could step out of the room in order to talk. Sunshyne got nervous.

"What's wrong?"

"Nothing is wrong, Ms. Morris. We would just like to speak outside away from your daughter," she said in a soft voice as not to alarm Maia.

"We'll be right back baby. We are going to talk to the nice lady."

"Alright, Mommy."

She and Marcus left the room while Desiree stayed with Maia.

Sunshyne realized why they didn't want to talk to her in the room as soon as she stepped out the curtains. The two officers were standing there, along with a stout Caucasian woman. One of the officers directed everyone to an empty conference room near the emergency room lobby. Once inside the conference room, the male officer introduced the unknown woman.

"Ms. Morris, this is Ms. Niemann from the Department of Children and Family Services. She was called in to help assess the situation further for us," he stated matter-of-factly. Sunshyne's face was now a mask of grave worry. She looked at Marcus and she could tell he was fuming.

Ms. Niemann officially introduced herself and handed Sunshyne her card.

"Ms. Morris, let me first start by saying I am here only to help you and your family figure out what happened and make sure that Maia as well as the other children are in a safe environment. Whether it be in your home with you or somewhere else. We can determine that after I have had to the chance to talk to with you and talk further with your other children."

What does she mean talk further with my kids? Does this bitch think she's talking to my kids without me around? I know they better not have said much to her. Those were just a few of the thoughts racing through her head. The last one was immediately erased from her mind as Ms. Niemann opened up the conversation with, "I had the chance to talk with the children for a little while and Mariah told us that she is left to watch the younger kids on a regular basis, sometimes they are left all day and can be alone during the night at times. To be honest, this is very disturbing."

Sunshyne looked over to Marcus who was shaking his head. He had told her several times not to leave them alone, but she did whatever she wanted and now it was coming back to bite her in the ass.

Ms. Niemann continued, "Your daughter is not old enough to be left alone to take care of her siblings, especially with one under the age of five. She also should not be cooking without adult supervision. I also understand you send them to the store when you are not home as well and that isn't very smart either."

Sunshyne was sitting there listening to this lady try to chastise her and tell her what to do with her children. She was ready to slap the taste out of her mouth. She doesn't know what goes on there every day, so she wanted that bitch to stop looking down on her.

"Do you have anyone who can watch the children while you are away from the house?" Before Sunshyne could open her mouth, Ms. Niemann continued with, "We would hate for something more serious to happen."

That was it. Sunshyne had had enough. Without letting her get another word out, Sunshyne quickly interjected, cutting her off.

"I know that this is a horrible situation, and I feel horrible seeing my baby like this. Before you come riding in here on your high horse with your judgmental ass, you need to understand one thing. I don't always have someone to watch my children for me all the time. Sometimes I can get my mother to watch them for me, and other times their father helps out."

By this time Sunshyne was up off the couch she had been sitting on and was getting louder as each syllable left her mouth.

"When I'm unable to reach either one of them in an emergency situation, I will leave my oldest in charge from time to time," Sunshyne continued, "She is old enough to watch her brother and sister. I was her same age watching my brother and sister while my mom went to work. I understand you have a job to do, but my children and I are just fine. This was a freak accident, one that I will take every precaution to make sure doesn't happen again."

With that, Sunshyne sat back on the soft tan leather couch. Ms. Niemann turned to Marcus, "Are you able to help her take care of the children more? She should not have to do this all by herself. "

"I haven't done as much as I should, but from here on out I will make sure that I am available to help more." Marcus replied guiltily.

Ms. Niemann turned back to Sunshyne, "It may have been a freak accident as you say, but it was a very serious one. I thank God nothing more serious happened to your daughter. I will need to discuss everything with my supervisor, but will let the both of you know what the plan will be before you leave the hospital."

Sunshyne and Marcus went back to Maia's room and awaited the outcome from Ms. Niemann.

Sunshyne just knew Marcus was going to have something to say, but before he had the chance Dr. Matthews came in to speak with them.

"Good afternoon. I am Dr. Matthews. You have one tough young lady here. She is doing much better than most adults given the circumstances. I have reviewed her x-rays, and nothing is broken. There are no internal injuries showing up at this time. However, we would like to keep her overnight for observations. Just to be on the safe side," she said pleased to share the good news.

"Thank you so much for taking care of my baby, doctor. I appreciate all you've done and am glad to hear she's doing well," Sunshyne beamed overjoyed knowing now that there was nothing seriously wrong with her daughter.

"You are welcome, and you have done a good job with her. She is well-mannered, bright and inquisitive. I wish you all the best. The nurse will be back when it's time to take her up to her room."

Doctor Matthews walked out of the room. Sunshyne and Maia talked a little while Maia played games on her dad's phone. Desiree stepped out to call her mom with the update. She had already spoken to their brothers. Damon was on his way up there. About fifteen minutes later, the nurse came in with the transporter and provided the room information for Maia's overnight stay.

As they were following Maia and the transporter, Desiree pulled out her phone to see if she had missed a text or phone call from Damon. She wondered why he hadn't made it up to the hospital yet. Right before she got ready to call to see where he was, he rounded the corner. She was the only one to notice them at first. Then Sunshyne looked and couldn't believe her eyes. Her jaw dropped and her eyes widen. Walking her way were Damon and Richard.

Richard was carrying a bag of takeout in his hand. Marcus looked at her, and every muscle in his body tightened. She could not believe he was there, and more importantly, she couldn't believe Damon was walking with him. She looked at Marcus and saw his reaction,

"I'll take care of this."

"You betta," was all he said in response and continued walking to the elevator. As soon as she approached the two of them, Richard immediately apologized.

"I did not know he had made it here already, or I wouldn't have come. I wasn't sure how long you would have to be here, so I brought you something to eat."

"Thank you. I appreciate it, but you should go. I don't need to add any more fuel to the fire right now." The smell of the food made her breakfast rise from her stomach to her throat. She could feel the heat filling her cheeks once the aroma from the bag hit her nostrils.

She pushed it back down, but not before Richard asked her if she was feeling alright. He asked how Maia was doing, and she gave him a brief rundown of her condition. When she saw that Marcus was out of sight, she kissed Richard on the cheek and told him she would call when she had the chance. She was going to get on Damon once they got on the elevator to go upstairs but realized it was not his fault.

She was just glad to have more support when she went up to the room to face Marcus. It was nice of Richard to bring her something to eat. However, she wondered if Richard really had her best interest at heart or if he was hoping Marcus was there and wanted to make his presence felt.

Once Maia arrived at her room, the grown-ups waited in the hallway while the nurses took Maia's vitals and got her settled in. Marcus and Sunshyne finally had the chance to talk. "You gon have to quit leaving the kids by themselves all the time, Jeanette. You are lucky shit wasn't worse than what it is. I know I could help a little more, but if I can't and you aren't able to get a sitter you just need to sit your ass in the house."

"Don't try and act like you ain't had a clue. You've even dropped them at the house when I'm not there, but now that shit has hit the fan you want act all holier than thou. You're right. You do need to come get them more. So until you do, Mariah is old enough to handle them for a couple hours when I'm not there. No, I won't leave them alone at night, but during the day they will be okay."

They all looked at her in shock. Even her siblings couldn't believe she was still willing to leave them alone after what happened today, but Desiree and Damon both decided to wait until they were alone to discuss it with her. They didn't want to address it in front of Marcus.

"Look. You do what you want, but if one of my babies get hurt again you gon be sorry."

This time Damon did have something to say. "What you mean *she* gon be sorry?"

"Just what I said. She got kids at home she need to take care of, but she wanna run up behind some cat that got a wife at home."

"You right, Bro. She does have kids, but they're yours too. So you need to step up and be a man and give her a break more than you do. Then you wouldn't have to worry about them being by themselves as much."

"And you need to mind your business," Marcus said stepping closer to Damon.

"These are my kids, and I say what goes on with them."

"Nette is my business so keep your threats to yourself," he closed the gap even more between them.

Then the elevator dinged and opened. Ms. Niemann stepped off the elevator and walked up to them.

"Ms. Morris. Mr. Thompson. Can we step over here for a minute to talk?"

"It's ok. This is my sister and brother. We can talk right here." Sunshyne told her.

"If you are okay with it then we can stay here. I have spoken to my supervisor and gone over everything with her. We have decided to remove the children from your household. At this time, we do not feel that is the safest environment for them. This can be temporary or permanent. It is all up to you. You will be required to attend parenting classes for starters. After we review your case futhr we will determine what additional requirements will be necessary. We will evaluate the progress after six months and determine if you are ready to have the children back or if further services are needed."

"This is bullshit," Sunshyne got loud and Damon tried to calm her down.

"Naw. Don't hush me. She come up here talking about they're taking my children because of one accident. Lady you act like this has never happened to anyone before," Sunshyne was getting loud. Her sister tried to calm her but it was to no avail.

"The accident could have occurred if I was in the house fixing lunch while the kids were outside playing," she snapped.

Ms. Niemann was trying to be calm. "I understand your frustration, but the fact of the matter is that you weren't at home. We can talk about all of the what-ifs, but you were not home with them and you aren't at home with them quite a bit."

"We can talk more when you come to the office, but the classes aren't just for you. You will have to attend classes as well Mr. Thompson. We understand that the kids were with their mother at the time, but we feel that the entire family would benefit from the services. We also feel that if you are not participating then you won't be able to assist Ms. Morris. You have my card. Please call me in the next couple days so we can get everything started. Again, I'm happy your daughter is doing well."

Ms. Niemann patted Sunshyne on the shoulder as to let her know things are not as bad as they seem.

"Is there someone who can get the kids today?"

"Yes. The kids can stay with my parents."

"Okay. Can we go to a private room so we can call to get everything set up?"

Ms. Niemann went to a conference room with Sunshyne and Marcus, and they called her mom. They explained everything that was happening, and Ms. Niemann confirmed the children could stay with Sunshyne's parents.

Mrs. Morris told her she was willing to help in any way she could and that it would not be a problem. Once they hung up, Ms. Niemann discussed a few more things with her and Marcus before they went back to down the hallway to Maia's room.

~21~

Renae had finally decided to go back home. She and Ruben had been spending more time together over the last few days. She still hadn't allowed him to pick her up from home yet. She thought it was still too soon, even if Paul had been an asshole about things. So, she either had him pick her up at her daddy's house or she met him at a neutral spot somewhere.

This evening she was just going to have him pick her up from the courthouse once she got off of work. Since she had her employee sticker in the window, the night patrol would not bother her car. It was 4:15 p.m., almost time for her to clock out. She glanced across her desk and saw her phone light up. It was a message from Paul. She immediately became irritated. She ignored it and started shutting down her computer.

He hadn't bothered her at all in a few days, but she knew he wouldn't leave her alone that easily. He was probably just occupied by the flavor of the week. As she was leaving her office, her phone lit up again. This time it was Ruben. He was running a few minutes behind but would be there shortly. Then she looked at Paul's message.

"I miss you Nae. I know you miss me too. You need to quit playing and let me show you how much I miss you."

She hurried up and deleted his message. She wanted to be petty and text him back to go show Moni Love how much he missed her, but she left it alone. She didn't want to start the back and forth with him and ruin the evening with Ruben. Nor did she want him thinking that she even cared. Renae got on the elevator and went down to the lobby. Donald, the night security guy was sitting at the desk.

"Hey, Renae. How have you been?"

"I've been good. How about you? Haven't seen you in a while," she replied.

"Yeah. The kids and I took a long vacation this year. We went to visit my parents down south", he said with a big huge smile.

Donald always talked about his parents and was disappointed he couldn't visit them as often as he would've like.

"How is your girl Dee doing? I know she is still fine and crazy as ever," Donald said. Donald was another one who had fallen victim to Desiree. They dated a couple of times and then she dropped him like a hot potato.

"She's good. Still being Desiree."

Just then her phone buzzed. Ruben was outside.

"My ride is here. Have a good night," she said walking toward the entrance.

"You too, Renae."

She was always excited to see Ruben and enjoyed hanging out with him. She placed her bag on the back seat and hopped in the front.

"Hey, Sweetheart. How was your day?"

"It was pretty cool. Got a lot of interesting cases in today, so it was pretty eventful," she said and sank into the warm leather seat relieved to be off.

"How has your day been?" she asked him.

"Mine was quite eventful as well. Probably not as exciting as yours, but nonetheless tiring," he said as he let out a sigh.

They were both glad to see each other and preoccupied with their conversation that they didn't notice the blue Chevy Malibu parked near the entrance of the parking lot. The driver watched as they pulled away onto Old Orchard Road. The driver wanted to follow them but stuck to the plan. He would wait. Sooner rather than later he would get her, and, more importantly get at that dude.

As they drove Renae could tell something wasn't right with Ruben. Something was off today. He wasn't his normal talkative self, but every time she asked what was bothering him he would tell her nothing. Only that he had a long day. She told him they could hang out another night, but he said being with her would make everything better. They continued to ride in silence listening to old school hip hop on the Backspin radio station on XM radio. When Wu-Tang's Triumph came on the radio, he was surprised she knew all the lyrics.

"You don't know nothin' about that right there."

"Man, you don't know who you rollin' with. Hip hop and house music are my life," she said confidently.

He turned off the radio, plugged in his iPad and played his Wu playlist. When she could recite almost every song he was convinced she had a real love for Hip Hop music.

"Not many women are into them. They were more into LL, Queen Latifah and MC Lyte."

"I just like old school Hip Hop period. It doesn't matter who I'm listening to."

About thirty minutes later they were pulling up to the Happy Crab restaurant. Ruben knew exactly what she liked. Crab legs were at the top of her list. The restaurant wasn't crowded at all so they had their pick of seats. They decided to sit at the bar since the Cubs would be coming on soon. They had a couple drinks and talked some more while they waited on their food.

Dinner was followed by a drive over to Belmont Harbor where they enjoyed a nice walk along the beach, before he drove her back to her car.

As they pulled into the garage, Harvey, the night patrolman was sitting at the entrance and peered into the car to see who was entering the garage at that time of night. Once he noticed Renae in the passenger seat he waved to her and backed up to allow them to enter. They pulled up to her 2013 silver Toyota Camry. Ruben noticed her licensed plate and let out a chuckle.

"Nae Baby 5, huh? I get the Nae Baby, but what is the 5 for?"

"Idk. It's just always been my favorite number," Renae replied.

He walked her to her car, he opened the door for her to get in just before giving her a deep passionate kiss on the lips.

He would never try anything more than a kiss. She knew after a few dates that she was sexually attracted to him and wanted to give him some. Maybe tonight she would make her move instead of waiting on him, but she didn't want him to think she was loose, as her mom used to say. Then there was the realization that she couldn't take him back to her place. She let the thoughts dance around in her head just a little longer before he broke them up.

"Looks like your back tire is on a flat. Do you have a spare in the trunk?"

"I believe so," she said with a taste of uncertainty in her voice. Her tires were just fine when she drove to work this morning. She wasn't sure how this could have happened. She gave him the key and he opened the trunk. Underneath the liner in the trunk was a pristine looking doughnut. Ruben changed the tire and told her it should hold until he could get it to the shop in the morning.

She kissed him again and got in her car. When she started the car they both noticed a funny noise but didn't pay it no mind because it went away almost immediately. As she drove over the expressway and got closer to Old Orchard Mall the car began to sputter and hesitate on her. The more she tried to accelerate the harder it became for her to drive. Ruben called her to find out what was going on and she explained the issues she was having. Since they were nowhere near her house, he told her to pull into the mall parking lot. He checked it out for her but couldn't figure out what it was. So he told her it would have to wait until he could get it to a shop in the morning. They figured it would be safe there over night. So they left it, and he drove her home.

He was at her house bright and early the next morning. She really wished he had called before he came, and she would have met him at the mall. All he was doing was coming to help her with her car, but she still felt a little guilty. As those thoughts were rolling around in her head, she could also hear Desiree's voice.

"Girl, why are you so concerned about Paul's feelings? He hasn't been worried about yours."

She still asked him to wait outside while she grabbed her stuff. Ruben was walking back to his car to call his boy that drove a tow truck to meet them at the mall to take it to Willy's shop for him. He called ahead to let Willy know it was coming and told him what was happening.

He was so involved with her car, they never noticed the blue Malibu lurking on the corner.

~22~

Marcus said he would stay at the hospital while Sunshyne went and got the other kids straight. They were going to stay at her parents' house tonight, but she wanted to get them a change of clothes. She also wanted to grab Maia some clothes to come home in tomorrow. While they waited for Marcus and Sunshyne to finish talking, Desiree told her twin she still needed for him to come by the house that night. Damon said he would call Terrell, and they would meet her there in a couple hours.

***

Damon and Terrell met at Desiree's house as promised. They talked about everything, including what was going on with Terrell and Michelle. Their baby brother gave them as much information as he could for the moment. Terrell promised them he was not sleeping with Michelle, but could not tell them anymore than that because he didn't want to involve anyone else.

Desiree and Damon ragged on him for a minute and told him they just hoped he knew what he was doing. She told him he better watch himself because Carlton didn't look very happy when he left the restaurant. They both told him to get his shit together and moved on to the pressing matter.

Desiree shared with them how she had been spending more time with Jerome, and he had done a little digging of his own to help her get some answers on the mystery man that showed up to the house. She played back what he learned and what she had uncovered from talking to their grandmother.

Jerome had found out his older sister was good friends with Desiree's mama back in the day. Although she was reluctant to get in the middle of what was happening, she could never tell her baby brother no. She told him the guy, Jesse Porter, used to live in the neighborhood and had a relationship with Mrs. Morris. The relationship didn't last long because Mrs. Morris found out early on that Jessie was abusive, a womanizer, and a cheat. He had several "baby mamas" around town and was not in a committed relationship with any of them.

Mrs. Morris stopped seeing him and moved away a couple months later. The rumor was he had gotten her pregnant. Her parents were very involved with the church. Her father was a trustee and deacon, and her mother was the leader of the Pastor's Aide Ministry and a Sunday school teacher. They believed her pregnancy would bring shame to their family. That is where her story ended and that's where Desiree's investigative skills began.

She also went on to tell them she went straight to the source to get the rest of the details. She shared the visit with them.

She stopped at Chicken Shack and got her grandmother some of their tilapia. Granny loved their tilapia so she knew she would be glad to get some. Her mother would be upset because she wasn't supposed to be eating fried food, but she didn't get it too often so Desiree figured it shouldn't hurt.

In between eating a fry or a piece of fish, Granny asked about her great-grandkids, her other grandkids, and her daughter and son—in-law. Granny always loved to talk even though she forgot some things at times. Desiree was able to get enough information to bring back to their parents.

"We had to send Barbara to go live with my sister, her Aunt Jean, in Cincinnati during her junior year of high school because that character she met wasn't any good for her. Got her knocked up and tossed her to the side like an old dirty rag, but then she met that fella, Darryl out there while she was in Cincinnati. Her life had turned around after she met him. 1He loved her more than anything in the world and couldn't wait to ask your granddad for her hand in marriage," her grandmother rambled on.

"You mean my daddy, Granny? Terrell?" Desiree let out a little chuckle.

"Oh, yeah baby. That's him. Your dad," she let out a loud laugh. "Baby, what's going on? Why does everyone want to talk about that low life and your mother's leaving town?" she asked.

"What do you mean, Granny? Who is everyone?"

"Your mama was up here the other day upset and worried about him. She babbled on about how she wished she would have killed him when she had the opportunity. She wouldn't tell me why, but I know it's bad because she only talked like this one other time. That time was awful," she said as she started dozing.

"What was awful, Granny," Desiree shook her. "Granny!" She said a little louder, startling her awake.

"Baby, my medicine is taking over, and I'm getting a little sleepy now. I need to take a nap," Granny whispered barely able to keep her eyes open.

"Alright, Granny. Get your rest, I'll come back and see you soon," she kissed her grandmother on the cheek.

After Desiree shared what she knew with Damon and Terrell, they both just sat there with their mouths wide open. They definitely were not the Brady Bunch, but they weren't sure what this would do to their family.

"Have you talked to mom and dad about all this?" Terrell was the first to talk.

"No. I wasn't sure how to bring it to them."

"I can't believe that. You've never had a hard time addressing any issues before." Damon mused.

"Yeah, but this is different. This ain't a chick trying to push up on my man or a co-worker going behind my back to steal my position. We're talking about mommy and daddy keeping a secret from our family. Again. Once we confront them about it there is no going back. So we have to tread lightly."

"We?" they both shouted simultaneously.

"I think maybe you should go talk to mom about it first, and see what she has to say. You may be able to get her to talk about easier than daddy would. If you can't get it out of her, then we can all get together and go at 'em." Damon said smoothly.

"Yeah. What Damon just said," Terrell leaned back on the couch and smiled.

"Y'all are some punks, but I will go talk to her because I don't think this Jesse character is going away anytime soon. Plus he is getting too close for comfort. I saw him out there the day Maia got hit by the car, but by the time I got ready to go to him, he had disappeared."

They all agreed on how they were going to deal with their parents. Years ago they abruptly find out they had a little brother. Now they realized that their dad was not Sunshyne's biological father, and it was just a matter of time now before she found out too. They all knew this would be way more devastating than Terrell's Jr's introduction.

***

Sunshyne spent the night with Maia at the hospital. Marcus was back there early the next morning. Not long after Marcus returned, the nurse walked in the room. Marcus and Sunshyne took the opportunity to step in the hallway and talk.

"Mommy and daddy will be right outside your door while the nurse is in here with you," Marcus told her.

"Okay, daddy. Don't be long cause I'm ready to go home."

"No problem, sweetie," and he closed the door behind them.

Marcus had been thinking all night about how they were going to make the situation better for the sake of their children. He still believed Sunshyne needed to be a better mother and pay more attention to the kids. Yet, he knew he needed to step his game up as well. He had to give her more help. They went back into the same conference room they met with the caseworker in yesterday.

"What is it now, Marcus." Sunshyne hissed and rolled her eyes.

"I didn't come here to argue this morning. I just want us to sit down and figure out what we're going to do so these people don't take the kids out the house permanently," he was trying to hold his temper, but she was making it difficult.

"Now you wanna worry about the kids? Where were you when I was asking for your help before? You were so bent on trying to keep me locked down while you were out there doing what you wanted to do."

"Jeanette just shut up and listen please. I'm trying to get it right now, and you should be trying to do the same thing. I know that dude isn't that important that you gotta leave the kids alone. You can sit down some time. You don't have to be gone as much as you do."

"I thought you said you were trying to get it right. All I hear you talking about is what I need to do. I don't need you to tell me shit about what I need to do. You not the one at the house with them all the time," she snapped back at him.

"Clearly your sorry ass ain't either," he came right back at her.

Their conversation went from bad to worse real fast. This was not the type of conversation he wanted to have to-day, but this is how it usually ended up.

"Fuck you, Marcus," she yelled before she was forced to take a seat.

Her head started spinning and she was feeling a little nauseous.

"Fuck me. That's cool. First, I don't know who you raising your voice at. You better calm that shit down."

She jumped up and got ready to walk out the room on him. As soon as she stood up her legs gave out on her.

The next thing she knew an extreme flash of heat came over her and she saw black.

~23~

Desiree couldn't believe an entire week had passed and she hadn't talked to Renae, her sister or Jerome. She hadn't even talked to her mom and they normally talked every day. She missed Sunday dinner at her parents' house the past weekend as well.

She called Renae, who was with Ruben, so she told her to get back with her later. She knew not talking to her older sister and her mother was because she wasn't sure if she could hold the news about Jesse Porter and wasn't ready to open up that can of worms.

However, today was the day she was going to see her mother. She called her to make sure she was going to be around and said she would stop by around lunch time. Her mother had a doctor's appointment that morning but would be home for rest of the day once it was over. She would have lunch ready for them around 12:30.

Desiree got to her parents' house around 12:15. She pulled into the driveway and saw her daddy's Cadillac pulled up by the garage. She sat for a moment to get herself together. When she got out the car she heard old school music coming from the backyard. When she got to the gate, Smokey Robinson and Rick James were singing, *Ebony Eyes*, one her mother's favorite songs.

The table was set with matching sunflower dishes and glasses. Her mother even had the yellow-handed silverware out. She knew it would not be a simple lunch because her mother looked for any reason to set up the table. The grandkids rarely ate off of plain paper plates or drank out of red Solo cups. Her mother always wanted to feel like she was entertaining. Her daddy had grilled some salmon and boneless chicken breasts for them. Her mom made some broccoli slaw and garlic mashed potatoes. She also had sweet tea and some apple cinnamon crunch cake left from Sunday. Her mom was carrying the bowl of slaw and a yellow ceramic platter with the salmon and the chicken out to the patio as Desiree walked up to the table.

"Hey ma dear."

"Hey, baby girl. How are you? I didn't know when I was going to get to see you again since you been so busy with work," she said as she hugged her youngest daughter, and they sat down at the table.

"I know, but they have been keeping me real busy at the office with a huge case we're working. I have to be at the office later this evening to prepare for a deposition tomorrow," she said already sounding exhausted.

"What was your doctor's appointment for?"

"I took a home pregnancy test that came back positive, so I went to see how accurate it was," she said with the straightest face possible.

"Bye, mom," Desiree said as she rolled her eyes. "You are not having any kids."

"Why not? You don't think me and your dad can have kids? We both have a few years in us."

"Y'all have grandkids and don't need to be thinking about having no kids."

"Oh ok, but don't think we ain't doing..."

Desiree interrupted her, "That's enough right there. I do not need to hear the rest. Where is daddy anyway?"

"He's upstairs napping. His allergies had been bothering him."

They sat and ate listening to the music floating from the wireless speaker. After they finished lunch and were eating dessert, Desiree figured she'd go ahead and get it out. She was a little nervous about even having the conversation with her mom but knew it had to be done.

"Mom, I'm not sure how to ask you about this, but I feel things are about to get real serious around here. Before I tell you what I know, I want you to know I am not holding anything against you, and I'm not judging you. I just think that things are about to get bad, real bad. I think it is going to be as bad as when Terrell came to stay with us, or even worse. I think Nette is going to be devastated," Desiree said already close to tears.

"What has happened now?"

Desiree began replaying what she had learned through Jerome's sister and her grandmother. She told her mother what she learned about her relationship with Mr. Porter, moving down south and when she met her father. She also let her mother know that he was asking everyone he knew about Nette. She went on to let her know how her granny started to tell her how something awful happened but didn't say much. A startled look came over Barbara Morris' face. Her eyes were distant, and Desiree could tell her mom was reliving things that had happened.

"I've seen him a couple times since he came to the house. He was at Jerome's bar asking questions and trying to enlist him with what he is trying to do. He was also outside in the crowd the day Maia got hit. I think it's only a matter of time before she finds out that he is her father."

Tears were falling from her mother's eyes.

"I should've known it would eventually come back on us. I thought since we had gone this long that we had weathered the storm, but I guess this *is* Glenmont.

Desiree reached over to hold her mother's hand as she began telling her the entire story.

"Jessie Porter was abusive, controlling, a cheater, and drank a lot. He was six years older than me and wanted to be in control of every aspect of my life. He didn't want me to hang out because I might run into him at the Gaslight or 1623 Club, two bars he frequented, and he didn't want me hanging with my friends anymore. I was okay with it at first because I was young and he would tell me things like, "they don't mean you any good" or "I don't want my woman hanging out in them type of places.

I eventually found out he had another girlfriend and that was the real reason he wanted to keep me hidden and didn't want me to show up where he was. One night I finally confronted him. He got mad and slapped me. He told me not to ever question anything he said again, and I didn't. I lost my friends, as well as my self-esteem. A couple months later I found out I was pregnant but couldn't tell my parents because it would've devastated them. I told my big sister and begged her to keep the secret until I told them.

When I told Jesse I was pregnant I thought things were going to changc, but thcy didn't. It just got worse. One night my sister took me to a party, and we ran into him. He got mad and beat me up bad. He accused me of sleeping around with somebody else and questioned if he was the father of the baby. That was the night I told your grandparents everything.

They took me straight to the police station and pressed charges. The next morning my mother took me to the doctor to confirm what we already knew was true. Since my parents didn't believe in abortions, the only option was for me to keep the baby. They didn't want me to stay up here so they sent me to live with Aunt Jean. They told me it was because I was too young, and they didn't want Jessie sweet talking me back in his bed. I think it was more about me being an embarrassment with their church members.

I was so grateful for Aunt Jean because she was more understanding and open-minded than your grandparents. She knew things happened, but she also believed that with God anything is possible. She let me stay with her for a couple years until I could finish high school, get a job and get out on my own. Then I met your father when your sister was about eight months old and from the beginning he was everything that Jesse was not. He didn't care that I had a child. He just wanted to see me smile," she said as a faint smile poked through all the sadness she was feeling remembering those days.

She freshened up their glasses of tea, "We dated for about a year and then moved into a small one-bedroom apartment. Your father eventually asked me to marry him, and once we were married we lied and said we had no idea who the father was. I told them I had a one-night stand and my daughter was conceived. We filed the papers for him to adopt Jeanette, and from that day forward she was *his* daughter."

After some time, they had to move back to Glenmont because his uncle had gotten real sick and needed help running his plumbing business, and things got a little tricky then. She said everything was going fine until she ran into Jesse coming out of a local store several years later. She had heard he was not only a drunk but had started using drugs heavily and was in and out of jail.

"His people told him I had a child, and that was the reason I had left town. He figured your sister was his, but I told him that day he would never see her as long as I had breath left in my body. He would come around every now and then and threaten to take us to court to prove she was his unless we gave him money so he could supply his habit. We did until he had gotten locked up again, and we didn't hear from him for a long time. Then one morning he showed up on our doorsteps claiming to be clean, but still asking for money again. Your daddy told him if he came around us or our family again he would regret it. So he waited until one night when he knew your daddy was at the bar and came by the house demanding to see his child. I made you kids stay upstairs and called your dad. He wasn't getting there fast enough, and I was afraid of what he might do. I went to the closet and grabbed your daddy's gun. When I was coming back down the stairs he kicked in the door. I aimed for his chest and hit him in the shoulder. Your dad was pulling up to the house by then, and one of the neighbors called the police. They took me in for questioning but said it was self-defense and let me go. Your daddy's reputation went a long way back then. He did a lot of good work around the city so no one wanted to charge me. Plus Jesse's reputation went a long way too, and they knew he was a piece of shit."

Desiree had not heard her mother curse since Terrell first came to live with them.

"What is going on out here? Why would you let me sleep like that, and why didn't anyone tell me my baby girl was here. I don't get to see her as it is and who knows when I will get to see her again?" His wife tried wiping the tears from her eyes before he got to the table.

"Hey daddy. Mommy said you weren't feeling well and we wanted to let you rest."

He sat down at the table. His wife's eyes were red and glossy, and her cheeks were tear stained.

"What's wrong with you, woman? What are you crying about? What's happened now?" He kept with the questions until she finally said,

"I think it's time, baby."

"Time for what?"

"Time for Nette to know the truth."

"Is that what this is about? I told you I would take care of it, and I plan to do just that," he said slamming his hand on the table.

"No. Desiree says he has been asking around trying to get in touch with us and even trying to find Nette. So it's only a matter of time before he does," she said on the verge of crying again.

"So now that he has gotten his life together some thirty-something years later, we are just supposed to let him come in and act like everything is cool? Hell no! Fuck him and whatever horse he rode into town on," he got up and was ready to walk away.

She grabbed his hand, gave him the sincerest look.

"It's time, baby. It's getting too close for comfort now."

The look she gave him melted his heart. As bad as he didn't want to tell *his* daughter about the man who gave her life, if his wife said she was ready then he would do as she wished.

~24~

Sunshyne woke up in a hospital bed.

"What am I doing here? What the hell happened?"

Marcus was sitting in the chair fiddling with his phone.

"You passed out upstairs. So, they brought you down to the ER to check you out," he said raising his head from his phone.

"Where is Maia?"

"I had Damon come get her and take her home."

"You didn't need to stay. I'll be alright."

"I didn't think you should be up here by yourself, but since you are alright I'm going to go and take care of some things. Despite what you think, I am not the bad guy. By the way, there was some man named Jesse Porter who was trying to see you. I told him he needed to wait until you woke up."

"I don't know anybody name Jesse Porter, so if he's still out there you can tell him to leave," she said with a twisted face.

"Oh. I thought he was another boyfriend of yours or your sugar daddy as old as he is, but I will make sure to let them know at the front desk," he said and walked out laughing.

~25~

Michelle was in the office first thing this morning waiting on Terrell to call. He had called her last night to tell her he had finally worked everything out and they would finally be straight. Carlton was still staying with Jacob, but tonight she had invited him over to talk. She wanted to let him know everything. Most importantly, she missed her husband at home with her. She walked to the front of the building only to hear Katie and Esther having a heated discussion, as they always did.

"Listen to this, Boss Lady," Katie said shaking her head. "Let's see what she thinks of this."

Michelle and Katie turned their attention to Esther as she told Michelle what she had just shared with Katie.

"Every year each member is asked to give a love offering for our Pastor Kent's birthday, his anniversary and for the church anniversary. Since Katie doesn't attend church regularly she can't understand."

"What's wrong with that, Katie?" Michelle asked.

"There is nothing wrong with giving your pastor something for his birthday, but they want $500 for his birthday. What happened a couple months ago is the kicker though? Let her finish," she said and looked back at Esther.

"This year they requested a Father's Day be given to the pastor. Not because he had children of his own, but because, as the Pastor's Aide put it, he was their "spiritual daddy.""

"Spiritual daddy?" Now Michelle had a confused look on her face. "If he is your spiritual daddy, who do you pray to when you say, 'Our Father...'?"

Katie looked at Michelle and gave her an 'I told you so' look.

"I know I don't go to church regularly, but that still doesn't sound right to me."

"He is our father, but the reverend is our daddy. He is the daddy of the church," Esther said firmly as if her words were the gospel.

Michelle couldn't with them right now because she knew this conversation would just give her a headache.

"I have to go check on a few orders, but will be back soon. I'm expecting a very important phone call from a Mr. Morris. Please page me if he calls, thanks," she said as she walked toward the warehouse.

It was 4:30 p.m. before Terrell finally called.

"I need you to meet me this evening so I can give you the plan on how we're going to have to do this," Terrell said with pure excitement in his voice.

"Not tonight. I can't."

"But you got to."

"I'm sorry Terrell. I can't. Carlton is coming by this evening and this will be the first time we will be able to have a real conversation since everything went down," Michelle explained.

She also had to run by the hospital to get Sunshyne, but she couldn't tell him because she had promised her best friend she would not speak a word to anyone.

"Alright, but we need to meet first thing tomorrow. We don't want to wait too long."

"No problem," she hung up. She wasn't going to have time to pick up Sunshyne and then cook, so she would have to stop and get Chinese food. She knew Carlton loved Hunan Kitchen's shrimp in lobster sauce. She and the kids would eat sweet and sour shrimp and orange chicken. She would also get some vegetable fried rice and egg rolls to top it off.

Michelle picked Sunshyne up from the hospital and took her home. They talked about all that had happened over the last few days on the way to her house.

"The doctor said the baby was okay. I just need to take it easy for a little while, but tell me what is going on with you and Carlton. What is the deal with you and little brother?"

Michelle let out a deep sigh, "He hasn't come back yet, but he is coming over for dinner tonight and for us to talk. I miss him so much. All I can tell you is that me and Terrell have a business deal going on to help the both of us, but that is all I can say. I hope you know I would never sleep with your baby brother. Hell, he couldn't be more of my brother unless Noreen gave birth to him herself. All this will be over soon, and I pray everything goes back to normal. Now tell me, what is happening with the kids?"

"Well basically the people told me and Marcus we need to get our shit together. Chelle, I knew I shouldn't have been leaving the kids alone as much as I did, but I never thought in a million years something like this would happen. Of course, Marcus wants to blame it all on me. He thinks I'm supposed to stay in the house with kids all the time while he rips the streets and does what the fuck he wants to do. I know I am the mother, and it always falls back on us but still. He needs to own up for his lack of responsibility and not try to continue to dictate me and my actions."

"Girl, don't worry about Marcus. You do what you need to do to get the kids back with you. The sooner you do it the better. It may be a little too late now, but sometimes when you need a sitter you know Kay will always be willing to come over just to get away from her brothers and sister."

"I definitely am, Chelle. There is no way my kids will be taken away permanently. Mariah is still a child herself, and I put too much on her. I got an appointment to see the caseworker tomorrow, and she will let me know the plan. My babies are my main focus now. I will tell you what is going on with Richard next time. "

"Alright girl, you get some rest and we'll talk later. I need to get home to the hubby."

"I hope everything works out for you guys. Thanks for coming to get me, and thanks for always being there for me."

Too much had happened in the last forty-eight hours, and Sunshyne had the feeling this was just the beginning. She put her iPhone on the charger and went to run a hot bath. She sprinkled some *Sleep Tight Scrubfusions* bath salt in her bath water and undressed. She turned on the Spotify app on her iPad and let the music shuffle. As she sank slowly into the water, she laid her head back and thought about everything that was going wrong in her life. What had she done to cause all of this to happen to her? She knew that you reap what you sow, but damn had she done that much because shit was coming at her like crazy.

She began praying to God to help her correct whatever it was that had all of this grief coming down on her at one time.

It was strange to be at home alone. She never had a minute when Maia wasn't calling her name or MJ and Mariah weren't arguing about something. She wanted to ball up and cry. Instead, she unlocked her phone and called her kids. Mariah and MJ knew what was happening and just kept saying they loved her and wanted to come home. Nobody had explained it to her baby yet. Maia just thought she would be spending time with Granny and Granddad. All she wanted to know was when Sunshyne would be coming to pick them up.

Sunshyne explained to her that she was going to stay there for a little while, but she would come see her soon. She told her she loved her and hung up the phone. Sunshyne noticed she had a few missed calls and a gang of texts from Richard, but she resisted replying and put her phone on the nightstand and tried to sleep.

She hadn't been sleep long before the nightmare started.

"You ain't shit but a trifling home-wrecker, you and that baby of yours. Don't think that little bastard is going to bring him to your bed for good because he will never get the chance to even hold it," the woman said right before plunging a knife into Sunshyne's round, stretch-marked filled belly.

Sunshyne sprang up and grabbed her stomach. She could hear the woman's icy voice, but the face was blurry. She knew it was Monica though. She went into the kitchen to make some tea and try to calm her nerves. She really wanted to throw back a shot of vodka but tea would have to do for now.

When she got back to her bedroom she saw Richards's picture lighting up across the screen.

"Hello," she answered sounding extremely irritated. What type of hold did this man have on her? Why couldn't she just leave him where she knew he should be?

"What did I do now, baby?"

"Nothing. What's going on?"

"I wanted to see if you if you were in the mood to let me lick on that thing the way you like."

"No. I'm good."

"Damn, that was quick. You didn't even think about it."

"There is nothing to think about. Now, is there anything else you wanted?"

"Well, if I can't have you, can we go get something to eat?"

She didn't really want to be bothered, but she was famished and didn't feel like cooking.

"I need a little while to get ready."

"I'll call when I'm close."

She thought now would be the right time to share the news of the pregnancy with him. She didn't want it to go on too long without him knowing. She decided she would tell him once they got to the restaurant.

A little over an hour later he was texting her telling her to come down the back. This made her feel shittier. But it was Richard and she could not deny him. No matter how unhappy she was, she never wanted to disappoint him. She knew it was crazy, but she still tried to give him everything, do everything for him in spite of all the things he promised and wasn't giving her.

Sunshyne went out to the back and stood on the lower landing waiting for him to pull up. When she saw his Mercedes turn into the alley she met him at the parking spots in the back. This was getting old. She should not have to sneak around to be with the man she was in love with. How could she continue to let this go on? She was going to have to figure it out soon.

Fifteen minutes later they walked into Claim Company in Northbrook Mall. The hostess showed them to their table. It wasn't long before a server arrived to take their orders. Richard ordered the 2-story meatloaf. Sunshyne ordered the pot roast. When the server asked about drinks, he ordered a double shot of Hennessy and she got an iced tea. He looked a little shocked because she usually had a drink anytime they went out, even if it *was* earlier in the day.

"You're not drinking. Is everything alright?"

"Do you really need to ask me a question like that? A whole lot of shit is wrong. My children are on the verge of being taken away from me, their father is giving me a lot of grief about it, and my man..." she said sarcastically, "...is married and it doesn't look like he is leaving his wife any time soon. Do you need more than that or is that enough?" She rolled her eyes and brought her attention back to the menu.

With the tone she had, he knew to leave it alone.

They ate most of the meal in silence. He asked about Maia. She shared news about what was going on with the whole situation.

"I need to get my shit together. I need my children back home with me. I felt I could use a break but not under circumstances like this."

He tried to console her, but it wasn't working.

The waiter came back to check on them and see if they wanted dessert. Sunshyne ordered the warm chocolate chip cookie, and Richard had another shot of Hennessy.

The waiter brought her dessert, and she devoured it.

Richard kidded with her, "Did you breathe at all?"

A faint smile briefly appeared on her face, "Shut up," she smacked his hand playfully.

Richard called for the check and paid the bill.

They were both so focused on each other when they were walking out that neither of them noticed Paul and Monica on the other side of the restaurant.

Monica wanted to get up and make a scene, but Paul stopped her from embarrassing them.

"I'm not in the mood to be fighting with your husband. Plus, how are you going to explain being here with me?" He said in an admonishing tone.

She thought about it for a moment. She would look pretty stupid starting an argument with her husband and his girlfriend while she was out with her boyfriend.

She calmed down and sat there working out her revenge in her head.

***

Sunshyne and Richard drove in silence for a few minutes before they both blurted out at the same time, "I have something I need to tell you."

They went back and forth telling the other to go first until Sunshyne finally folded her arms and sat there silent until Richard conceded.

"I love you, baby, and you know I want more than anything for us to be together," he started out.

She knew it was about to be some bullshit. She looked over at him, and he looked like a deer caught in headlights. He pulled over into the lot at Lovelace Park. He wanted to be able to look her in the eyes when he said what he had to say. When he pulled in the lot and parked, he sat there for a couple of moments, silent.

Sunshyne rolled her eyes and said, "Just say what the fuck you got to say. It can't be any worse than the rest of the shit that is happening right now."

"Well, I know things are bad right now. I don't want to add to it, but I wanted you to hear it from me before you heard it in the streets."

Sunshyne's body was feeling warm, no she was feeling nervous.

"Baby."

"What the hell is it, Richard. Just say it," she snapped.

"Okay. Okay. Monica told me last night that she's pregnant." Richard blurted it out before he knew it.

Sunshyne's chest started hurting, followed by her head. She knew it was going to be bad, but she didn't think it was going to be devastating. She couldn't speak. Tears were pooling in her eyes, but she couldn't blink enough to keep them back.

Richard reached over to hold her, and she slapped his arms away.

"Take me home!"

"Baby, can we talk about it?"

"What the fuck is there to talk about Richard? Your wife," she said with malice, "is pregnant. So that means all the promises you have been spitting were nothing but pure bullshit,"

She was fuming.

"No, Nette. It wasn't. I really do..."

She cut him off.

"You really do what? Want to have me and your wife? You want to have me on one side of town and continue to build your family on the other," she slapped his face so hard his head jerked back and hit the head post.

"No. I promise you, it's not like that," she put her hand up to stop him from saying another word.

"Just take me home. Now!" she screamed.

He didn't say another word. He started the ignition and headed toward her house.

As he got closer, he asked, "What was it you wanted to talk to me about?"

She rolled her eyes and told him, "Never mind. It doesn't even matter. Enjoy your family," she got out of the car, slamming the door hard behind her and marched up the stairs.

Her life had become a total mess. She sat on her bed rocking back and forth, crying uncontrollably.

How could she be such a fool to ever think he was leaving his wife? She rubbed her stomach. She thought the baby was going to be her and Richard's answer to everything, but now she was going to have another baby by a man she was not going to be with. She laid there completely drained. Thinking about everything all over again, she could no longer keep her eyes open and her body surrendered to the sleep.

~26~

By the time Michelle made it home, Carlton was pulling into the driveway in front of her. As soon as the kids saw him, they ran to meet him and started asking him when he was coming back home.

"Can I at least get a 'Hi, daddy.' 'I miss you daddy?'"

"Of course we miss you daddy. That's why we wanna know when you're coming back. I know there are some things you and mommy need to work out," Chloe said. "So, I hope that's what you're here for tonight..."

What did she know about working things out? He thought.

"Girl, go get cleaned up for dinner. You are starting to get a little too grown," he said and turned her toward the stairs.

Everyone filed into the house. They ate dinner, caught up on things that had been going on with the kids and then Michelle and Carlton went out on the porch while the kids cleaned the table and dishes.

"I miss you, Carlton."

"I miss you too Michelle, but you need to tell me what the hell is going on with you and Terrell."

Just then, nosey Ms. Parker came outside with her German Sheppard,

"Hey, Carlton. Glad to see you. You must've been out of town or something. Haven't seen you in few... several days." Ms. Parker said, sounding too concerned.

"Yeah, works keeping me pretty busy got me all over the place."

"Alright, you kids have a good night."

"You too, Ms. Parker." They both looked at each other and shook their heads.

Jason came out to let them know the kitchen was clean and they were all going upstairs. Carlton acknowledged his son and then turned his attention back to his wife.

"So, what's up, Michelle?"

Michelle told him everything - how she was helping Terrell to go legit, how they couldn't tell anyone because they didn't want to get them involved and how he had helped her come out of a deficit and keep the company afloat.

Carlton started to raise his voice, but calmed down so the neighbors and the kids wouldn't hear him.

"You mean to tell me that you jeopardized everything you built to help him clean his drug money?"

"Yes. I thought it was a good idea at the time. But after it had gone on too long I told him this was all I could do. I was tired of sneaking behind your back," she explained, her voice pleading with him, hoping he would understand.

You could tell he was fuming on the inside. He could not believe she put everything in jeopardy.

"Say something, Carlton."

"I don't know what to say. I understand you wanted to help your best friend's brother, but what hurts the most is that you didn't trust me enough to come to me before you made that kind of decision for our whole family. You thought taking drug money to help your company was better than coming to your husband to work it out," he scolded her.

"I know I made some serious mistakes. It wasn't all about helping Terrell either, but it will all be over tomorrow. He wanted to meet this evening to get everything taken care of, but I felt this was more important," she said wishing he would just hold her and tell her everything would be okay.

"I don't know how, or if, we're going to get past this, but I'm not willing to throw sixteen years of my marriage away. It's going to be a long road ahead, but I'm not giving up my family that easy. You have damaged my trust, but I'm relieved to know you aren't sleeping with him. Plus I'm tired of sleeping on Jake's couch," he grabbed her close, tilted her head up to his and gave her a forgiving kiss.

"This is far from over, but we can finish up another day. Let me go tell the kids good night before I go."

Michelle had a shocked and pleading look on her face, "You're leaving?"

"I don't have to."

"Then don't"

Carlton went upstairs to say good night to the kids while Michelle made sure the kitchen was cleaned. Bryson wouldn't let him leave his room. He had to give him a play by play of the days he missed.

Michelle was showered and in bed by the time Carlton made it to their room. She was glad to have him back home, where he belonged. She would never do anything else to cause him to spend the night out again, let alone for as long as he did this time.

She hadn't realized she dozed off until she felt Carlton's fingers moving the crotch of her black, lace boy shorts over and sliding his fingers inside of her from behind. She was already warm and moist. The touch of her husband excited her body beyond imagination. She didn't turn over right away. She let his fingers dance inside her from behind. He finally slipped off her shorts so he could look at that perfect round ass of hers he fell in love with when they first met. He lifted her thighs and hid his face inside her. He let his tongue pleasure her secret treasure while his finger seduced her clit. She let out a soft moan of pleasure. She tried not to scream in ecstasy because she knew the kids were still awake. When she couldn't hold back any longer, she buried her face in a pillow and let it go.

She definitely missed the way Carlton took time with her body, and her body was craving every single touch from him right now. When she couldn't take it anymore, she turned over and pushed him on his back. She took his shaft and engulfed it in the wet heat of her mouth. She massaged it with her tongue as she rubbed his scrotum. He wanted to let it go immediately but didn't want to waste the moment. It had been way too long since he felt his wife and wanted to enjoy every second for as long as possible. So he begged her to let him taste her pussy again.

She swung her body around and put it in his face. He sucked and licked her until her juices flowed. After she came, he flipped her on her back and entered her hungrily.

"Ooh, baby. You are so wet. I have missed you so much."

He was deep inside her, hitting that spot only he could touch. That place reserved for only him. He began to hit it a little harder, and this time she couldn't hold back.

"Oh my God! Don't stop, baby," she yelled out before she realized it. She grabbed the pillow and placed it over her face.

He didn't stop. He continued to move in and out, stroking it methodically, and allowing his queen to come several more times before finally asking,

"Can I come?"

She didn't have to say a word. He knew he had permission when she held her hips in position for him to work it in and out, making it more intense with each thrust, until he couldn't take it anymore. His body stiffened, and he held her tight as their fluids mixed together. They laid there overcome with exhaustion until Carlton moved down and nestled his head in her bosom and fell fast asleep.

Michelle laid there for a minute thinking about all that had happened and finally fell asleep with a smile on her face.

~27~

Renae and Ruben were getting along pretty well, spending quite a bit of time together. He found out she had never been to the Chicago History Museum and figured she might enjoy it. He planned the day around the museum. He took her to the museum and then a walk-through Lincoln Park to end it with a summer evening picnic by the lily pool hidden away from everything. This was a place Ruben would frequent as a child, but yet another one Renae knew nothing about. She felt a little embarrassed that she had lived right next to such a beautiful city that she never really explored.

Another day he picked her up and they went to an arcade. They played all the games she remembered as a child. She even beat him at a few games he bragged about being the champion of like Mortal Combat, Ms. Pacman and pinball. She just couldn't do anything with Centipede and Galaga though.

No, they weren't the extravagant dates and trips Paul had taken her on. Like the times they went to Punta Cana or the Dominican Republic. However, they meant just as much to her because Ruben put a lot of thought into them.

She was still staying at her dad's, and Paul was texting her almost every day to let her know how much he loved her and missed her. She ignored his calls and was thankful he hadn't been back by her father's house stalking her.

Even her dad liked Ruben. Some days he would be at the house kickin' it with her dad, waiting for her to get home. They talked about everything from old movies to football to baseball. That was the main subject that kept them both talking. She felt like she was acting out the beginning of a love story from a movie and was waiting for the hammer to drop anytime.

She told her dad that she would probably be moving back to her house next week. He hated for her to go because he was enjoying having her around, when she wasn't with Ruben. When she told him her plans, he immediately took her to the gun store to purchase a Ruger .380 automatic, and then to the range to make sure she could handle herself. She wanted to purchase a revolver like the one Dirty Harry carried, but her dad and brother agreed she should have something she could handle a little better. They also had a new security system installed at the house while she was away.

She had just walked out her office to go grab some lunch when her phone rang.

"Hey, Dee," she squealed into the phone excited to talk to her best friend. What's going on with you girl? It feels like we haven't seen each other in forever,"

"I know that's right, but you seem to be keeping yourself busy. It's a wonder you answered your phone, but I guess Ruben can't sit up there with you on the job." Renae laughed out loud, and people stared at her like she was crazy.

"Hush, but for real, girl. Ruben and I have been together almost every day. When he's not at the club and I'm not at work we are either going out to eat, walking on the lake or just sitting somewhere talking."

"I'm glad you're having a good time," Desiree said with a smile in her voice.

"I am. For real I am, but I feel like he is too good to be true. If not, all I wanna know is why didn't you ever introduce us sooner?"

"Girl, bye. Everybody knew yo ass was stuck on Paul and not goin' nowhere, and Ruben is too nice of a guy for me to even let you mess over."

Hypocritical seeing as how Desiree didn't have a problem with how she treated men.

Renae couldn't help not to remind her of it, "Girl, you got a lot of nerve. You go through men like tricks go through money."

"Whatever. What you doing tonight?"

"I'm moving my stuff back home, and then going to see Ride Along, the movie with Kevin Hart and Ice Cube. Ruben doesn't really care for Kevin, but I've sat through two boring ass movies with him, so tonight's my night," she said with a little attitude in her voice.

"Okay. Well maybe we can get together to do some shopping and go to lunch tomorrow," she said sounding a little sad.

Desiree missed her friend but didn't want to intrude on her happiness. Renae could hear it in her voice so she told her no matter what they would hang out tomorrow. They said their goodbyes and hung up the phone.

Renae didn't have much time for lunch, so she decided to grab a turkey sandwich on wheat, a bag of BBQ chips, and a sweet tea from the cafeteria in her office building and head back to her desk. As soon as she stepped out of the cafeteria, she saw Paul going up the escalator.

She had had it with Paul and his bullshit for real. She had talked about getting a restraining order against him in the past, but now she was going to put it in action. She walked straight to Judge Millner's chambers. She knew how tough he was on men/women who stalked or abused their partners. His daughter was stalked by an ex-boyfriend, and by the time he found out it was too late. Her teenage son came home to find her battered body lying on the kitchen floor. Ever since then Judge Millner had a very low tolerance for that type of behavior.

Renae's office worked closely with him, and she had been in his chambers for different cases on a regular basis. His clerk said he had an important matter to deal with this afternoon but she would make sure she told him and told Renae to come back once the afternoon call was over.

Renae went back to her office hoping Paul had left. When she got there he was nowhere in sight. Her co-worker told her a gentleman had been by looking for her. She was new and didn't know Paul, so she told him Renae was out of the office. Renae figured she should tell her boss what was happening as well. She explained everything that was going on and ended with Paul coming to the office today. She told him she had already been up to see Judge Millner to give him a heads up.

Ron assured her he would get started on the paperwork and make sure an order of protection was entered before she left the building that day.

Judge Millner's clerk called down at 4:00 pm to let Renae know that he was ready for her. They did it the official way. She stood in the courtroom before the judge. There was a court reporter and clerk. They went through the process as any other citizen would have gone through. Ten minutes later it was done. Paul was now forbidden to come within 100 feet of Renae. She wasn't sure if he would adhere to it, but it made her feel a little safer. She didn't want to have him arrested, but she would if he refused to leave her alone.

She thanked Judge Millner. He told her the same thing, "Be careful."

She went back to her office to grab her purse, thanked Ron for his help and went outside to meet Ruben. Ruben was standing at the entrance waiting for her. He kissed her.

"How was your day?

Renae gave him a rundown of everything that took place.

"Do you think it is a good time to be moving back home?"

"I have been at my daddy's house too long. I feel like I'm back in high school. Plus, I think him and Ms. Loretta need their space back. I know he doesn't mind having me around and doesn't want me at the house by myself either, but I think I'll be alright. My alarm system works just fine and so does my new toy," she pointed her fingers at him like she was holding a pistol in her hands.

"Maybe you could come stay with me for a little while," Ruben said, hoping she would accept the invitation. It would be nice to wake up to her in the morning.

"I have a spare room and it's all yours, unless you think you'd feel safer in my arms," he said shyly.

"That is great of you to offer, but I want to be home, in my bed."

She went on to tell him she could handle the gun her dad got her and reminded him that she had a new alarm system.

"I won't push it, but if you ever feel like it's too much you are more than welcome."

"Thank you."

She kissed him as they got in the car to drive to her dad's to pick up her stuff.

***

Renae was upstairs getting the last of her things together. Ruben and her dad were downstairs chatting. They're Cubbies weren't doing so well this year so they were talking more general and about the history. Ruben told him that his granddad lived next door to a man by the name of Theolic Smith who was a pitcher for several teams in the Negro and Mexican League.

Of course her dad had already heard of him, "Yeah. Yeah. His nickname was Fireball."

"That's right!" He was the first person he talked to that had ever heard of him.

Renae came down the stairs with the last of her belongings. Her dad's face instantly became sullen.

"Young man you are welcomed here anytime. I don't get to talk this kind of baseball too often. I love my boy to death, but he just was never this into it."

"Thank you, sir. I will keep that in mind."

They carried Renae's bags and Muffin's dog gear out to the car.

Renae walked her dad back to the house.

"Baby girl, you know you don't have to leave."

"I know daddy, but I can't live here forever. I'm not gonna let that fool run me from my house. I have my protection so I should be okay," she said as she tapped her purse.

She had gone back to the range a few times by herself and felt comfortable handling it.

"Okay. You're a big girl, but you're still my little girl. If anything happens, I'll be there Johnny on the spot."

He kissed her forehead. She hugged him.

"I love you, daddy."

"I love you too, baby girl."

She got in the car, and Ruben drove her home.

Paul had watched them earlier at the courthouse. He was now sitting down the block, watching their every move. The more he watched them, the more enraged he became. Now was not the time or place, he thought.

He had something planned for both of their asses and couldn't wait to see the look on their faces when he finally caught up with them. She wasn't just going to leave him like that, and especially not to be with that dude. No matter what he'd done to her, she was his.

He started rubbing his hands on the steering wheel.

"That is my pussy and another motherfucker will never get the chance to see what it feels like." He thought as the anger built.

He waited until they were off the block and her dad went in the house.

"Sooner or later," he said, as he pulled away.

~28~

Desiree was still burdened by the case she'd been working on and didn't have time to think about much else. She woke up that Saturday morning groggy but decided to still do some work from home. While she was writing up her notes to give to Jonathan Mason, their lead investigator, it hit her. She thought about having Jonathan get everything he could on Porter so when her parents finally did talk to Sunshyne she might be able to give them some stuff to help her see why they did what they did.

She knew if anybody could do it, Jonathan could. He had the resources to find things you didn't even know existed. Hc was the type of person Olivia Pope would have on her team. Most of the cases where she came out on top were because of Jonathan's help. He found hidden money, secret lovers, and high rollers' vacation homes that her clients' spouses thought would never be found.

She had him look into Jerome's dealings when she found out about his daughter to see what else he had been hiding from her. He didn't find anything worthwhile that Jerome hadn't already told her.

She texted Jonathan to tell him she had something for him to look into. He immediately texted her back, telling her to email as much info as she could. She did a little more work before getting ready to spend the day with her BFF.

As she was stepped out the shower, she saw her phone light up. She'd forgotten to turn the ringer back on after she finished working. Jerome's name was flashing across the screen. She had deleted his nickname "Papa Bear" out of her phone a long time ago. He was simply Jerome now, but he still had his ringtone, *We Both Deserve Each Other's Love* by LTD. If she was honest with herself, and Jerome, she would tell him that she never stopped loving him and wanted him back in her life.

She just couldn't allow her heart to be crushed again. She would do whatever necessary to guard it from the pain she felt before. She answered.

"Hello," she said beaming with a child-like smile.

"Good morning, Baby Bear. How are you?"

"I'm good. How are you?"

"I'm well. I was calling to check on you and see if you had gotten any more info to help you with your issue," he said with pure concern in his voice.

"I got a little more information from my granny the other day and talked to my parents about what I had found out, but I'm rushing to get ready so Renae and I can hang. Can I call you later?" she asked while lathering her body with lotion.

"Sure. That was the other reason for me calling. I was hoping we could get together and go out for an early dinner later.

"Yes," she said without hesitation.

She couldn't believe she had agreed so fast. She knew she missed him. She realized a long time ago she had made a mistake when she walked away from Jerome, but her pride wouldn't allow her to open up again. She knew it was immature, but she kept telling herself, "to just let it be..." until today.

She told herself it was just dinner, and she felt obligated since he was trying to help her with her family situation. They made plans to meet up after she was done hanging with Renae and said they're goodbyes.

As she was applying her NYX lipstick, she felt those butterflies, not only in her stomach but her pearl was pulsing with excitement. She cursed herself for feeling this way, but deep down inside she couldn't wait to see him.

Desiree was riding, listening to WGCI. Dani D was playing all the jams from the 90s. She was stuck at the light and in the middle of helping SWV sing "Rain" when a police car went flying past her with its sirens blaring. Before the light changed she tried to call Renae and got no answer. She sent her a quick text to tell her to come on outside.

She drove a little further, and another police car passed her before turning onto Renae's block. As soon as she hit the block she saw that very police car that passed her just a few minutes before, parked in front of her best friend's house.

She drove as far as she could and jumped out the car. She ran up to Renae's house and met her and a couple officers at the bottom of her porch. She was facing the female officer with her eyes filled with tears and jaws clenched listening to the officer tell her they were going to make sure they pick Paul up for violating the court order. As soon as she noticed Desiree walking up, she interrupted the officer to tell Desiree what happened. The officer went to finish talking to the neighbor.

"Girl, this motherfucker brought his ass over here smelling like weed and liquor with the 'he loves me and we need to talk' bullshit. He must have been sitting somewhere watching me because Ruben had just dropped me off about ten minutes before."

Desiree gave her a sly look.

"It wasn't like that, but we can talk about that later. I told his ass he needed to leave, but I guess he thought it was like every other time we went through our shit. So, when I wouldn't let him in he tried to kick in the door. I'm so glad my dad and Dougie put in a new security system and installed a reinforced door."

She was no longer crying. Her eyes were now red with rage. She was clapping her hands together with every other word like she did every time she got upset.

"He wouldn't leave, so I told him I was calling the police. He kept trying to plead his case, and when I wouldn't let him in he threw one of my flower pots through my kitchen window and left."

Desiree had never seen Renae this mad before. She would usually get mad, but whenever she talked about what she was going through there was more hurt in her voice than anger. This time she was speaking with more venom instead of the hurt little girl from every other time before.

"Well, I'm glad you got that order of protection when you did."

"Yeah, but what good did it do. He still came by, and he still fucked up my house."

"Have you called Ruben?"

"No. I don't want him to get involved anymore. I'm going to handle this myself. Let me finish talking to these officers so we can get our shopping on."

"You still want to go to the mall?"

"Of course. This dude is not going to ruin the rest of my day. Plus, you and I got some catching up to do. First, I gotta wait for the guy to come fix my window and then we can leave," she walked over to the police and finished her conversation.

After Marty's Glass Repair left, Renae locked up and activated the alarm. They decided to go to Woodfield Mall. They wanted to go to the Aurora Outlet Mall, but with all the drama, they didn't have time before Desiree was going to meet Jerome for dinner.

They barely started driving before Renae started telling Desiree all that had been going on with her and the "men in her life". She was so excited. "Girl, I'm glad I didn't take my butt in the house after that picnic or I may never had met Ruben. He is very sweet and protective. Sometimes he can be a little too protective like I'm a child of his, but it is better than the alternative. I really do like him to the point that it's kinda scary."

Desiree looked at her, "What are you scared about?"

"He is too perfect. That kind of perfect that is too good to be true. When we are together he acts nothing like the tough guy in the club. He is nothing like any other guy I've dated." Her eyes got brighter with each word she spoke. "It has been a short time, and I'm already daydreaming about the future with him. What if God has only brought him into my life to show me what I've been missing? What if he is the one who is going to get me over Paul?

Desiree looked at her again and rolled her eyes. “Girl, here you go sabotaging the relationship before it even gets started. You’re enjoying yourself. You’re having a good time. Don’t over think anything. If that’s all it is you will know it. Right now, enjoy it for what it is, and if your dreams turn to reality then that is even better.”

“You’re right… as always. No matter what happens Paul is *definitely* a thing of the past.

"So, tell me about him dropping you off this morning," Desiree said twisting her lips and giving her a suspicious look.

"Girl, it wasn't nothin'. I told you we were supposed to be going to the movies, but plans changed. Actually movies were never the plan as far as he was concerned. After we dropped my things off to my house, he said he needed to stop by his house. He told me it would only take a few minutes and to come up. When we got upstairs he had prepared a nice dinner and had the table set up like we were at a fancy restaurant."

Renae was grinning from ear to ear.

“He noticed the shocked look on my face and assured me it was just dinner. He said he would drop her off after dinner, but instead we watched movies and talked until we fell asleep. When I woke up, I was on his couch with a blanket over me.”

Desiree gave her another skeptical look.

"What? I don't have a reason to lie to you. He didn't get none last night, but you can bet I'm gonna give him some when we spend next weekend together," she looked at her with the side eye.

"Ooh, girl, you nasty."

"Naw, I'm grown. Stella got her groove back. Why can't I?"

They both busted out laughing.

"Girl, I am just glad to see you smiling again. Whatever it is you're doing with him, keep doing it. It looks good on you."

Desiree proceeded to tell her a little bit about what was going on with her and her rekindled feelings for Jerome. When she first broke up with him they talked a little bit about the subject, but then Desiree clammed up and wouldn't say a word about him after that. She had made it clear to everyone that the topic was not up for discussion.

Now that Desiree had told her about these feelings and that she was meeting him for dinner, Renae took the opportunity to get some clarity.

"So what made you decide to go out with him after all this time? I thought his name would burn your tongue if you ever spoke it again. You haven't talked to him in I don't know how long and now you're going to dinner."

She paused and waited for her to shut the conversation down. A somber look came across Desiree's face as they pulled into the parking lot.

"I'm really starting to think that I made a big mistake when I pushed him away. I mean I always knew it, but I let what Billy did to me destroyed any hope for me and Jerome. I let what he did cloud my judgment when I found out about Jerome's daughter. I put that hurt and pain on Jerome. He is not Billy at all, and being around him these last couple weeks has stirred something up inside of me and I want to see if I can make things right between us."

"Does he know what actually went down with you and Billy?"

"Not the whole story. He just knows that Billy hurt me beyond belief."

Desiree still hadn't gotten over the hurt he caused her. Renae knew how bad it had been between her and Billy, and she didn't want her to go back there.

"Well, I'm glad you finally came to your senses. I'm sure Jerome will be glad you decided to come back where you are meant to be."

They high-fived each other and headed towards Windsor and Akira.

Desiree and Renae had bought enough stuff for five people. They had bags from Bebe, Forever 21, Michael Kors, Agaci, DSW, and a few other stores. Desiree bought a turquoise halter jumpsuit to wear to dinner with Jerome that evening. Not that she needed it, but she couldn't help herself. She dropped Renae off and went home to get ready. They had taken longer than she wanted, she texted Jerome on the way home to let him know what time she would be ready.

He told her to take her time because this was her night. He had gotten Darnell to take care of the bar for the night, and she had him all to herself.

She got home, soaked in the tub, and took her time getting ready. After she dressed, she called her sister. No answer. She left her a voice message and told her she was thinking about her and would see her tomorrow.

By the time she put her make up on, Jerome was ringing her bell. He was always a gentleman. He didn't believe in that texting or calling to let you know he was downstairs. He still came to the door, opened car doors and pulled her seat out when she sat at the table. He was one of the older gentlemen who didn't get caught up in this new age stuff.

Desiree opened the door. Jerome was standing there looking as luscious as ever. His tall, dark physically fit frame, his salt and pepper mustache and goatee were trimmed perfectly, and his fade was on point as always.

Jerome's eyes lit up when he took in his Baby Bear's beauty. It was all he could do not to grab her into his arms. Her long, black curls hung just above the halter top of her jumpsuit. Her makeup was flawless. She invited him in and offered him a drink while she finished getting ready. Twenty minutes later, she was ready. They headed out for their night on the town.

~29~

Sunday morning. New Light Baptist Church was packed. The parking lot was filled to capacity when Sunshyne pulled up looking for a place to park her car. She didn't want to block anyone in because she knew how she felt when she came out of church and was boxed in. She pulled out onto the street and got lucky. There was a space practically right in front of the church.

When she walked in, the choir was ending their last song as Pastor Collins took the pulpit.

"Aren't you glad you came to church today? If you would just give me fifteen minutes I promise to have you out of here. I don't want to be before you long. I don't want you to shout and then get mad," he said as he looked to the clock at the back of the church, right over the usher's bench.

"Go with me to Esther 1:10-12 where the Lord has a word for us this morning."

He read the scripture passage, prayed, and went right into his sermon.

"You are designed to handle where you are. Has anyone ever been in a place where you looked up and said I can't take this? I can't handle it. Well, I come to tell you this, wherever you are God knew you were going to be there because he is an all-knowing God. Before you got there, He gave you everything you needed to handle it. Three of y'all are looking at me like 'Naw. I don't believe that Reverend. I can't handle this.' Well I got to tell you, if you couldn't handle it. You wouldn't have made it."

Sunshyne's mind started wandering. Reviewing the details of everything she'd been going through the last month or so. She tuned out Pastor Collins. Before she knew it, she was crying a river. She got up and went to the bathroom. When she came back out Pastor Collins was almost done.

"Listen. Listen. You can't let the pain you feel now make you miss the glory that's coming. Let me finish when I tell you this. You don't have to trade yourself based on what anybody thinks about you because it's what God says about you. If it costs everything, it's not worth it. You may wanna live like that, but it's not worth it to live in disrespect."

By the time she made it back to her seat the worship team was up singing "*Worth.*"

Sunshyne wasn't feeling well, when offering time came, she gave her money and left.

After church she went home so she could lie down for a little while before going to have Sunday dinner with her family. She called her mom, "I'm gonna be a little later, but I will make it in time for dinner."

"Alright baby. I will hold dinner until around 4:00 for you, but make sure it's no later than that. You don't want to disappoint the kids.

That was partially the truth. She didn't want her to let the kids down because they were excited she was coming today. They hadn't seen her in a few days and Maia kept asking when she would be over. They had talked to her a few times, but understandably that wasn't enough. The main reason her mother wanted her at the house today, though, was so that her parents could finally sit down with her and her siblings, and reveal the lie they had been living all these years.

Richard had been texting and calling her non-stop but she totally ignored him. Her soul ached every time she thought about the fact that Monica was pregnant. She had hoped the news of her pregnancy would make things move faster, but she had enough time the last few days to think.

She realized she had been dreaming. Deep down she knew men only do what they want, when they want. As long as they had been seeing each other, and he hadn't left her by now, she did not believe he ever would. Now was the time for her to do what was best for her. Monica could have her husband. She was not going to continue to play this game with Richard.

The sermon from earlier that day replayed in Sunshyne's head, and, at that moment, she deleted his texts and blocked his number. She rolled over until sleep consumed her.

“Let him find someone else to play with.”

***

The house was packed when she arrived at her parents'. The mouth-watering aroma of her mother's cooking wafted from the kitchen and hit her as soon as she walked through the door. Damon was already there with the kids. Lauren had to work a double shift today and wasn't gonna be there. She knew her mind had been elsewhere for a while when she saw Jerome sitting in the front room watching the game with her dad and brothers. She walked into the kitchen to see her mom and sister preparing the food to set out on the table.

It looked as if her mom had fixed most of her favorite dishes - fried pork chops, cube steak, candied yams, macaroni and cheese, and a caramel cake was sitting in the corner. She was glad she forced herself out of bed to make it. Now she just prayed that evening sickness didn't creep up on her. Her upset stomach didn't bother her in the morning. It usually waited until late afternoon or evening. So she hoped it held off until after dessert, at least.

"Hey, Nette."

"Hey, little sis. What's going on? she said as she walked over and gave her mom a kiss on the cheek."

"Nada. What's up with you?"

"I see Jerome on the couch. So you got something going on."

"Yeah, girl. I haven't had a chance to talk to you," she beamed. "We have some catching up to do."

"Yes...we...do," Sunshyne laughed and turned to her mother, "Do you need me to do anything?"

"Sure. Take these to the table," and placed a bowl of greens and a plate of fried chicken in her hands. When Sunshyne left out of the kitchen she gave Desiree a worried look. Desiree mouthed, "It will be okay."

Maia came running in the house when Sunshyne walked in the dining room.

"Mommy," she said with excitement in her voice, waiting for Sunshyne to put the food on the table before jumping in her arms.

"Hey, baby girl. Where is your brother and sister? Go get them and your cousins so you can wash your hands before you eat."

Maia ran to the back door and yelled for them to come in. Terrell came in right before everyone sat down to eat. He grilled Desiree and Jerome about their relationship until their father told him to mind his business.

After dinner was over and the kitchen was cleaned, Mrs. Morris told the kids to go down to the basement and find a movie to watch because the adults had some business to discuss.

Since Jerome thought it best that he not be there for this conversation, he volunteered to take the kids to the game room downtown.

"That would be great," said Mrs. Morris in a very shaky voice.

The kids were out the door and on the porch before anyone could say otherwise. Terrell and Damon volunteered to give him money, but he refused. He unlocked the door for the kids and watched them pile in his Escalade like they were getting on the bus for a field trip. He told her to text him when they could return, kissed her, and hopped in the truck.

Desiree walked back in the house and gave her mom a nod of assurance to go ahead and get on with it. She sat down on the couch and held her mom's hand. When her dad seen she just couldn't get the words out, he stepped in.

"You kids know we love you all the same. We all know things got a little rough for us when Terrell joined the family, but after a while we all adjusted to the new situation. It was hard on everyone. However, we all became family and remained family. We are always family no matter what anyone else has to say about it."

He didn't know how to say it and was babbling.

Damon busted out, "Pops, did you find out Terrell really isn't your son?"

"No boy," and Mr. Morris gave him a good whack on the back of the head.

"Mom, can you tell us what is going on around here. I'm sure I'm not the only one getting anxious," Sunshyne interjected.

"Well, when I was younger, and before I met your dad..." she squeezed his hand tight, "... I dated an older guy. Your grandparents didn't approve, but I thought I was grown and kept seeing him anyway," her voice trembled. "I ended up getting pregnant by him and they sent me to go live with Aunt Jean."

"Isn't that where you said you met daddy before moving back here?" Sunshyne asked.

"Yes, sweetie. It is."

"So are you now gonna tell us you have another child out there, did you get an abortion?"

"No, I don't, and I didn't." Sunshyne could feel her skin getting warm. She could feel her skin getting hot and her chest getting tight.

"So, then what are you trying to tell us? I'm not daddy's child. That this other man, whatever his name, is my..."

Her father cut her short, "I am your father. No one will ever take that away from me." The room had become eerily silent. No one said a word until Sunshyne broke the silence.

"Really, you're not, and for all these years we have been living another lie. Can you be honest about anything? What else don't we know, and are you only telling us now because he done came back," she jumped up screaming and then went outside for some air.

Sunshyne's heart was feeling as though it had been ripped from her chest. Mrs. Morris was now crying inconsolably. Sunshyne ran out of the house to get away. Desiree and her dad followed her. The boys stayed to attempt to comfort their mom.

Sunshyne was sitting on the swing crying with Desiree and their dad standing on either side. They tried to say something, anything, to help relieve some of the pain she was feeling at the moment, but there was nothing anyone could say right now. They just rubbed her back to console her. After a few minutes passed, her mom came out to see about her. Sunshyne couldn't even look at her mom. Mrs. Morris got ready to say something and she put her hand up to quiet her.

"Just leave me alone. I have nothing to say to you right now."

Her dad interrupted, "That is still your mother, and you will not talk to her that way."

"You too, Daddy. I cannot believe y'all kept this from me all this time."

"We did what we thought was best, Nette," her dad said.

"You thought it best to lie? I guess that's what you do," she barked. "You lied to me. You hid Terrell. What else are you hiding...?"

"You watch your tone. I understand you're angry, but your mom and I thought we were doing the right thing. That man was a drug addict and treated your mother horrible. When he found out you were his child, he threatened to go to court unless we gave him some money to go away. After time and time again, I told him if he ever brought his ass around our family again he would regret it," he was fuming now. "He had stayed away until a couple weeks ago when he showed up here out of the blue."

By now everyone was out on the porch and looked at each other. "So is that the only reason you are telling me now? Because he's back?"

Mr. Morris told everyone to go back in the house before their nosey neighbors came out. Sunshyne reluctantly agreed, and they all went back in the house. When they were all seated again around the table, Mrs. Morris answered her daughter.

"That's right. I prayed he'd never come back and if he hadn't we would have never told you," she said trying to hold her first born.

Sunshyne jerked away.

"What is his name?" she demanded.

Her parents hesitated.

"Tell me his name. I deserve to know."

Barbara looked at her husband and murmured, "Jesse Porter."

"That was the man here looking for daddy that day at dinner, and the same man who came up to the hospital the other day."

"He did what! Came to the hospital when?" her daddy shouted.

"The day I passed out at the hospital. Marcus told me he stopped by to try and see me, but he told him he needed to come back when I was awake."

Her dad was livid now. “I’m going to kill this motherfucker.” Terrell and Damon told him to calm down, but Sunshyne wasn’t concerned with his feelings at the moment. That is all she could handle right now.

"Tell my kids I'll be back to see them tomorrow or something. I gotta go."

She jumped up to go.

Her siblings yelled after her to come with her.

"No. I need some time to think, get my head together."

"Sunshyne." Mrs. Morris pleaded, and her daughter just looked at her and rolled her eyes.

Mr. Morris told her to let her have her space.

Sunshyne hopped in her car and sped out of the driveway not paying attention. She didn't see the van coming down the street. By the time the driver saw her it was too late. He slammed on his brakes, but it did not stop his Astro Van from barreling into the passenger side of her car and spinning it around until it careened into a parked vehicle pinning her in the car.

It seemed like the ambulance and fire department took forever to get there. Desiree and Mrs. Morris panicked. The men ran to the car to attempt to get Sunshyne out. They had gotten the doors open by the time the fire department made it. They didn't move her because they didn't want to make things worse.

The firefighters removed Sunshyne's limp body from the car and rushed her to North Shore Hospital. Mrs. Morris rode in the ambulance with her daughter, and everyone else drove with their dad.

Desiree called Michelle. Her voice was shaking and filled with panic. "Michelle. Nette was just in a bad car accident. We are all on our way to the hospital now. I think you should get up there."

"Where was she at? How did it happen?"

She couldn't go into detail, "She was upset and was leaving the house in a rush. A van was coming down the street and broad sided her." She felt like she was going to hyperventilate, "Jerome has the kids. Is Kay Kay home? Can he drop them off to her?"

Michelle didn't hesitate, "She is down the street at a friend's house, but I will call and let her know they need to come down to the house. I will see you in a minute." She told Desiree she would be there as soon as possible.

Michelle hung up with Desiree, and immediately called Kay Kay to let her know that something bad had happened to Auntie Nette and her and her dad were on the way to the hospital. She would let her know what was happening as soon as she could.

Desiree called Jerome next to explain everything. He said he would drop the kids off and be on his way. She also noticed she had missed a couple calls from Renae and a text asking her to call. She tried calling and didn't get an answer. She would try again later, but now she had to focus on Nette.

~30~

The scene at the hospital was chaotic. There was an elderly lady suffering from a heart attack, a kid who was riding a bike down a makeshift ramp who fell on an old rusty pipe that was now lodged in his shoulder, a gunshot victim had just went up to surgery and a young child suffering from, what seemed like, years of abuse. Lauren didn't think the day could get any more hectic, but then they got a call that an ambulance was on the way with a woman who was in a horrible car accident. Unfortunately, she had not been wearing a seat belt.

Damon didn't have time to give Lauren the heads up. Unbeknownst to her, she was part of the team waiting on her sister in law. When the paramedics rushed the gurney into the hospital, Lauren's legs almost came out from under her. She could not believe her eyes when she saw her sister-in-law covered in blood and glass with tubes coming out of her body. She quickly regrouped and took her mother-in-law over to talk to intake.

"I'll be back as soon as they get Nette settled." she told Mrs. Morris.

It was a blessing the paramedics were able to regain Sunshyne's consciousness. The attending physician spouted out orders to everyone around. He wanted everything moving fast. One of the nurses was working to remove the glass from Sunshyne's arms, forehead and hair. Another was wiping the blood so they could better assess her injuries. He wanted to ensure there were no serious or life-threatening injuries.

They let Sunshyne's parents back to first to talk to the doctors. Lauren hugged them.

"Try not to worry, she is in the best care." Lauren tried to assure them. "'I'm going to go out and update everyone else."

When she got out to the main ER waiting area, she held Damon for a minute before she updated everyone on Sunshyne's status.

"No one else is able to go back there with her right now. Nette is going through a bunch of x-rays and tests. I will come get you all as soon as she comes back. Desiree do you want to go upstairs with Renae while you wait?

"Renae? What the hell happened to her? Is she al-right?"

"Calm down, sis," Lauren held her arm. "She's do-ing fine. Her boyfriend...What's his name?"

"Ruben," Terrell blurted.

"Yeah, him. He was brought in not too long before we got the call about Nette . He's still in surgery so she might need someone to sit with her while she waits."

"What happened to him?" Damon asked.

"I don't know the specifics, but he came in with a gunshot wound."

"I'm going to go up. Sis, can you text me as soon as Nette is done with her tests?" Terrell said.

Desiree and Damon followed Terrell in the direction of elevators to the operating waiting area. Renae was pacing the floor when they stepped off the elevator.

"Hey, girl. What the hell happened?" Desiree asked as soon as she stepped out the elevator.

"It's a long story. I've been trying to call you all even-ing," she said looking exhausted and distraught.

"I know girl, but we're taking care of some family drama," Desiree said with a look that said I would tell you about it later. "By the time I saw your calls we were on the way up here," she said close to tears.

"How did you find out about him getting shot?"

"We didn't until we got here. Nette was in a bad car accident and is down in emergency."

"Oh my God, no."

"They're running all kinds of tests on her right now, so we came up here to see about you. What's going on?"

"Ruben got shot in the shoulder, but they haven't been able to tell me much else yet. His parents are out of town, but I talked to them. They're getting on the first plane back," Renae said in almost a whisper, her voice shaky.

"Did you get in touch with Kenyatta?" Terrell asked.

"Yes. She was waiting on the neighbor's daughter to come over and sit with the kids."

They all looked at each other. Kenyatta was Ruben's younger sister, but you never knew where her head was. She may be on her way up to the hospital or she could be sitting at her girl's house smoking and drinking.

"So, what the hell happened?" Damon asked, his voice laced with anger.

"That motherfucker shot him. I know it was him," Renae said with complete hatred in her voice.

"Who?" they all asked in unison.

"Paul. He kept calling my phone last night. I kept sending him to voicemail. I finally blocked him. When I went out to my car this morning to go to eight o'clock service my tires were flat. I called and texted Ruben, but he was sleep since he worked at the club last night. Dougie was at work, and I didn't want to upset my daddy. Ruben eventually woke up and saw all of my calls and texts and came over around 3:30," she was becoming real emotional.

"To make a long story shorter, I told him what I saw. As we were walking out to talk to his boy that came to tow the car for us, shots rang out of nowhere. One caught Ruben in the shoulder," she was more furious and worried now than sad.

"Did you see Paul?" Terrell.

"No, but one of the officers that was on the scene asked if I or Ruben knew anyone who drove a blue Malibu."

"Do you?" They all asked again in unison.

"Yeah. His sister drives one now."

Before anyone else had the chance to ask, Damon blurted out, "Did you tell the police?"

"No. I wanted to wait until Ruben came out of surgery to ask him what he wanted to do."

"Cool," Terrell said. "Don't let anybody else know about the car until you talk to him."

Just then Rufus came running up the escalator.

"Hey, y'all." He was out of breath and sweating. He looked towards Renae. "What the hell happened? Where is Ruben? What are they saying?"

"Are you going to give me a chance to answer?"

"My bad, mama."

She told him the short version of what happened. He asked the same question Damon did and she gave him the same answer she gave a few minutes earlier.

Damon's phone started buzzing. It was Lauren letting him know Nette was back in her room.

"She's back."

"Alright, girl. We gonna head back down. I'll come back to check on you before we go. You gonna be okay?"

"Yeah, I'm cool. You go check on Nette."

"I'll stay here with her until he goes to his room."

They left to go back downstairs, and then the doctor came out soon after.

"Hello, ma'am. The surgery went well. Thankfully the bullet hadn't done any major damage. He is in recovery know, but the nurse will come out shortly so you can go back with him. I am sure he would love to see you. He will stay down here for about an hour and then go up to a room."

Renae let out a long sigh of relief, "Thank you very much doctor."

Rufus let out a soft, "Yes!!!"

His boy was gonna be alright, and as soon as he was well enough they were gonna handle Paul. Renae knew she wouldn't be able to reach Ruben's parents yet, so she left them a voicemail so they would have it as soon as they were able to turn their phones back on.

Jerome and Michelle had made it by the time Desiree got back downstairs. Sunshyne was up talking as much as she could. You could tell she was in extreme pain. Her mother was sitting at the side of her bed and wouldn't move.

After a few minutes, the doctor came in to talk to Sunshyne.

He got ready to give her the news and stopped, "Would you like to speak privately?"

"No, sir. Please go ahead. They can hear whatever you have to say. I just want to hear what is happening.

"Well as you know, we performed a few different tests on you. We didn't see any broken bones. It seems as if you were just knocked around very badly. You're going to have a headache, and your body will be sore for a while. You will probably be taking your pain medication for the next couple of days."

Michelle looked at Sunshyne suspiciously, knowing she shouldn't be taking any type of serious medication right now.

The doctor went on to say, "I'm not sure how much of the information you want me to share at this..."

She interrupted him, "Go on doc. This is my family, and I don't keep secrets," emphasizing the "I".

"Okay. Well the ultrasound showed that you have experienced, what we call, placenta abruption, or more commonly known as a miscarriage."

Just as the doctor spoke those words a nurse entered her room with Richard. Everyone in the room looked a bit bewildered, except Michelle. She was more hurt for her best friend than anything.

"Miscarriage!" Richard was the first to speak.

"I'm sorry, sir, who might you be?"

Before he could answer Sunshyne spoke up, "That's the baby's father."

The room turned quiet as a library in that moment.

"Father? When did you find out? Why haven't you told me?" His voice was getting louder with each question and was moving closer to Sunshyne.

Terrell had to grab him, "Calm down partna. This ain't about you right now. You need to go home and tend to your wife and let my sister get her rest. Matter fact, we all need to get out of here and let her get some rest."

"Yes, that sounds like a good idea. She's had a rough day and needs her rest. She will be receiving her medicine shortly, and then we'll take her up to her room. It's nothing serious, but we do want to monitor her overnight," explained the doctor.

Richard hesitated for a minute, "Nette, can we please talk about this?"

Terrell shot Richard a glance, and Sunshyne saw the look on his face. "I got this little brother." She turned her attention to Richard, " I am tired and not in the mood. We can talk soon, but for now you need to leave."

The men in the room gave him the look to let him know that was his cue to leave and there was nothing else to be said right now and Richard obliged.

Mrs. Morris told everyone they could go ahead; she would stay behind to wait with her.

"No. You can go, mom. I'm okay."

Mrs. Morris looked hurt, as if she had lost her best friend. Her husband gave her the look that meant she shouldn't force it on her right now. She kissed her daughter on the forehead and left to go home. Everyone else said their goodbyes and let her know they would be back to check on her tomorrow. Richard tried to lag behind, but Damon made sure he left with everyone else.

"I just wanna talk to her really quick."

"Now is not the time, Bro."

"I just can't believe she didn't tell me."

"Well she has been dealing with a lot. I'm sure she will call you if she wants to talk."

Richard conceded and left.

Damon stopped to see Lauren on his way out.

"Can you follow up with the floor nurse and ask her not to let anyone up to bother Nette except family and Chelle."

"I will let them know, but I can't guarantee they will accommodate the request," Lauren advised.

She kissed him and let him know she had a few more hours on her shift.

The family found out what room Ruben was in and went upstairs to check on him and Renae. She had dozed in the chair next to his bed. He was laying in the bed half sleep watching tv.

"What's up, bro? You getting' to be a little slow these days", Terrell joked.

"Man, when I find that ninja his ass is dead," his words were slightly comprehensible. The meds still had him a little groggy, but everyone in the room knew that as soon as he was up out that bed and moving around he was going to deal with the situation.

Ruben did what he had to do to live on the right side of the law now, but he was not the one to be messed with when he was in the game. Once he got out though, he was completely done. It cost him a lot, but he walked away and never looked back.

Terrell told him, "I ain't gonna try to talk you out of it because I know I can't. Just be smart when you go at him, and if you need anything let me know."

"I'm cool, B. You ain't gotta worry bout me. How's your sister doin'? I heard she was in a bad accident."

"She's doing okay. They're moving her upstairs so they can watch her for the night," Desiree told him.

"Cool. Tell her I said what's up," he was barely keeping his eyes open now.

"We gon' let you get your rest. We just wanted to check on you to make sure you're straight, Damon told him.

"Nae, let us know if you need anything," Michelle said as they left.

~31~

It had been a little over a week. Sunshyne was out of the hospital. Her relationship with her parents was still strained. She didn't show up for Sunday dinner and had very few words for them when they did try to call. She was thankful her sister brought the kids to see her. Today was her first day back at the salon. She had bills to pay and couldn't stay home any longer. Marcus was nice enough to come take care of a few things for her while she was down in spite of everything going on between them. She was glad she could still depend on him.

She still had Richard blocked, so she hadn't heard from him. Michelle and Desi would share his messages when they came by until she finally told them to keep them to themselves. She was done with him and didn't want to hear anything about him. As soon as she walked into the shop, Lollie, the receptionist gave her a handful of messages and told her that the "married man" had been here every day looking for her. She said if it was like any other day, he would be pulling up in about twenty minutes.

Sunshyne didn't have time to think about him right then. Her first client was in the bowl. She threw away the stack of messages and went to get her station ready. She colored Kimberly's hair and watched the clock at the same time. About forty-five minutes had passed by and no Richard. As soon as she finished washing Kimberly and putting her under the dryer to set, Richard walked through the door.

Her book was too busy for this shit right now, she thought. She had the shampoo girl wash her next client and took Richard to the back room. She didn't want it to turn into a yelling match. She knew he was upset.

Before he could say anything, Sunshyne spoke. She wanted to control the conversation.

"Look, I know you're upset, but I don't need you doing all that yelling up in here", she waited for him to say something and he just nodded in agreement.

"Maybe I was wrong for not telling you what was going on, and maybe you had every right to know that you had *another* baby on the way", she made sure she emphasized another. "Honestly, I wasn't sure if I was going to keep the baby, and then when you let me know your wife was having a baby I made up my mind."

She was really saying those words to hurt him. She had no intention of getting rid of the baby, but maybe it was for the best now that she had lost it. She thought she was only thinking that, but then heard the words come out her mouth.

"Maybe it was for the best."

"How can you say that? I love you. The baby could've been the best thing for us", he said grabbing her hand.

She jerked her hand away from him.

"I'm tired of playing second. I deserve better. My kids deserve better than what I've been giving them. So that means there can be no more us. We are done, Richard."

He walked closer to her.

"You don't mean that. You and I are meant to be together forever. You are my soul mate. I don't know what I'd do without you in my life, and I don't want to know," he grabbed her in his arms with a weird look in his eyes.

She tried to pull away from him, and he held her tighter.

"Let me go, Richard. I need to get back to work, and it's time for you to leave."

"I'm not going anywhere until you say that we're going to work through this."

"I'm sorry, but I can't tell you that. Leave now!"

The shampoo assistant came to the back to check on her.

“I’ll be out in a minute.”

When she left the room, Sunshyne turned back to Richard.

"You need to go, and when you leave out that door don't come back. If you do I will call the police and have you arrested for trespassing. Better yet, if you come back I will call your wife."

"You don't mean that, but I'm leaving. We're not done with this conversation though. I told you we were going to be together, and I meant it."

"I meant what I said. Don't come back up here again."

He bent down to kiss her, and she pushed him out towards the front. This time he obeyed and left the salon.

Sunshyne got herself together and went back out to the front. She apologized to everyone and went back to working her magic. She apologized to Ms. Wilson for keeping her waiting, but she told her there was no need to. She was in love once and knew how it went.

"I couldn't help but over hear you. You were right, if you feel you deserve better, don't let anyone else make you believe any different. That is where we go wrong. We allow these men to do what they want, when they want. I'm here to tell you he’s not the end all be all. There is someone out there who is going to love you the way you need to be loved. He will make you his priority and show you what true love is meant to look like. Okay. That's enough old lady wisdom for now. Let's see what spectacular style you got for me today."

Ms. Wilson got a few amen from some of the other ladies in the salon, and they started a much lighter conversation. After Sunshyne finished Ms. Wilson and her next client, she went to the front to check her book for the rest of the day.

"I almost forgot. You also had some older fine ass man looking like he could be Denzel's father come in for you a couple times last week," Lollie said.

"Did he leave a name?"

"Nope. He just asked for you, and when I said you weren't in, he left. You got you a sugar daddy too?" she said with a chuckle.

Sunshyne rolled her eyes and walked to the back. She had about thirty minutes before her next client so she decided to take a break.

She wondered if the man Lollie described was the man she recently learned is her real father. She wasn't sure how she felt about the whole situation. One minute she was mad because she couldn't believe her parents would keep it from her for so long, or mad about the fact that what they said may have been true. Her father was willing to sell their relationship for money and drugs. She realized couldn't be upset with her parents because they were both looking out for her wellbeing, and Terrell had stepped up to be the man Jesse couldn't or wouldn't.

The more she thought about everything, the more the tears streamed down her face. She had to get herself together. She couldn't be up in the shop like this. She decided she would take the kids to school tomorrow. Afterwards she would go back to her parent's house to talk to them and let them know how she felt. Hopefully she would be able to move towards forgiving them. She didn't like the feelings she had towards them now because they had been very close up until this point. She went into the bathroom and threw some cold water on her face. She decided to run out to get something quick to eat before her next appointment.

~32~

Michelle was on her way to the bank to sit down with Mr. Beasley to discuss how they were going to handle moving the money. She met with Mr. Beasley for about an hour, going over every little detail. He assured her everything would be taken care of in a couple days and her worries would be behind her. She somewhat explained to him the urgency to finally get this done without letting him know all her personal business.

During their meeting, her warehouse manager had called twice and sent a couple of texts. The meeting concluded and she headed to the warehouse. She got lucky and caught all the green lights. She didn't notice the black Mustang pull in behind her when she pulled in to the parking lot. She hopped out the car and rushed to put out the fire inside.

~33~

Sunshyne finished her last client and called her sister. She wanted to finally talk about all that was going on with their family and also share her thoughts about going to stay with their cousin Rita for a little while.

"Hey, Nette. What's going on with you?" Desiree answered on the first ring.

"Hey, girl. Nothing. Just calling to see if you wanted to go grab something to eat. I really need to talk to you," Sunshyne said, sounding desperate.

"Me and Jerome were going to dinner tonight, but let me call him and cancel."

"You two have been spending a lot of time together lately. Every time I talk to the kids they're always telling me you and Uncle Jerome just left or y'all had taken them here or there. Go ahead to dinner. We can talk later."

"No ma'am. You need me, and we got a whole lot of catching up to do. Jerome will be alright for a night. I'm leaving the Maywood courthouse in a few minutes. How bout I grab us some Joe's barbecue on the way in and meet you at your house? That way we don't have to worry about nosey motherfuckers in a restaurant staring when you start crying because we both know you will eventually."

Sunshyne sucked her teeth.

"Whatever, I have some wine at the house. I'll see you in a couple hours."

"Cool."

Sunshyne hung up. As soon as she got in the car, Michelle called.

"Hey chica, "Que pasa?"

"Nothing girl. What's up with you?"

"Leaving the shop. On my way home to hang with Dee. We haven't seen much of each other lately and need to spend some sister time."

"That's cool. I was calling to see if you wanted to hang out later. Carlton and the kids are going to visit his dad for a couple days, and I can't get out of here early enough."

"Well call me when you're done and maybe we can hook up after Desi leaves."

"Okay. Well let me get back downstairs and make sure everything is flowing smoothly. We had a few hiccups this morning and some orders were backed up. I swear if it ain't one thing... Love you and will hopefully see you later."

"Alright. Love you too." Sunshyne hung up and turned up the Backspin station.

MC Search was interviewing KRS One and Chuck D. She was almost home when the radio was interrupted by an anonymous call. She didn't have time for whoever it was and let them go to voicemail.

When she got to the house she was exhausted. Her body still wasn't at a hundred percent. She took a hot shower and decided to lay across the bed until Desiree got there. As soon as she let her head hit the pillow, everything going on in her life flooded her mind. She laid there with tears streaming down her face knowing that her children were living with her parents because she put a man before her them. Then after all this time she found out the true identity of her father. For whatever reason, he decided to move on with his life and not include her. Her parents felt they needed to hide the truth from her, even as an adult. As she dozed off she thought about Richard. She thought about the baby and their relationship. Then she thought about the new addition his wife was carrying. She still loved him, but she needed to let him go. She wouldn't allow him back in her life no matter how much her heart ached right now. Her body gave in to the sleep it had been crying for.

"Bitch, you thought you were going to destroy my marriage and live happily ever after. You tried to take my husband from me, but now I'm going to take your fucking baby." She could hear the woman's sinister voice but could not see her face. Sunshyne was laying on a gurney with her arms and legs strapped to the sides. She felt a sharp pain in her abdomen. It was a pain she had never felt before.

"Get the knife off the table. It's time," the woman ordered the man in the room with her.

They started walking closer to her, and now she could see them both. Sunshyne couldn't believe her eyes. It was Monica and Richard.

She yelled at him, "Don't let her do this. You told me you loved me, and we were going to be together for the rest of our lives," Sunshyne pleaded with Richard.

"Bitch, stop talking to him. He is not the one in charge here," Monica said as she took the knife from Richard.

Sunshyne let out a loud, piercing scream as soon as the scalpel cut across her belly. Monica cut the cord and snatched the baby from her womb and walked over to a nearby cradle. Sunshyne could hear her baby crying, but there was nothing she could do about it. She kept calling for Richard, but he had disappeared. Monica walked back over to where she lay, and now she was swollen with a baby bump.

She cuddled her stomach in her hands, "Now, Bitch lay here and die. I will make sure to take good care of your baby."

Monica grabbed the infant from the cradle.

Sunshyne was snatched out of the nightmare as her ears filled with the ringing of her doorbell. She jumped up and surveyed the room to make sure she was really in her own bed. Her heart was pounding so hard in her chest she thought it was going to bust out. She rarely had bad dreams, but she couldn't seem to shake this one.

Her doorbell kept ringing. She found her bearings and remembered Desiree was coming over. She rushed to the door and buzzed her sister up. She left the door unlocked and went to the bathroom to get herself together. At least now

Monica didn't have to worry about her having her husband's baby anymore.

~34~

After Michelle hung up the phone with Sunshyne, she called Terrell. He had been trying to reach her all day to see how everything went at the bank, but she was so caught up with an emergency at the warehouse that she didn't have time to return his calls or texts. He was around the corner and suggested they meet at the Wing Stop by Food for Less. He was stopping by his parents' house and was grabbing the kids something for dinner.

"Mom and Pops have been at the doctor all day so I told her she didn't have to worry about cooking. Nette needs to hurry and get her shit together, Chelle. Mom and Pops are too old for this."

"Yeah. I'm sure she will soon, but she is going to need support from everyone. She has to see that we got her back. Especially with the devastating news about that Mr. Porter guy."

"I know. That shit is crazy. I kinda know what she is going through right now, but we made it through once before. We'll do it again."

"I'm sure it will work itself out sooner or later. I'm heading out now. Catch you in a few minutes."

Terrell was waiting for his order when Michelle got to the restaurant.

"Do you want anything?"

"Nope, I'm good. Thanks."

Michelle began telling him the run-down of her conversation with Mr. Beasley.

"We should be good in a couple days."

Terrell sat there with a slick grin on his face the entire time she was talking.

"What boy? What you smiling like that for?"

"Well, if you would've answered your phone earlier you would've known that it's all done. Beasley called me a couple hours after you left to tell me that he had talked to a few people and pulled some strings and moved the process along. We're all good. All of the accounts have been set up and the money is there. Your money and business is safe and sound."

Michelle squealed like a child. The few patrons in the restaurant looked at her. The lady behind the counter let him know his food was ready, and he nodded to acknowledge her.

Michelle calmed down and got quiet.

"I'm so glad. I was tired of all the sneaking around. I had to tell Carlton for the sake of our marriage but I haven't told Nette everything yet."

Michelle's phone started ringing Kay Kay was texting to let her know she needed a ride from work. Terrell walked her to her car and noticed the Mustang again.

Who the fuck was this, and why the fuck did they keep following him. They said their goodbyes.

Before Michelle could leave, she told him, "Next time you have another bright idea like this one, don't call me. I can't put my family in jeopardy like this again."

"No problem. I understand, sis. I pray I never need to come up with another one of these bright ideas again."

Michelle pulled off, and he put the food in his car. He couldn't see through the dark tint on the windows so he started walking toward the Mustang. As he got closer, the driver's side door opened. He couldn't believe his eyes. It was his boy Jamie.

When they were away at school, he and Jamie had the weed market on lock. In the middle of their junior year, somebody started hating and snitched on them. They had just got a new shipment in when campus security and Fayette police raided their rooms. Terrell got lucky because they had stored everything in Jamie's dorm room and hadn't split it up yet. When they came for Jamie he took the weight. They kept questioning him about his "partner" and he acted like he didn't know what they were talking about.

He became the example for the small, college town and was expelled from school and sentenced to three years in prison. Terrell visited him several times over the years. He also sent money regularly to Jamie's sister to make sure he was well taken care of. Jamie's parents blamed Terrell for getting their baby into trouble and refused to talk to Terrell after Jamie's sentencing.

"Man, Joe. Why didn't you tell me you were coming home, and what's with all this sneaking around shit?"

They did the official black man hug.

"I tried calling, but I don't have a current number for you and Sherrell didn't have one either. So I figured I would just pop up on you."

"Yeah, man. I had some shit come up and forgot to shoot her a text. Anyways, I'm glad to see your ass."

"Every time I was going to ride down on you there was always someone around you, and I didn't know what you had told anyone."

"Where did you get that car?"

"I had Sherrell save some of the money you were sending so that I would have a little to fall back on when I came home. I know you said you had me whenever I did touch down, but I needed to have my own just in case something went wrong. You know what I mean, but hey isn't that your sister's best friend I keep seeing you around? You sleeping with her? I thought she was married?" Jamie remembered her from pictures.

"Oh okay. Yes. That's her. Yes, she is married, and no I'm not sleeping with her. We just got done working on a business plan."

"Gotcha. It seems you're doing pretty well for yourself."

Terrell didn't want to seem all soft, but he couldn't tell Jamie enough how grateful he was that he didn't turn him in back in college.

"Man. I can't thank you enough. Some people would have given me up quicker than it took them to get to the station. It still stands. Whatever you need... I got you." Terrell's voice sounded like it was starting to crack so he left it like that.

"Dude. I ain't never been on no snitching shit. No matter what my parents thought, I made my own decisions. You didn't force me to do anything, but enough of all that. I'm back now and a nigga need some serious help. I need to get some money."

"You came back at the right time. I told you whenever you got home that I had you and nothing has changed. I'm bout to start up a club and now that you're back you can help me run it. You were always good with those numbers."

Jamie thought, "Did he just say help him run it. Naw, nigga. How about you give me my own bread and let me do what I want with it? If it wasn't for me your ass would have been sitting right next me in a cell."

He decided to leave it alone for now. That would be a conversation for a later date.

"Cool, but for now I need have some fun and grab me some digs."

"Alright. Follow me to my crib. I'll give you some ends to get what you need. Then tonight we celebrating. Where are you staying?"

"I'm out at the Super 8 out on Waukegan Road."

"Oh hell naw. You either coming to stay with me or we can get you a room at the Extended Stay or Hampton Inn until we can figure out the next moves."

They got in their cars and drove out of the parking lot. Jamie's wheels were spinning in his head. He wasn't sure if he wanted to wait for the club to get up and running or not. For now though, he would roll with his boy for as long it lasted.

~35~

Ruben and Renae were getting something quick to eat before he needed to go to the club. As the waiter returned to the table with their food his phone rang.

"Baby, I got to take this call."

He stepped away from the table.

"Yo. What's up, Bro?"

The call lasted for just a couple minutes. When he hung up, he was calling for the check and two to-go containers.

"Baby I'm sorry, but I gotta take care of something."

"Is everything alright?"

"Yeah. Rufus needs me to come help him with something."

Renae got a weird feeling in her stomach. She knew if Rufus was calling there was nothing good involved. There had been plenty of stories about the two of them back in the day. He had told her, and Desiree confirmed, he was done with all that. So now she was concerned. They got their food, paid, and Ruben took her home.

He walked her to the door, "I'll call you in a few."

"Alright. I know there is something more than what you're telling me. I just want you to be careful", she gave him a long kiss.

He made sure she was in the house and then went to meet Rufus. He hadn't seen Paul since he'd gotten shot. They heard of a few places he was hanging out but could never catch him. This time they had his ass. They had him laid up at Boney's house, one of his dips that also fucked around with Rufus. She knew they both had a woman at home and several others in the streets but wasn't concerned with that. She was simply in it for what she could get. She knew they were looking for him, and Rufus told her she could get paid as well.

She hadn't heard from Paul in weeks, and was actually glad. He was not all that good in bed, but he was a payer. Plus, his head game could win him a gold medal in any competition. He called her last night and asked if he could come over this afternoon. He told her some lame ass story about his girl put him out and he needed some love and affection. She didn't hesitate to tell him yes because she knew when it was all over with she was getting paid either way. After she hung up with him, she immediately called Rufus from the burner phone he had left her a few days ago.

Paul showed up with it all – food, liquor and weed. He said he wanted to have a "Netflix and chill" type of day. Boney would have rather been outside enjoying the weather, but lining her pockets was more important. They were lying in bed watching Belly and smoking when her phone rang.

"Hey, Girl. Naw, I'm not coming out. I'm booed up for the night. I'll check y'all out tomorrow night. Yep. It sure is. Alright. Bye."

She got up to put her phone on the dresser, and he smacked her on her ass.

"Who said we going anywhere tomorrow night. I told you I came for some love and affection, and I ain't leaving til I'm done," he said and pulled her back towards the bed.

"Whatever you say, Boo. Them hoes will be there whenever."

He tried to start playing with her by rubbing on her pussy.

"Not yet. Let me go use the bathroom. You lay right there, and I'll be right back."

Boney walked towards the bathroom then eased around the corner to unlock the door. Rufus told her they were on their way, but was coming from the other side of town. He told her not to let him leave — no matter what. She went in the bathroom flushed the toilet and washed her hands. When she got back in the room Paul was in his boxers. She turned the TV off and turned the music up. He pulled her down on the bed on her back.

"Baby. I thought you needed the affection today."

He unbuttoned her shirt.

"We got all the time in the world. I'm gonna make you beg for me to let you fuck me."

He lifted her bra and swallowed her A-cup breast. He began licking her nipples while his hand moved down her stomach into her shorts and started massaging her clit. He pulled her shorts down and took his index and middle fingers, moving them in and out of her pussy. He took turns sucking and licking her titties. Her moans got louder. He traced his tongue down the middle of her body until he found her clit, keeping his fingers inside her wet pussy and sucking on her clit. He knew that was going to be all it took before she squirted her juices down his throat, but she wasn't ready for that yet.

She pushed his head back and moved him around the bed so that her ass was on the edge. He knelt down on the floor in front of her, and she threw her legs up in the air and pushed his face into her snatch. He pressed his fingers on her G spot sucking her clit harder until she couldn't hold it anymore and gave out a loud scream as her walls tightened around his fingers. Neither one of them saw Rufus and Ruben watching until it was too late.

"That must have been what it was that kept Renae with your bitch ass all this time."

Ruben and Rufus both let out a chuckle.

Paul jumped up, "Mother...," Ruben clocked him with the butt of his Kimber 1911.

"Nope it's not your mother. Although I think she would have even been proud of what just took place. I hope you at least fucked her or got your dick suck with a performance like that because where you bout to go I'm not sure if they allow that."

"Bitch, you set me up," Paul yelled jumping towards Boney, and Ruben clocked his ass again. He was out.

***

Rufus kicked him a couple times and Paul came back to, but it took him a few seconds before he realized where he was.

Rufus threw his clothes at him, "Put your shit on. We going for a little ride."

"You motherfuckers must be crazy. If you gon kill me it's gonna be right here."

"Who said anything about killing you, but if that's how you want," Ruben said reaching into his pocket and pulling out a silencer.

"Naw, Man," he said putting his clothes on as fast as he could. "Tell me what you need to make this straight."

Ruben turned to Rufus, "Look at his bitch ass. He was tough the other day when he pulled up on me. Now he pleading with me like I'm the man wearing the robe in a courtroom. I don't need your money or anything else you got to offer."

Paul was moving too slow for them. "Man, hurry the fuck up. Taking all day isn't goin change shit. You just making me mad." Rufus pointed his gun at Paul to give him a little motivation. As they were walking out Rufus told Boney she had done good and he would be back to take care of her later. They took Paul down the back entrance where they had parked Rufus' beater, and Rufus knocked him out with the butt of his gun after putting him in the trunk. Ruben got in Paul's car, and that was the last time Boney or anyone else ever heard from or seen of Paul.

Ruben called the club and told them he wouldn't be in tonight. After they finished up, Ruben had Rufus drop him back at Renae's. Renae was glad to see him when she opened the door. They looked at each other for a few seconds until he finally said, "It's all over now. You have nothing else to worry about." She knew exactly what he meant. She threw her arms around his neck and kissed him passionately. Tonight was going to be the night she finally rewarded her knight in shining armor. She lead him upstairs to the bedroom she had once shared with Paul. Halfway up the stairs Ruben paused, "Baby, this is not what I want; not why I did any of this. I know we haven't been dating long, but I knew the first night I saw you at the club I wanted you to be my old lady. I heard things about you and dude so I never thought it was gonna happen. I also heard things about you personally that made me want to pursue this relationship even more. Then the more we hung out and I got to know you for myself... well that was it. I knew if I played it cool and waited, you would eventually see that cat wasn't worth it. I knew the type of dude he was, and I also know the type of man that I am. Sweetheart, I want to do this right. I don't want this to be like any other relationship I've had in the past, and I'm gonna make sure it is nothing like your last. To make sure we keep moving in the right direction there are some things I need to tell you, but first I need to know this is what you want as well."

"I want us to keep moving forward like we have. I want to know everything about you, I think," she said with a sly smile. "... and I want you to know everything about me."

"Good," he said before pulling her close to him and smothered her lips with his in a hungry kiss. That night they talked until Renae could no longer keep her eyes open, and she fell asleep on her sofa with her head laying in his lap.

~36~

Desiree could tell something was wrong with her sister the moment she walked out the bathroom, but she didn't say anything. Whatever it was she was sure they would talk about it sometime tonight.

"You must've been knocked out. It took you forever to answer the door."

"Girl, I don't think I am completely recovered from the accident. I'm sleeping every chance I get," Sunshyne told a half truth.

"You and your body have been through a lot lately. Maybe it need the rest. I just hope you got an appetite because I got us plenty of Joes."

Sunshyne pulled out some plates and wine glasses. They ate, drank and talked. Sunshyne talked about everything from her feelings about Jesse, her relationship with Richard and their baby and she told her Monica was pregnant.

"Dee, I need to get my life straight. I need to be a better mother for my kids, and I need to figure out who I am and what I really want in life. I don't want to wait on Richard's sorry, no good ass anymore. I am better than that and deserve so much more. I'm sorry I didn't get the chance to tell you about the baby. Really, I wasn't sure about keeping it, and then there was always one thing after another. I did decide I'm going to talk to mommy and daddy. The more I've thought about it the more I realize why they did what they did. I would still like to talk to Mr. Porter. I don't want a relationship, but he does need to know my feelings."

Desiree wiped the tears creeping down her cheeks, "I'm so glad you see that for yourself now. We all get caught up in our feelings and emotions and throw logic out the window. Just like the old folks used to say... Love is blind but the neighbors ain't. The main thing is that *you* finally see it, and I know you are gonna get it right. I know I haven't been much support lately, but I am here. Whenever you need a break just call. Don't think it will be every day," she said with a smile. We all got your back. You just have to let us know. I'm also glad you're starting to see things from mommy and daddy's point of view. As for Mr. Porter's ass… that's on you."

Sunshyne hugged her.

"That's enough of that. Tell me what's up with you and Jerome. What made you give him another chance?"

Before she told her about him, she had to let her know that she knew about Jesse. "I hope you don't get mad when I tell you, but I knew this Jesse cat was in town looking for you. He had come by the bar to ask Jerome about you."

Desiree wanted to stop there because she could see Sunshyne getting more upset.

"Not you too."

"Wait. Let me explain. I got all the information I could and went to mommy and daddy to tell them they needed to tell you. It wasn't fair that they kept this secret for so long, but it wasn't my place to say anything until I had given them a chance. I just hope you will forgive me."

"I forgive you," Sunshyne assured her. "It's not your fault they lied."

"So when he came around asking questions, Jerome was there with me to help me get to the bottom of this. I wanted to tell you, and I threatened mommy to tell you. If she hadn't told you when she did I was going to. Anyway, we got closer, and the more time we spent together I realized I should've never left him in the beginning. Nette, I really do love him, and I know he loves me."

Sunshyne was happy for her sister, but it was hard for her to really celebrate with her while she had all she did going on in her life.

She forced a smile, "Girl, I am so happy for y'all. I know Jerome is happy you finally came back to your senses.

I know you were fighting it because of what you went through with Billy, but I'm glad you let it go."

Desiree's eyes started to glisten and the look in her eyes held the hurt she had been through. Sunshyne changed the subject really quick.

"So what you gon do? Y'all gonna move in together?"

"Naw. I'm not quite there yet. I want to keep my place for now, even though I'm spending most of my time at his condo."

"Well whatever you do, I wish you the best."

They talked the whole night. They talked about the incident with Michelle and Terrell and her marriage. They laughed about her fine ass daddy. They talked about Ruben and Renae. They also talked about what she was going to do about their parents. Sunshyne wasn't sure how she was going to handle it, but she knew it would be soon. Sunshyne told her about Jesse also coming to the shop.

Desiree started dozing off. So Sunshyne told her to go get in the bed and cleaned everything up. The wine was taking over. She closed her eyes and before she knew it the sun was shining on her face. Desiree was up and getting ready to go home. She didn't need to go into the office today, but she promised Jerome they would go to lunch.

She hugged her sister. "I love you, Nette."

"I love you too, girl. Thanks for last night."

"I'm glad we hung out, but now I gotta get out of here. I'll call you later."

Sunshyne called her mom. She tried calling MJ first, but he didn't answer his phone.

"Hello. There is my Sunshyne. I didn't think you were going to ever call."

"Hey Ma Dear. Don't be so dramatic," she laughed so her mother would know she was joking. "Where is MJ? He isn't answering his phone."

"He's in the shower. Carlton and the boys are coming to take him down to the Bears training camp to watch them practice."

"That sounds good. He needs some time away from his sisters."

Her mother got quiet for a minute.

"Maybe you can come get the girls and spend the day with them."

"Mom, it's Friday. You know it's one of my busiest days. I don't have to be at work until eleven though. How about I come get them and take them to get some breakfast."

"That sounds like a good idea. I think they'll enjoy the time with you. How have you been? You have been through a lot, and I know I didn't make it any easier for you. Baby, I'm sorry for not letting you know, but I thought I was doing what's right. Jesse was a horrible person. Maybe it was me being bitter, but most of all I didn't want his corrupted self around you. Even worse, he refused to love you. So I decided I wouldn't let him hurt you the way he hurt me."

"I really don't wanna talk about it right now. Can you get the girls up? I'll be by in about forty-five minutes."

They hung up.

Maia was sitting on the couch looking out the window when Sunshyne pulled up.

"Granny my mommy is outside," she said as she went running to the door.

She swung the door and ran to her mother.

"Are we going to get pancakes, Mommy? Granny said we were going to get pancakes."

"If you want pancakes then you can have pancakes." Mariah didn't say much to her. She went and got straight in the car.

"Alright Lil Mama. Let's go get your pancakes."

Maia ran to get in the car and put on her seatbelt. Sunshyne turned to her mom, "I'll have them back in a couple hours. I'll come up and see daddy then."

Barbara Morris hated the way her relationship was with her daughter right now, but she would give her the time and space she needed.

"Enjoy yourselves."

When they got to IHop in Skokie, it was practically empty. They always ordered the same thing, so they didn't need menus. Baby girl wanted the create-a-face pancakes, Mariah ordered the silver dollar pancakes, and Sunshyne got the BLT with extra bacon.

The waitress took their order and walked away.

"How have you been?" she asked Mariah.

She just kept drawing.

"Do you hear me?"

"When do we get to come back home?"

"I'm not sure sweetie. I'm working on it."

"That lady came to the house and told granny that we would have to stay there indefinitely."

"I'm going to have you back with me soon I promise."

"I hope so. It is fun at granny's. We have fun with our cousins and Uncle Jerome and Auntie Dee, but we miss you. When we come back home I hope you spend more time with us. You never spend time with us. You are either at work or with your *boyfriend.*

In between bites of pancakes, Maia chimed in, "Yeah, Mommy. I'm ready to come home."

Sunshyne's heart sank to her stomach at the sound of those words. She needed to get her life right ASAP. There was no way she could not have her children with her. Her daughter had every right to feel the way she did, but it hurt knowing that was how they felt. She probably would have never had a conversation with her mother like this, but she was glad Mariah was being honest with her.

"Baby, I'm sorry I haven't been doing a very good job lately. I promise I'm going to do whatever I have to do."

"Okay."

Maia asked, "Does that mean daddy will be back too?"

"No sweetie. Daddy is still going to live at his house."

Mariah looked at her sister and rolled her eyes. They finished their food in silence.

On the ride back to her mom's, Sunshyne tried to reassure Mariah that she was going to do everything in her power to get them home soon and things were going to be different. As soon as they pulled in the driveway, the girls jumped out the car and ran into the house. Maia went to tell her granny about the face she made on her pancakes. Sunshyne went upstairs to see her dad.

"Hey, daddy. How are you?"

"I'm doing better today. Yesterday was a rough one, but I'm Terrell Morris. I refuse to let this get the best of me. How are you?"

"I'm good."

"That doesn't sound too convincing, but if you say you are then I guess you are."

"Gotta a lot on my mind, but I'm Jeanette Morris. I can't let it get the *best* of me either."

He let out a slight laugh. "I'm glad you're still referring to yourself as a Morris. It gives me some hope that we will be okay."

"I think we will, Daddy. I just need a little more time to process all that I've learned. I have a lot I'm dealing with right now."

"I know sweetie. Things are going to work themselves out. You said it yourself...you are a Morris. Plus, all things work together for good to them that love the Lord."

"That's what it says, Daddy, but I gotta go. I need to open the shop today."

"I was hoping you would stay a little longer. I miss you and wanted to talk."

"We will. We'll talk real soon. I just have to get to the shop before my customers."

She kissed him on the cheek and headed downstairs. When she got downstairs, her mom was out back tending to her garden. Sunshyne opened to the sliding doors.

"I'm gone. I have a full day tomorrow, but I will be over for dinner on Sunday. I also want to take the kids to church with me."

"Okay, baby. I'll see you on Sunday. Maybe if your daddy is up to it, we'll come with you."

"That sounds good."

She drove to the shop thinking about what Mariah had said to her at the restaurant. She was frustrated with herself. She had fallen so deep for Richard and didn't realize what it was doing to her family. She called Ms. Foster and got her voicemail.

"Ms. Foster, this is Jeanette Morris. It's important, can you please give me a call?"

She wanted to figure out what the plan was going to be. She hadn't given herself a chance to deal with it all. She pushed herself to work and hadn't dealt with any of it. She sat at the red light replaying the last few weeks in her mind. It wasn't until the car behind her laid on their horn that she snapped out of her thoughts. She felt horrible and really didn't feel like going in now, but she drove on to the shop anyway.

Her heart was still sitting in the pit of her stomach. She could get over Richard. It would take time, but he would eventually become a memory of her past. Finding out she had a father who only saw her as a cash cow was very painful. Her daughter expressing herself hit her below the belt and losing the baby was devastating. Together it was too much at one time. She felt as if her world was crumbling around her.

~37~

Desiree finished up the work she needed to get done that morning and decided to spend the rest of the day with Jerome. When she called him to tell him, he couldn't mask his excitement.

"Don't worry about anything. I will plan the entire day." He beamed through the phone.

By the time she got home, showered, and dressed, Jerome was downstairs waiting for her. He had texted her to let her know to dress casual because he knew she always dressed like she stepped out of a fashion magazine no matter where she went. She came out in some white walking shorts, a light denim button up and light tan boat shoes. Her braids were up in a bun, and face was softly made up.

Jerome was always awed by her beauty. He looked at her like she was an angel who had fallen from heaven. He got out to open the door for her and could not take his eyes off of her.

"What?"

"Nothing baby. You're just so beautiful."

A sexy smile covered her face. The way she smiled, made butterflies dance in his stomach. It made him feel alive again. They got in the car and he drove off.

The Museum of Contemporary Art was displaying an exhibit by Mickalene Damon. Her work is inspired by powerful women. So he knew Desiree would love to see some of her art, and she did. She had been to the museum once before to attend a function hosted by one of her clients.

He always managed to surprise her with their dates. He knew just how to make her days special. After the museum they grabbed food from Big & Little's and went back to his place. He hooked up his Firestick and they watched old movies until it was time for him to go to the club. He offered to take her home, but she told him she would stay and be there when he got home. She walked him to the door, and he instructed her to make sure all the doors were locked behind him. Before he shut the door, he pulled her body into his and planted a long passionate kiss on her lips.

She locked the door and laid against it for a minute. She was excited for their second chance, and this time she wouldn't let anything ruin her happiness.

~38~

Carlton was home when Michelle got in. MJ decided to spend the night with Jason and Bryson. They took the girls over to hang out with Maia and Mariah. The boys were down to the park playing ball. Michelle was placing her Tupperware in the sink from lunch. Carlton came up behind her and put his arms around her waist. She melted in his arms. They were working towards their happy place again. She let him know that everything was alright and assured him there would be no more sneaking around behind his back.

He turned her around and kissed her uncontrollably.

"Babe. We can't do it right now. The boys may come back in the house."

He wasn't listening to a word she said. He held her face in his hands and took his time kissing her soft and slow. She could never resist her husband. She moved her hands up and down, massaging his back, pulling him closer until she could feel the bulge in his pants. He scooped her up and carried her to their room. He laid her on the bed and unbuttoned her blouse.

He knew they didn't have much time before the boys were back and he wasn't going to waste a second. He lifted her bra and nibbled on her breast. He sucked her nipple and put his hand into her skirt massaging her clit just the way he knew she loved him to. The moans escaped her mouth, and he continued flicking her nipple with his tongue while he unzipped his pants. He raised her skirt and slid her thong to the side. She was already moist.

He plunged inside of her. She let out a loud groan. He moved in and out of her with swift motions while she gyrated her hips in rhythm with his. She felt her body quivering, and she pulled him deeper into her. She grabbed his ass and started grinding hard into his body. Her body tensed and locked to allow her to be overcome. He made her keep his gaze. He loved looking in her eyes as she cried out his name. The sound was like sweet candy on her lips. When he felt her body relax, he grabbed her hips and held her steady. He began moving faster and harder.

"Ooh, baby. I'm bout to co...," before he could finish, he exploded. His juices filled her, and his body fell limp. They laid there for a minute until they heard the front door slam. Carlton jumped up and ran for their bathroom first. He opened the door back up.

"Don't think that's it Mrs. Jennings. We will finish this later."

She smiled and laid her back against the headboard. Her life was gonna be alright.

~39~

Sunshyne headed home after she finished her last client. She wasn't in the mood for anything else. She stopped at Herms and grabbed dinner, a polish and fries. As she was pulling into the parking lot, she noticed Richard's car in front of El Tipico. She had a brief thought to go get tacos, just so she could see him, but she let it go as quick as it entered her head.

She got her food and went straight home. She only ate half her polish and very few fries before she laid back on her couch and fell asleep.

She woke up nervous and scared. She had another nightmare, but this time she saw the baby's face and it was Maia. Monica had taken her from her womb and had given her to Marcus this time. She laid there. Her heart racing. She didn't move. She didn't want to go back to sleep for fear of another nightmare.

She just stared into the dark room until she had no other choice but to sleep. When she woke up again it was nine o'clock Saturday morning, and she was late. She needed to be at the shop for her first client in thirty minutes. She called to let them know she was running late and to have Ms. Washington washed and put under the dryer. She made it there just as Ms. Washington was being placed under the dryer.

***

Mr. Morris decided to call the number Jesse Porter left for them. He came by one day earlier in the week and Barbara couldn't believe her eyes when she went to the door. They were sitting on the couch watching baseball when he came to their door. He looked as if he had been on a binge and apologized for coming to their house unannounced but knew if he called first they wouldn't allow him to come. Mr. Morris was ready to knock his head off, but instead told him to meet him at the bar around the corner. They didn't want the kids or grandkids to see him there. He had already caused enough trouble in their household.

When Mr. Morris sat down Jesse came right out with it. "You don't want me to be in my daughter's life, and after thinking about it long and hard I don't think I would be good for her either. I want this to work for everyone, me included." Terrell, Sr. jumped in really quick to hurry along what he knew the conversation would eventually come to.

"We aren't giving you shit else. Jeanette already knows everything so we are done.

"Are you sure about that? Maybe I can catch her at the beauty shop to make sure she knows both sides of the story," he said taunting Terrell, Sr.

Since Mr. Morris wasn't exactly sure he had up his sleeve, he asked, "What is it you want this time? Just know, this will be the last time you ever darken my door. I don't need you to keep hurting our baby girl."

"I think twenty thousand would do it this time. If you could get me that I will never bother you or her again."

Terrell wanted to knock fire from his sorry ass.

"Are you crazy? Where are we supposed to get that much money from?" Ms. Morris couldn't believe she ever loved this monster.

"You are one of the worst kind of human beings, using your daughter to fund your habit. You know what, I'm going to get it for you so you can be out of her life for good, and if you ever come around here again I will kill you myself."

Mr. Morris told him he would call him as soon as he got the money, and left him sitting at the bar alone.

Barbara Morris sat at the house antsy the entire time. When her husband walked through the door she was anxious to hear what he had to say, and Mr. Morris replayed their conversation. They needed to figure out how to come up with that type of money. They wanted this to be done and over with once and for all. They knew they could not make him stay away, but they knew he had a price. Hopefully this time would be it. The little twos and fews they had given him in the past was small change compared to what he was asking for this time. They had known for a long time what their baby boy had been into. They had given him plenty of speeches on how nothing good would come of what he was doing, but he was grown and would need to live life and learn his own lessons. Thankfully nothing had happened over the years. They would never take any money from him for anything because they didn't want him to think they condoned anything he did, but this time they were desperate. Terrell, Sr. and Barbara knew he was the only person that could give them the type of money they needed.

They came up with a story that their house needed some work and asked him to loan them $20,000 dollars. They prayed that Jesse would take the money and leave town. They knew God's blessing would not be on their plan and there was chance their daughter would ever understand why, but they knew it was best if Jesse was nowhere around Nette. He was like poison and they worried he would only infect her.

They called their son, and he obliged their request with no hesitation and said he would get it after work. They told him the contractors would contractors would be by later that day. He told them he would have Larry drop it by for them shortly. Mr. Morris thanked him before he hung and nervously dialed Jesse's number. When he answered, there were no pleasantries. He told him what time to be at the house. No one would be around. The girls were going to the pool with the neighbors. Desiree was still busy working on her case, and Damon and his family were at The Dells. Nette would be at work all day, and Terrell was at the job working on a special project. It was perfect. They would have the house to themselves for a few hours, at least.

~40~

Two of Sunshyne's clients had cancelled. She was glad her day was over early. While lying on the couch last night, she decided she needed to talk to her parents. They needed to clear the air and she was ready to have that conversation with them. Deep down she was hurt, but she knew her parents truly loved her. She was not one to judge anyone for their mistakes. Lord knew she had made enough in her lifetime. She heard Pastor Collins in her head, "Anyone here who has never sinned can throw the first stone." He quoted this passage of scripture in several of his sermons.

On her way to her parents' house she called Michelle. She missed her best friend.

“Hey girl. Carlton and I are on our way to tennis lessons we just recently signed up for, but I’ll be around afterwards if you want to get together.”

“Okay. I’ll call when I’m leaving my parents”

When Sunshyne got to the house she walked in and saw her parents sitting in the living room with a handsome older man. They were all shocked to see her.

"I'm sorry. I didn't know you had company. I thought we could have a chance to talk."

"Give us a minute. We will be done here soon."

"Okay. I'll go into the kitchen to find something to eat."

The man looked familiar to her, but she couldn’t recall where. She found some meatloaf and mashed potatoes in the fridge. She fixed her a plate and put it in the microwave. It didn't take long for her to realize how she remembered him. She used to see him in their old neighborhood. He used to come to the park with a young boy, and then she remembered the conversation with her sister. She wondered if this handsome man was Jesse Porter. She went back in the living room.

"Mr. Porter?"

He turned his head in her direction by instinct. She thought she was coming to have a peaceful conversation with her mom and dad. Instead she blew up.

"I can't believe this. What the hell is going on? I guess y'all are doing what's best for me again."

Barbara was the first one to speak.

"Baby, I know it doesn't look good, but it's not what you think. Your dad and I were really trying to do the right thing this time."

Jesse had only been there for about ten minutes before she showed up.

She thought real fast.

"We didn't want to hurt you again. Jesse showed up here today demanding money again."

Both men looked at her in shock, but Barbara kept talking.

"He said he needed a lot of money. He knew we didn't want him to see you again and that he wasn't in a place to have a relationship with you so he thought he could work out another deal. Your daddy was just telling him to take his raggedy suitcase and get his ass out our house."

Sunshyne looked at the bag by the door that her mom pointed to and then at Jesse.

Before she knew it, she snapped, "Get the fuck out. Do just what my daddy said and leave their house. Don't you ever bring your sorry ass back around here again. To think, I was going to try to talk to you to get your side of the story."

Tears were running down her face like a waterfall. Her body was trembling. She didn't know if the tears were from the hurt or the anger. Just then Terrell, Jr. came through the door with Jamie behind him.

"What's going on here? I heard the yelling all the way to the street

He had gotten off earlier than expected and stopped to see if Larry had brought the money and also to bring Jamie to the house to introduce him to his parents. They heard a lot about him when they were in school but hadn't met him. Terrell Jr. didn't know what he was walking into.

"Meet the infamous Mr. Porter. This bastard brought his no-good ass up in here trying to get money from mommy and daddy again."

Terrell Jr. gave his parents a perplexing look but didn't say anything. That's what they needed the money for he thought to himself. His dad had a mortified look on his face, and his mother wouldn't even look at him. He went along with the charade.

"Man, you heard my sister. You need to bounce."

Sunshyne held the door open for him and threw his bags on the porch with Terrell and Jamie staring at him letting him know it wasn't a game. He took the hint. He got to the door and just said sorry to Sunshyne. Now was not the time to try anything. When he got on the porch he turned to say something else, she slammed the door in his face.

Terrell, Sr. took his baby in his arms to comfort her. She wasn't sure what she believed at that moment, but it always felt good to be in her daddy's arms. She relaxed and cried into his chest.

Their son looked at them and mouthed, "This isn't over."

Barbara went over to her husband and daughter and held them both. She prayed this was the last time she ever heard from Jesse Porter. After some time Sunshyne got herself together and went upstairs to wash her face.

Terrell took the opportunity to reprimand his parents about what they had done and told them they were lucky it didn't backfire. His parents agreed.

"Now who is this young man?"

"This is my boy from college I used to tell you about."

"It's nice to meet you. Terrell always spoke of you and told us what happened at school, how your roommate left his drugs in your room and you got caught with them.

That was horrible that he didn't step forward to say it was his."

That was the story he told, Jamie thought. Well, whatever helped him sleep at night. He wasn't going to destroy his parents' image of him.

"It is very nice to meet you. Yes. It was horrible, but I'm glad to be home."

Sunshyne came downstairs. In spite of her intentions, Sunshyne was no longer in the mood to talk.

"I gotta go. I'll talk to y'all later."

"You can't stay for a while?"

"Naw. I'm not really up for being around anybody right now."

She lied. She just didn't want to be there.

"Alright." Her mama hugged her. "I love you, My Sunshyne." She hadn't heard that in a long time and it kinda felt good.

"I'll check on you later, Nette," her brother told her.

"Okay."

Terrell, Sr.'s phone buzzed. He picked it up to see he had a text from the number he called Jesse on earlier that day. It simply said, "This isn't over." He deleted the message and never said a word to anyone about it.

***

Sunshyne thought about driving to the lakefront because she was always able to get a clear head down there, but she knew it would be full of people this time of day. She went home instead. She wanted to get herself together before Michelle called. She ran a hot bath as soon as she walked through the door. She grabbed two pink rosebud Scrubfusion aromatherapy candles, and got undressed. Her thoughts were all over the place. She couldn't shake the look on Mariah's face when she told her they wanted to live with their father yesterday at breakfast. She still couldn't believe those were the words her daughter said to her. Thoughts of

Richard filled her head. She missed him. As much as she tried to fight it, she wanted him back. She wasn't happy with him. She wasn't happy without him. The more she thought about him, the harder it was to hold back the tears welling up in her eyes.

She thought about today's events and became more and more depressed. She started to feel like everyone might be better off without her around. She remembered she still had Demerol in the cabinet that she didn't really use after her short hospital stay.

She grabbed the bottle out the medicine chest and played around with it for a few minutes. She couldn't bring herself to open the bottle. Instead she put her head back and began praying. She had not prayed in a long time.

"Today, Father God I come to you asking you for strength. I know what it is that I should do, Lord, I need you to give me the power to do what is necessary. I know you would never give me anyone else's husband, and I ask you to remove the desire from my heart. Help me to make my relationships with my children, my parents and the father of my children better. Most importantly Father, help me to realize the person you want me to be. I am tired of crying and to be happy." The more she prayed tears poured down her face. After she prayed, she let James Fortune, Yolanda Adams, Tasha Cobbs and other singers soothe her soul.

While she prayed, it hit her. She wasn't sure if it was her voice she was hearing or if it was God speaking to her, but she would get away for a little while. Her cousin, Kim, had been asking her to come to Cincinnati to visit. She was Aunt Jean's oldest granddaughter, and they were thick as thieves growing up. They still talked on occasions, and she extended the invite for her to visit whenever she wanted. Well, she wanted. She let the water out the tub and showered.

She ran to the room and dialed Kim's number.

"Hey Jeanette."

"Hey Cuz. How are things going down there?"

"Things are excellent. I am about to open my own boutique. Y'all will be getting invites soon."

"That's great news."

Kim had wanted to design clothes ever since she was a little girl. She'd been selling pieces here and there to other shops around Cincinnati, but it was good to hear she was getting her own shop.

"You remember when you said I could come visit whenever I wanted to. Well, I need to get away for a little while."

Kim squealed into the phone.

"Hell yeah," she said exaggerating the yeah. "When you coming? It would be good to see you and the kids."

"This time I'll be alone." Kim could hear the distress in her voice.

"Is everything okay with you?"

"Not really but we'll talk more when I get there."

Sunshyne didn't feel like going into details about it all right now.

"Ok sweetie. Call me when you have your flight details."

"Cool. Thanks, cuz."

She hung up the phone and texted Michelle to tell her she was exhausted and hopefully they could get together tomorrow.

She didn't want anyone to know she was leaving or where she was going. She would call when she got there and let them know she was safe. She needed to get away to think. Here, she felt like she couldn't breathe. She felt guilty leaving, but she justified it as just taking a trip. Although everyone else probably would have thought now was not a good time for a trip. Still, she was going. She called Meechie to see if they could help with her clients the next couple weeks. Her phone beeped. It was her mother. She asked Meechie to hold.

"Hello."

"Nette. You need to meet us at the hospital right away."

"What is wrong? Is daddy okay?"

"Yes. Your dad is fine. It's Maia."

"What's wrong with her?" Sunshyne was asking questions as she frantically looked for her keys and purse.

"We're not sure. The girls were in the back playing, and Maia came in crying because her head was hurting. She said hear stomach wasn't feeling well and felt like she wanted to throw up. Before we could get her upstairs to the bathroom she blacked out on us. The ambulance is here with her now, and we are on our way up there now. Just hurry."

~41~

Sunshyne was having an out of body experience. She was moving, but it was like she wasn't in control. She called Marcus to tell him what her mom had told her. He told her Desiree called him already, and he was on his way. She called Michelle.

Sunshyne took every side street and back road to avoid as many stoplights as possible on her way to the hospital. She drove so fast that she beat her parents and the ambulance there. She had been there so much in the past month she felt like it was her second home.

The paramedics rushed her baby in before she finished her conversation with the nurse sitting at the desk. She ran over as soon as she saw them. Maia was awake but still in some pain.

"Hey, baby. How are you?"

Maia tried to smile back but strained.

“Is she ok? What took so long for you to get here?" Sunshyne was yelling at the top of her lungs.

"Take it easy, baby. They had to work on her some before they left the house," Mrs. Morris tried to calm her down.

One of the nurses recognized Sunshyne from her last visit to the ER.

"Please ma'am. Let us get her to the back so the doctor can look at her. We want to have the doctor look at her the sooner the better."

Sunshyne calmed down, "Alright but I need to be back there with her."

“Come on. I’ll take you back."

Sunshyne was a little hesitant because she did want to impede on what the doctors needed to do. However, she wanted to be close to her baby.

After they examined Maia, the doctor came out to talk to Sunshyne. By this time Marcus had made it and was waiting outside the room with her.

"Hello Mr. and Mrs. Morris. My name is Dr. Jarvis."

Neither one of them corrected him.

"They're going to take Maia to get a CT scan. That may better help us to figure out what is going on with your daughter. I understand she was recently struck by a car?"

"Yes, sir. They kept her overnight for observations and said it was safe for her to go home the next day. Are you going to tell us now that they should have kept her a little longer?"

"No ma'am. I don't think one extra day would have made a difference. From the symptoms the EMT explained to me there is a possibility your daughter may have an aneurysm that was caused from the impact of the car, but we won't know for sure until we do a CT Scan. Because an aneurysm can form deep within the brain, it did not show up on any of the tests from that day so there was nothing to be alarmed about."

"So what does that mean, Doc?" Marcus asked.

"Well to make it as simple as possible, a brain aneurysm is an enlarged part of a vessel. The artery weakens and fills with blood resembling a balloon. It is more common in adults but can occur with children when there is a head injury. In your daughter's case, the car accident could have possibly caused it."

"What will you have to do if it is an aneurysm?" Sunshyne asked.

"The best way to treat it is through surgery."

"So you mean you would have to go inside my baby's head?" she asked nervously.

"Yes, ma'am. Surgery will be necessary to alleviate the pain she is experiencing. I understand you're nervous, but the longer we wait..."

The technician was bringing Maia back. He placed the films at the nurses' station and took Maia into her room.

"Please excuse me. I need to go take a look at these."

He went over to view the images while Sunshyne and Marcus went back to the room with Maia. The nurse that recognized her earlier came back to let them know there was a waiting room full of anxious family members wanting to know how Maia was. Sunshyne asked her to let everyone know what was going on and that they would be out as soon as they knew exactly what was happening.

As soon as the nurse walked out, Dr. Jarvis came in with a distressed look on his face.

"What is it doctor?" Sunshyne asked anticipating the bad news.

"It seems that the accident caused some cerebral damage. Our top pediatric neurosurgeon is reviewing the images and will then come down to explain our options. She may decide to watch it as it is not that big or she may choose to go in and close it up. Nevertheless, we will be back shortly to discuss everything with you."

Dr. Jarvis left.

The nurse checked to make sure Maia was still comfortable and asked if the parents needed anything. Sunshyne turned to Marcus.

"Step outside with me for a minute please."

He followed her out of the room.

"I'm sorry for all that is going on right now. I haven't been taking any of this as serious as I should, but it finally hit me the other day. I can't have anything happen to our baby," the tears were falling uncontrollably. "From here on out I'm going to make sure I do better as far as the kids are concerned. I'm going to need you to step up and spend more time with them too. I know your business is booming right now, but you said the reason you came back was to spend more time with them and you haven't."

Marcus told her, "I will, Jeanette. I promise. Don't beat yourself up about this. Accidents happen all the time. Our little girl is tough and is going to be alright. Let's just see what the specialist has to say before we jump to any conclusions."

"Thank you, Marcus, but it's enough that she has to go through any of this at all. I appreciate it though. I'm going to go out front for a minute to talk to my family. Come and get me when the doctors come back."

He nodded his head.

Everyone had made it to the hospital. She asked where the other children were. Her dad told her they were with the neighbors. Ms. Wilkinson said they could stay as long as needed. She was glad to have her family there with her. She couldn't imagine that just a few hours ago she was thinking about up and leaving them without a trace or any notice. She filled them in on what was going on with Maia and told them she would come back as soon as the surgeon gave them a better diagnosis of the situation.

They wanted to go back to her room to see her, but Sunshyne thought it would be better if she didn't have much excitement right now. As soon as she turned to walk back toward the room, the nurse was coming out to get her.

“The doctors are back in the room ma’am.”

Maia was up talking to the doctors when she entered the room.

"Ms. Morris, this is Dr. Prescott."

"Hello. Dr. Jarvis has brought me up to speed on what has happened over the last few weeks. This young lady has been through a lot, and I'm here to do what I can to ensure she doesn't have to go through much more. I want to explain what is needed. Do you have family in the waiting room?"

"Yes," Sunshyne replied.

"Is it possible to have someone come back and sit with her while we go somewhere private and talk?"

"Sure. I'll be right back." Sunshyne went to get her parents and came back to the room.

She and Marcus followed the doctors to the same room off to the side that they sat in only weeks ago with the social worker when this all started.

As soon as they were seated, Dr. Prescott explained, “Maia’s condition is so severe that surgery is the only option at this time. I believe that if we don’t perform the surgery there is a likely chance the aneurysm may rupture and cause serious damage. I don’t want to scare you, but it’s crucial that you come to a decision quickly. We want to get things moving as quickly as possible.

Sunshyne sat in silence with tears streaming down her face. Marcus asked the doctor to send the rest of the family in to the room with them.

"If you could also get her parents that would be great."

He knew it was ultimately their decision to make, but he still knew she would want her family in there with them.

Sunshyne still could not find the words to speak. The information was too overwhelming for her. Marcus let everyone in the room know what the doctor had to say and the decision they were facing.

Mr. Morris interjected, "This is a hard time for you, but before you make your decision you need ask God for the answer. If you pray to hear His voice and ask to be on the same page as one another, He will direct your path."

Sunshyne finally spoke, "You are absolutely right, Daddy. So, if you all don't mind we need some time alone. You all can go into the back with Maia now, but please don't get her too excited... Terrell."

She eyed her baby brother because she knew he would go in there trying to make her laugh. Sunshyne did not want to bring further stress on her.

Everyone gave them hugs and got ready to leave the room, but before they could leave Mr. Morris spoke. "We should all pray together. There is power in the prayer of the group." They gathered close. Her father began,

"Father God, we come to you today asking for your healing powers. Prayer that is said with faith will make the sick person well, and the Lord will heal that person. Well father I come to you on behalf of our baby asking that you help the parents to make the right decision. We know that you are in control of everything and we rely on you to direct them. In Jesus name. Amen."

Everyone left. They both spoke at the same time. They would have the surgery.

Sunshyne got herself together before going back in with Maia and headed straight for Maia's bedside. Marcus mouthed to everybody that they decided on surgery. They did not want to risk it rupturing and causing severe brain damage. The family went back into the waiting room. Mrs. Morris gave her daughter a reassuring hug and let her know everything was going to be okay. On her way out, Barbara asked the nurse to inform the doctors that the parents wanted to speak with them.

When the doctors finally returned, Marcus and Sunshyne informed them of their decision to go through with the surgery. Dr. Prescott advised them that she thought that was a good choice and went over everything that would take place. She explained the preparation, the surgery and recovery. She told them they could talk more about follow up and any therapy that may be required later. She went on to advise them they would get prepped and someone would come to get Maia shortly.

The whole time, Maia had been as upbeat as possible. Sunshyne explained to her that the doctors were going to put her to sleep and get rid of those awful headaches she had been feeling.

"Thank you, Mommy. I am so glad because those headaches hurt so bad and are the worst thing I ever felt. Even worse than daddy's whoopins." Sunshyne just smiled.

"You won't get any whoopins from me for a long time," Marcus promised.

They spent a little more time with her before the attendant came to take her up for surgery.

"We will be right outside waiting for you baby," Sunshyne said doing her best to hold back her tears. "When you come out of there you will be feeling so much better."

Doctor Prescott came back one last time to answer any other questions.

"Just take care of our baby." They both replied nervously.

"I promise, I will handle her with special care. The surgery will last about three hours."

Sunshyne and Marcus went to the front to get the others and they all went upstairs.

Sunshyne was on pins and needles the entire time. She was either focused on the black-framed clock on the wall or pacing the slate-gray carpeted floor.The family tried to bring her into the conversation, but she couldn't stay focused. She just wanted somebody to come out and let her know her baby was going to be okay.

After about an hour a nurse came out to tell Sunshyne the surgery was going well and would report any updates. After she left to go back in the operating room, Sunshyne went off to herself to pour her heart out and pray to God.

"Father, I come to you first to say thank you. Thank you for always being there for me even when I don't realize it or don't appreciate it. Lord, I need you to shine down on my family. I ask that you guide the doctors' hands while they work on Maia. I don't want my baby to suffer for anything I have done. This has been a rough time for me lately. Nothing seems to be going right in my life right now. This cannot be what you have for me or her. When will I get to see the day of light? When will my morning come? I know that I should not be bargaining with you, but I promise to do whatever it is you want me to as long as you bring my baby out safe and sound. Help me appreciate the joy that comes after the pain and remind me that from bad comes good and this is one of those times. Give me the grace to overcome the person I have been. I need you to help me. I give it all up to you. I want it to be done. Please Lord let it be enough. I ask all of this in your son's name."

After what seemed like an eternity, Dr. Prescott finally made her way out to the waiting room.

~42~

SIX MONTHS LATER

Maia's surgery had been a success. She made it through therapy better than expected. Sunshyne's prayers had been answered, and now her baby was running around like nothing had ever happened. She could not thank God enough. This whole ordeal had turned Marcus and Sunshyne around. They were just about done with their parenting classes and had been getting along better. Of course they weren't the Cosbys, but they were both taking their responsibilities as parents more serious. Sunshyne's routine was work and home with the kids. God had given her another chance, and she was going to do everything to get it right this time.

Sunshyne and Richard were no longer seeing one another, but they remained cool. She had not been able to get him out of her system completely and would talk to him every now and then. She knew they would never be together again romantically but wanted to keep in contact. She didn't hate him but realized he couldn't give her what she needed and deserved. Sunshyne's phone chimed to let her know she had a text message.

She hadn't spoken to Richard in a few weeks and opened her message app to see it was him.

Can you talk? It's kinda important.

Yes, but it has to be quick.

No sooner than she hit send, Richard was calling.

"What's going on? I don't have much time to talk."

"I'm not trying to burden you with my problems but Monica had the baby, and turns out it's not mine. The baby is as dark as Tyrese. I had a DNA test done, and it is conclusive that he is not mine. When I confronted her about it, she told me everything about her and that dude Paul. She says she believes he is the father. She wants to work things out, but can't… not another man's baby."

He sounded so hypocritical, but Sunshyne thought to herself, 'That's how most men are. They can dish it out but can't take it.'

Then she remembered Monica was messing around with Paul, Renae's man. He was dark. Maybe *he* was the father. "Wow. She is early, isn't she? How are you doing?" She said with sincere concern in her voice.

"Yea. She was having complications throughout the pregnancy. I will be fine. I knew our marriage was going to end soon, but I just didn't think it would be like this."

I am sorry this happened, and I hope it all works itself out. I don't mean to cut you short, but I gotta go. Maybe we can talk later."

"Thank you for listening. I will let you go, and I would like that. I miss you. Maybe we can get together for dinner or something? I really need to talk to someone."

"I'll let you know, but it probably won't happen tonight."

"Well just let me…"

"I gotta go," and she hung up the phone.

Sunshyne stood there for a minute with thoughts racing in her head. She should have never answered the phone. She felt bad for him, but she knew dinner was out of the question. She wasn't even sure why she gave him hope. Things had been so much better since she left him alone, and she was not going to go back to the person who caused her the most hurt. Although it was hard, she knew that missing him was just part of moving on. Now she needed to focus on her and her family. Building the relationship with her children and parents was her priority.

THROUGH IT ALL
Coming Winter 2019

Heartache and pain are things that Sunshyne, Michelle, Desiree, and Renae know all too well. Prayer, sacrifice, and their faith will be what helps them receive what has always been destined for them. Will they all finally reach out and grab the happiness that is right in front of them before it's too late? Will they stay true to themselves and leave their baggage behind or will they give into their weaknesses and let hurdles continue to get in the way?

Through It All will take you deeper into the lives of these four ladies and answer these questions and more. Sign-up to receive updates on the new release, upcoming book signings, and other special offers at my website, www.ShellyKewWrites.com.

Jeanette Morris, also known as Sunshyne, has been working to get her life back in order. After the devastations and tragic events that came crashing down on her world all at once just months ago, she could now see a little light at the end of the tunnel. After discussing her issues with Pastor Collins and attending bible study regularly, Sunshyne had started seeing her life from a different perspective. Instead of a woe is me attitude and wallowing in her misfortunes, she had begun to look to God even more for her strength.

She had depended on Jeanette Morris for far too long to work things out in her life. She had stopped trusting Him. However, now, as soon as she couldn't handle what was coming at her, it was "Dear Lord please help me." That was the reason why she was trying to get out the shop right now and make it to bible study, but her last customer wanted to talk about the trip she had just returned from. So Sunshyne went ahead and cleaned up while Rhonda told her all about it.

"Girl, Paris is such a beautiful city. You have to go there one of these days," she said. Talking with pure excitement in her voice.

"I just might make it there one day," Sunshyne half promised herself.

"When you go, don't worry about riding up the Eiffel Tower. I know that is usually what everyone wants to do. The view is great, but you can see the same view from other places with less hassle."

That really didn't matter to Sunshyne. She was terrified of heights anyway.

"I recommend you take a river boat cruise at night. The Eiffel Tower is absolutely beautiful when it's lit up." You could see Rhonda's mind go back to her boat ride. "Let me show you the suite he had us staying in." She pulled her cell phone out of her Louis Vuitton tote hobo bag.

Rhonda opened her photo app to show Sunshyne her luxurious room. The room was decorated with 18th-century inspired furniture. As they were looking at the marbled bathroom, they noticed a moving truck pulling up to the building across the street. It had been vacant for over a year since the previous owners retired to the south and took their mom and pop shop with them. There had been a crew working in there for the past few weeks, and since they had paper up to the windows you couldn't tell what was going on inside. No sooner than the moving truck parked, a black Cadillac XT5 pulled up along with two more cars. The ladies stood in the window to watch what was happening. Maybe now they would get the chance to see. The guy driving the moving truck got out and used a key to open the door.

Rhonda turned to Sunshyne, "What do you think they are doing over there?"

"I am not sure, but it looks like we are about to find out soon enough." Sunshyne replied.

"I guess Pastor Collins won't see you tonight."

"Nope. I need to see what's going down around here. See who my neighbors are gonna be. They both laughed but turned their attention back to the activities going on across the street.

All the men from the cars were helping to carry items into the building. They could see it was mostly furniture, couches, chairs and tables, but couldn't figure out what the place was going to become.

"I say it's gonna be a hooka lounge or maybe just a lounge," Rhonda was the first to give her opinion.

"I think hooka lounge is a good idea. It seems like those are popping up everywhere. I can't tell what it will be by the furn…" Then she saw what she knew could only be a stylist's or a barber's chair. She just knew they weren't coming in her trying open another salon right across the street. Who the hell do they think they are coming into their territory? No sooner than the thoughts entered her mind, the guy in the passenger seat of the Cadillac truck pointed over to her shop. Then he and the guy from the moving truck started walking towards them. Sunshyne and Rhonda jumped out the window like they had just been busted doing something wrong. Sunshyne got it together real quick. She opened the door, and they stepped out to greet them.

Sunshyne had not been able to get a full view of him from across the street, but as soon as she opened the door she saw how stunning he was.

"Hi. My name is Kody, and this is my little brother Nico."

Kody was short. She was sure he couldn't be more than 5'6" with wide shoulders. His light brown complexion was as smooth as caramel syrup being poured on a sundae with eyes the color of deep, rich brown coffee beans with reddish flecks. His black curly hair afro was very short and neat.

Nico cleared his throat and clarified things. "Younger brother." The ladies understood there was nothing little about Nico. He was much taller than Kody and looked like he weighed well over 300 pounds.

Sunshyne was having a hard time getting her thoughts together. "Hi. My name is Sunshyne, Jeanette"

Rhonda stepped in, "Actually, her name is Jeanette, and my name is Rhonda."

Kody extended his hand to Sunshyne, and she politely shook it never taking her eyes off of him, not even to acknowledge his brother. So Rhonda shook Niko's hand.

Sunshyne finally came out of her trance. "I am part-owner of Kuts and Kurls. I've been watching things going on over there, and was wondering when someone was going to finally move in. I haven't seen you around here at all. What is it you're opening? Where are you all from?"

Nico turned to Kody like the ladies weren't standing there. "Man, I don't know if she is the owner or if she is working undercover." Both men let out a laugh.

"We stay in Bellwood. Our shop recently burned down, and a partna' of ours told us about an opportunity in the beautiful City of Glenmont. He said the sun always shines on Glenmont."

Now it was the ladies turn to laugh.

"What's so funny?" The brothers spoke in unison.

"Well, my nickname is Sunshyne, with a "Y" though instead an I. So I guess as long as I'm around there will always be sunshine."

"I guess you're right. In that case, I hope you will be around for a while. I love the sunshine," and gave her a teasing wink.

"Hopefully you will too. I mean, hopefully your shop does well for you."

"Well, we better get back and make sure they ain't broke nothin'. It was nice meeting you ladies, and I'm sure we will speak again. Before I forget, do you mind if I give you some flyers for our grand opening?"

"No. Not at all," Sunshyne said.

Kody ran across the street to grab the flyers while Nico stayed to get more acquainted. Kody came right back with the flyers and handed Rhonda one and gave the rest of the stack to Sunshyne.

"Thanks. Make sure you give one to your man." He had already noticed she wasn't wearing a ring.

Sunshyne made sure it was clear. She noticed a small glint of delight in his eyes or at least she hoped she did, "I don't have one of those right now, but I will definitely make sure to tell my brothers."

"Alright. You ladies have a good night and be safe out here."

"You too." With that, Kody and Nico were headed back to the shop. Halfway across the street Nico turned to his brother, "My bro is smitten. I seent it all over your face." Kody gave him a playful nudge with no real effect and went back to supervisor mode.

Sunshyne and Rhonda waited until they had gone back across the street. Rhonda turned to her, "Somebody is sweet on Kody. I could hear it all in your voice."

"Well, let's hope he could too."

Rhonda gave her a high five, "I know that's right."

"Let me get back in here and finish cleaning so I can grab my children from my mom and dad." The ladies went back in and Sunshyne swept up the pile of hair that she had left. She locked up and the ladies went to their cars.

Kody stood in the doorway and watched her leave thinking that he couldn't wait to make love to the beautiful Jeanette, Sunshyne or whatever else she would let him call her.

***

Sunshyne stopped at 7-11 to grab a couple Pure Life teas and then called her mom. Her mom answered almost immediately, "Hello."

"Hey Ma Dear."

"Hey Baby. Is bible study done already?"

"I didn't get to make it. You remember the shop Mr. and Mrs. Berry used to own. Well some fellas have remodeled it and turned it into a barbershop. So my last customer and I were welcoming them to the neighborhood. I figured I had missed enough of bible study, so I'm on my way home. What are the kids doing? Y'all done baking cookies?"

"Child. These kids know they get me every time. We were only supposed to be making chocolate chip cookies. Then MJ and Mariah wanted peanut butter. I am all baked out for another month, at least. Hopefully they are too. Maia and Mariah have bathed and are getting ready for bed. MJ just got in the shower. They asked if they could stay the night, and of course daddy and I agreed. You don't have to come get them tonight. Either daddy or I will take them to school in the morning."

"Are you sure, mama?" Sunshyne asked.

"Yea, baby. There is no need to wake the girls. They will be fine." Her mama enjoyed whatever time she got to spend with her grandkids. Even if it was breakfast at the table in the morning.

Sunshyne thanked her mom and drove home thinking about Kody and where things will.

II

Renae woke up to her cell phone ringing. She thought she was dreaming at first so she didn't move right away. Then she realized it was the playtime ringtone she had set on her cell phone. She rolled over and saw that it was only 3:00 in the morning. She had to be up in a few hours and could not understand who would be calling her at this time of night. She immediately became worried. She prayed it wasn't about her daddy. She jumped up and grabbed her phone and saw it was Paul's baby sister, Tanya. It had been several months since she had spoken to her. They were pretty tight while she was with Paul, but once he went missing and his body was found she distanced herself from Renae. So it was odd for her to be calling her, let alone at this time of night. Ruben got up to go to the washroom when she reached to grab her phone.

She answered the phone sounding half sleep and a little puzzled, "Hello?"

"Nae. What are you doing?" Tanya yelled and slurred into the phone. This is why she was calling at three in the morning. She was drunk.

"Do you know what time it is? I am doing what most people who have to get up to go to work are doing. What do you want? Is everything okay?"

"Girl. I just had to call you. Mama and Kenyata told me not to. They said you never really loved Paul and are glad he is dead. I know that was a lie. I know you loved him with all you had in spite of everything he did. I just wish you and him could...," Renae knew she didn't want to hear anything she was about to say after that. Plus, it was enough to try to understand her.

"Tanya, it's 3 a.m. What do you want? I have to be up for work in a few hours." Sunshyne was beginning to get irritated.

"The police called mama last night to let her know they had gotten a break in the investigation. Somebody had finally came forward to give some information. There is a lady who says she saw some people driving away from the forest preserves around the time Paul's car was burning." Her voice was shaking like she was about to start crying.

A queasy feeling came over Renae's stomach. She tried to hide the disappointment when she spoke. "That's good. Did they say what kind of car it was?" She tried to remember what kind of car Rufus drove that day. Just then Ruben walked out the bathroom. Renae put up a finger to tell him to give her a minute and continued the conversation with Tanya.

"No. They didn't give her much information but said they would be by the house tomorrow, well I guess later today, to talk with her more. Nae, I hope this is something that will lead them closer to my brother's killer. Whoever the coward or cowards were that shot him in cold blood like that need to die too." Now she was crying. Renae felt bad for her. She never wished the pain of losing a loved one on anybody, but she really did not miss Paul at all. Was she glad he was dead? No. Had she been losing any sleep over it? That was a negative as well.

"Tanya, you need to get home. You shouldn't be out by yourself in this type of condition. Text me when you make it home, and I'll give you a call later to see how you are. Maybe we can get together and figure out the driver of the car was after you get more information."

"Okay. I will. Stay strong, Nae. Hopefully all this will be done soon. Love you, girl"

"I will. Get home safe," and she ended the call.

When she hung up the phone she turned to face Ruben.

"What was that all about?" He asked.

"That was Paul's baby sister. She said someone has come forward to identify a car leaving the forest preserves where they found Paul's body and his car. She didn't have much information, but I told her I would call her back. Baby, I am getting nervous all over again. I hope everything will be alright."

"Don't you worry about a thing. Everything is going to be just fine. We are going to be just fine." He turned off the light and moved in closer to hold her. He snuggled closer to make her feel more at ease. "Since you gotta be up in a little while anyway, how about I help ease your tension. I got something for you to help take your mind off of all this," he slid down under the covers and raised her nightgown. She had a million thoughts racing in her head, but they started dwindling with each flick of her pearl by his firm but gentle tongue.

ACKNOWLEDGMENTS

I would first like to thank God for giving me the talents to create this story. It is through His grace and mercies that I can fulfill my dream and be intentional in my purpose, and I am grateful for the people He put in my life to make this book possible. A HUGE thanks to my support team.. my family and friends who have been there to push me when I wanted to call it quits. This book has been a long time in the making, and your dedication to my dream means the world to me. I would also like to thank my editor, C. Nzingha Smith for SNC2 INK, LLC., for your insight that helped expand and enhance my creativity. Finally, to everyone who has bought the book, I hope it was worth the experience.

Thank you for your purchase.

About the Author

Shelly Kew, born Nichelle Renee Askew was raised in Evanston, IL. She graduated Summa Cum Laude from Robert Morris University and has worked in the legal profession for over ten years. She has been writing as a hobby for years, until she finally decided to make her dreams reality and turn those writings into published work. Shelly Kew is creating stories her readers can relate to and portrays characters that are dealing with some of the same complex issues that are dealt with in everyday life.

Connect with her on: Twitter: @AuthorShellyKew, Facebook: Shelly Kew Chronicles, Instagram: ShellyKew and at ShellyKewwrites.com.

Cic,

I am so grateful and thankful for our friendship. Your support means a lot to me, and I appreciate your advice during our talks. I am so glad He saw fit for us to cross paths. I hope you enjoy every page!

Love,
Shelly Kew